Pale
Shadow

Other books by Robert Skinner

Ficton
Skin Deep, Blood Red (1997)
Cat-Eyed Trouble (1998)
Daddy's Gone A-Hunting (1999)
Blood to Drink (2000)

Non-fiction
*The Hard-Boiled Explicator: A Guide to the
Study of Dashiell Hammett, Raymond Chandler,
and Ross Macdonald* (1985)
The New Hard-Boiled Dicks: A Personal Checklist (1987)
*Two Guns From Harlem: The Detective Fiction of
Chester Himes* (1989)
*The New Hard-Boiled Dicks: Heroes for a New
Urban Mythology* (1995)

Edited Works
With Michel Fabre:
Plan B by Chester Himes (1993)
Conversations with Chester Himes (1995)

With Michel Fabre and Lester Sullivan:
*Chester Himes: An Annotated Primary and Secondary
Bibliography* (1992)

With Thomas Bonner, Jr.:
*Above Ground: Stories About Life and Death by
New Southern Writers* (1993)
*Immortelles: Poems of Life and Death by New
Southern Writers* (1995)

Pale Shadow

A Wesley Farrell Novel

Robert Skinner

Poisoned Pen Press

Poisoned Pen Press
6962 E. First Ave., Ste. 103
Scottsdale, AZ 85251
www.poisonedpenpress.com
info@poisonedpenpress.com

Printed in the United States of America

For Glenda Williams and Louise Smith,
my right and left hands
(and sometimes my brains)

It was the third of September,
a day I'll always remember,
yes I will...
The Temptations, 1972

He discovereth deep things out of darkness,
and bringeth out to light the shadow of death.
Job 12:22

Each substance of a grief hath twenty shadows.
William Shakespeare
King Richard II
II, ii, 14

"I became Wesley Farrell's partner at the age that most boys are only thinkin' about cars and young gals. He trusted me from the beginning, and I did my best to live up to that trust. Yeah, we did some questionable things to make money, but I played by the rules and was as honest as I knew how. One thing about bein' the partner of a man like Wesley Farrell, though—you never knew when you might have to kill…or be killed…it was part of the cost you paid for makin' a living in the dark side of this city…. Some call New Orleans 'the city that care forgot.' (laughs) Those folks don't know what I know…"

Marcel Aristide, President of Farrell and Aristide, Incorporated, age 73. From an oral history tape in the Archives at Xavier University of Louisiana dated 3/24/1992.

Prologue

Tuesday, September 3, 1940

In a large brick house on Mirabeau Street in the northeastern sector of the city, a man stared at the naked dead woman tied to the chair in front of him. In a quiet, savage voice, the man cursed the corpse, the corpse's mother and father and grandparents, the sky, the earth, and the heavens above. He cursed until he'd used every foul combination of words he knew, then stood breathing heavily as he tried to calm himself. He set the electric iron he was holding on its end, then jerked the plug from the wall outlet, wrinkling his nose at the odor of burnt flesh.

With his mind restored to calm, the man tore the room to pieces, unshelving books, rolling up the rugs, dumping desk drawers, shoving his hands down inside the cushions of the chair and love seat. When he finished with that room, he went upstairs to the bedrooms where he continued his search.

He continued on into the bathroom, going through the linen closet, the dirty clothes hamper, and the medicine cabinet.

The man realized he shouldn't have resorted to the hot iron on the woman's feet so quickly. He should have begun with the knife. The sight of blood will frighten most people into saying anything, but he had been in too much of a hurry.

With his expectations at zero, he pulled the rope to a disappearing staircase in the hall. Climbing up into the dark, he found a light that revealed a lot of dusty junk that had not been touched in years. He backed down the stairs, shutting off the light as he descended.

After searching all the downstairs rooms, he returned to the kitchen to retrieve a bottle of bonded bourbon uncovered by his search. He found a glass, then took them into the library and sat down in an armchair. He poured the tumbler about half-full and drank it down, sighing as the hundred-proof liquor loosened the tight muscles in his neck and back.

A few minutes later, he left through the kitchen door, pausing at the back porch. The neighborhood was quiet but for a dog barking a few blocks away. Pulling his hat down over his face, he walked quietly through the darkness to the service alley. There, he continued through to the next street, where his car waited. Within seconds he drove away from the neighborhood, leaving his headlights off until he was at least three blocks away from the house on Mirabeau Street.

When he reached the edge of the campus of Dillard University, he pulled up in front of an all-night pharmacy on Gentilly Boulevard. Leaving the car running, he entered a telephone booth just outside the drugstore. Feeding a nickel into the slot, he gave the operator a number on the other side of town.

※※※

On Sherwood Forest Street at the edge of City Park, a black-haired woman with skin the color of old gold dug her nails into the back of the man on top of her as he finally hit the spot he'd been probing at for the past quarter hour. She shuddered as the orgasm contracted the muscles inside her. He shook and shuddered along with her, completely caught up in the completion of the sex until the telephone on the nightstand began to ring insistently.

"Ah!" she cried out, mostly in frustration. The man ignored the phone as he continued to plow the same furrow with single-minded devotion. Finally, he collapsed on top of her, at the same time reaching out a searching hand that eventually fumbled the phone from its cradle.

"This," he said in a voice lightly accented with Spanish, "had better be good." He was a long, slender blonde man with bold, sharp features and a widow's peak that grew to a precise point on his broad forehead. His slanted eyes contributed to the somewhat demonic cast of his face. The glittering eyes stared a bit madly as he bared his teeth at the telephone receiver.

"It's Dixie Ray," the caller said. "Sorry if I interrupted anything, Spanish." He didn't sound particularly sorry. There was, in fact, a hint of a smile in his voice. Spanish hadn't wanted to hire him, and he knew that.

"Did you find them?" the blonde man asked, a different kind of excitement now trilling along the edge of his voice.

"No."

"Why not?" The excitement was suddenly gone. Now his voice had an edge of steel.

"She wouldn't play ball so I had to get rough with her. She kinda died in the middle of things—must've been a heart attack or something." The words came from Dixie Ray's mouth flatly, without emotion. Death was his stock in trade. He expected people to die when he went to see them.

The blonde man swung his long legs over the edge of the bed and uttered a profanity. Whatever pleasure he'd derived from the dark-haired woman had evaporated with the other man's news. "Did you search the house?"

"From top to bottom. I tore everything there to pieces. They're not in the house, and probably never were. I just went there to make sure of things."

The other man was silent for a moment. "I should have known it wouldn't be that easy. Did she tell you where Martinez is?"

"It's too bad I'm not a priest, Spanish. Once I went to work on her, she confessed every fuckin' sin since the fifth grade, but she didn't seem to know where Martinez is. You can believe I was tough enough to make her talk." He laughed in a softly indulgent way.

The other man snorted. "That's rich, my friend. So now we have nothing." He bit the words off clean and hard, fighting to keep the rage in him from boiling over. "What are you going to do now?"

"I'm gonna keep lookin'. See, I went to the trouble to find out about him. He's got friends here, places to hide. I'm gonna use that against him."

The blonde man snorted derisively. "If you know him so Goddamned well, why haven't you gotten my plates back yet? Those are more than just engravings, my friend. They're part of an important plan, more important than you know."

"Yeah, things are tough all over, *hermanito*. Course, if it was any of my business, I'd be askin' why you decided to cross Martinez after he set everything up for you. Now you got a mess, and it takes a man like me to clean it up."

"It *isn't* any of your business," the blonde man said angrily. "I've got a stockpile to work with, but it won't last forever. I need to produce more bills, and I can't do that until you get those counterfeit plates back. I don't care if you have to tear this damned town apart brick by brick until you find Martinez. Just find him."

The man in the booth seemed unabashed by the blonde man's angry impatience. There was still a hint of laughter in his voice as he responded. "Sure, Spanish. You're the boss. Just relax, *entiende?*"

"I'll relax when you bring me back the plates. Now get them." He threw the receiver back into the cradle.

The woman stood at the bureau, nude, pouring gin into a couple of glasses she'd filled with ice while the blonde man spoke into the telephone. She wasn't very tall, but the curve of her hips and the elasticity of her round, dark-nippled breasts made up for it. She brushed a strand of long, black hair away from her eyes as she pretended to ignore the telephone conversation. The name Martinez had a particular meaning for her. She recognized a strange indefinable pleasure in knowing Martinez had stymied the blonde man in some way.

"You've been mad long enough, Spanish. Have a drink and let me take your mind off of it—whatever it is." She returned to the bed, unconscious of the provocative roll of her hips. She stopped just short of him and reached out with the drink in her left hand.

Still scowling, the blonde man took the glass and drank about a third of it. "Stay out of it. It's nothing to do with you."

She walked to her side of the bed and climbed back into it, fluffing the pillows so she could lean against them comfortably. When she'd taken a taste of her gin, she looked at his back. "Don't be so sure, sugar. That was Luis Martinez you were talking about, right?" As she stared at his broad back, she saw the muscles tighten, as she'd expected them to. He treated all women as though they knew nothing. It pleased her to make him wrong in something. In anything.

"What if it is? He's got something of mine, and I've got to get it back. It's important."

"Of course, honey. Everything you do is important."

He turned to her, his eyes hot. "What do you know about it? This is man's business."

Her full, soft lips smiled. "Baby, would it interest you to hear that I used to know Luis Martinez?"

He looked at her, his eyes like shards of glass. "How did you know him?"

She ignored the look in his eyes, even though she knew from experience he would only take so much ragging before he lost his temper. For some reason she didn't care. "We had some laughs a few years ago before I left him."

"So you are not friends now?"

She gave him the full benefit of her large eyes, smiling sweetly into his face. "How could I be, sweetheart? I'm a one-man woman, and you're the man."

He nodded, interested in what she had to say. She enjoyed that. "But how well did you know him?" he asked.

"I got to know him real well, like I've gotten to know you, Santiago. I know where he goes, what he does when he gets there, and what he thinks while he's doing it. I could find him, if you made it worth my while." She sipped her gin to cover the look of calculation in her eyes.

Santiago blinked at her self-assurance, and for a moment he wondered if she was talking sense or just trying to rag him. "Do you think you could find him, even if he doesn't want to be found?" For once his words did not drip sarcasm. It was a message to her just how badly he wanted Martinez found. She liked to see desperation in him.

She nodded seriously. "If it's worth my while."

He returned her seriousness with interest. "All right, Jelly. Is ten grand enough?"

Jelly. She hated that name. She had once entered a bar while the jukebox blared "It must be jelly 'cause jam don't shake like that." After that, wherever she went she was Jelly. "Ten grand would be swell." And then you won't treat me like a dumb twist anymore. She hadn't realized until now how just much she hated him and everybody like him. She wanted to hurt him, to get away from him.

He drank his gin, examining her as though she was a different species of woman, somebody he hadn't met before. He patted the covers beside him. "Come here. Let us finish what we started before the telephone interrupted." He put his empty glass on the nightstand and took her by the arm, pulling her insistently to him.

She wasn't in the mood, but the game had changed for her. Everything she did from now on would be a blow she struck against him. The name Luis Martinez had reminded her of another life she'd had, a life she'd given up for reasons she could no longer remember.

Her face flattened and sparks began to jump in her eyes as she crawled into his lap. She grabbed his head savagely, raking the nails over his scalp. Santiago grunted in surprise and pain, tried to push her off. She twisted his head up and mashed her lips down on his, chewing on them with predatory abandon. He was startled by her strength, and his inability to shake her loose. As they struggled, the feel of her hot flesh in his hands distracted him from his worries. But it didn't dispel them. He was in trouble and he knew it.

⊗⊗⊗

The man called Dixie left the stifling booth and stood on the sidewalk, letting a cool breeze dry the sweat from his face and neck. He looked up into the darkness at the faint flickering of stars, and for a long moment he enjoyed his anonymity, and the feeling of complete freedom he knew at this moment.

He had freedom in the work he undertook, as well. Dixie Ray Chavez liked to think of himself as a bullet which stayed on course until the job was done. He had some mixed feelings about this job, however. He didn't like Santiago Compasso, not because the man was handsome, sophisticated, and powerful, but because Dixie Ray already knew he wasn't smart. The other man—now that was a different story. That was a man you could stick with, a man who knew which end was up. Compasso wouldn't last, but the other man would.

Dixie Ray took in a deep breath and let it out. He had tried to find Martinez in all the easy ways he knew, and nearly three weeks had gone by. Now it was time to put a more complicated plan in motion. He got into his car and drove away.

※

Uptown, a frail, white-haired man drummed his fingers on the desk in his study as he stared at the telephone. His watery blue eyes reflected both impatience and worry, but there was a grim determination on his lined face, as well.

The telephone bell broke the tense silence at last. He waited until it had rung twice before he slowly picked it up. "Yes?"

"Mr. Leake, I have your party. Go ahead, please." The operator spoke with impersonal courtesy.

"This is McCandless, Marston. What's so damned important that it couldn't wait another couple of days?" McCandless's voice was an impatient rasp.

"This *is* important, A. J.," Leake replied. "Treasury agents began crawling all over the bank yesterday. They're looking for counterfeit money. I thought I'd better tell you immediately."

McCandless was silent for a long moment. "Christ on the cross. Who else knows?"

"Right now, just you, me and the vault manager," Leake replied.

"Keep it that way. Make like it's something routine from the Federal Reserve."

"All right. What about you?"

"I'll be home when I planned. If I raced back, it might create an impression we'd find difficult to change."

Leake's eyes narrowed. "I see."

"Keep the lid on, Marston. Keep it on good and tight. I'm depending on you."

"All right, A. J. Whatever you say. Good night."

"Good night, Marston." McCandless hung up in the same decisive way he did everything else.

Leake replaced the telephone receiver in the cradle then sat there thoughtfully, fingering his chin.

Chapter 1

Wednesday, September 4, 1940

Sergeant Israel Daggett of the Negro Detective Squad got out of the passenger side of his Dodge police cruiser and walked up to the red-brown young man who stood in the open door of a large two-story frame house. He wore a carefully trimmed mustache that little disguised his youth and a stylish Wilton fedora tipped over his right ear.

"Hiya, Park. Tell us what you got."

Park showed Daggett a lopsided grin. "The housekeeper come in this morning, found the back door unlocked. She went inside and began lookin' around. That's when she discovered the body. She pitched such an ing-bing it brought some of the neighbors a-runnin'. Lady next door's the one who called us."

Detective Sam Andrews came up behind Daggett. "Give us the tour, Eddie."

The wide-shouldered young cop led the two detectives inside to the staircase. Andrews stared, shaking his head. "Damn. This place looks like a cyclone hit it broadside."

Daggett looked but said nothing as he continued up the stairs behind Park.

Park paused at the open door to the upstairs parlor. He turned to the older men, his face stiff. "In there, boss. It's bad—real bad."

Daggett walked through the open door with Andrews on his heels. What he saw stopped him.

"Sweet Jesus." Andrews's voice was a harsh whisper.

Daggett picked his way through the debris, stepping around the corpse. He went to the window and opened the drapes, then stepped back. A rectangle of early morning sunlight fell across the dead woman's body like a pale shadow. She had been stripped naked, then bound hand and foot to a wooden armchair with strips of her underwear. Dead eyes blared from her face and her jaw line was lumpy with contorted muscle. Her hands were clenched fists.

Nearly two dozen burns were visible all over her light brown body. The worst of them had bled, leaving strings of dried blood down her skin. The smell of burnt meat hung in the air like the dregs of a nightmare.

Daggett knelt, looking at her hands, checking the rigidity of her muscles with his fingers. "Been dead a while now. Skin's cooled off." He cupped a hand around one of her heels and lifted the foot off the floor. The sole was like a slab of raw ham. He winced, shaking his head.

"Looks like this is what he used on her." Park pointed to an electric steam iron propped on its end. "Some of those burns are shaped just like the point on this thing."

"Whoever did this wanted somethin' from her," Andrews said. "She probably croaked before he could get her to talk, which is why he tore the house to pieces. The question is what did he want?"

Daggett turned to the younger officer. "Do we know who she is, Eddie?"

"Driver's license in her purse says Linda Blanc."

Andrews' head snapped up. "You remember her, Iz. She ran with Straight-Flush Henry Alford's gang in the early '30s. She was just a joy gal in those days." He looked around the room, taking in the furnishings. "She's come up in the world since then."

"Yeah, but where would she get this kind of money?"

A new voice spoke. "Invite me in, maybe I can suggest a theory."

Daggett turned to a lanky white man in his middle forties. "What brings you to a homicide, Agent Ewell?"

"One of my guys caught the squeal and recognized the address," he replied. Paul Ewell was the Chief Resident Treasury Agent, and Daggett had worked with him before. "We've been keeping an eye on Miss Blanc because she's involved with a counterfeiting ring we're investigating."

Daggett frowned as he stroked his chin. "Involved how? Her rap sheet is a string of prostitution beefs and other penny-ante stuff."

Ewell stepped into the room a bit farther, his eyes dispassionately examining the dead woman. "Her connection to the gang is more personal than criminal. She's the girlfriend of a man named Luis Martinez. Know him?"

"Sure. He used to be head of a bootlegging mob. Dropped out of sight after they repealed the liquor law. I haven't heard of him for a while."

"He's been in and out of New Orleans for the past six or seven years," Ewell said. "We kept tabs on him because we never got enough evidence to jail him during Prohibition. But word came through informants earlier this year that he was recruiting talent for a counterfeiting mob."

"That's a new wrinkle for Martinez," Andrews said.

Ewell turned a thoughtful gaze on the trio of negro detectives. "This case is trickier than any I've seen. Martinez was hard to track, but he's been seen or reported in places as far apart as Dallas and Atlanta."

"Doing what?"

"In Memphis a master engraver named Hardesty disappeared after a visit from Martinez. In Birmingham it was a chemist named Appleyard. In Atlanta a printer named Stevenson. And there are others. A crack crew of phony money guys all visited by Martinez." Ewell shook his head, and his eyes took on a troubled look. "We've been getting some strange whispers in this investigation, Daggett. Hints that this gang is bigger, better organized, and better led than any we've seen before. Phony bills have turned up in most of the major banks in the South and Southeast. The engraving technique is so good that the Bureau of Engraving and Printing is jealous. And the paper is good enough to fool ninety-seven percent of the people who touch it. We don't know how much of it's in the currency pool already."

"I wouldn't think they could find paper good enough to fool bank employees," Daggett said. "Only one company makes it, and they don't sell it to anybody but Uncle Sam."

"Like I said, this gang is different. It's made up of experts good enough to analyze Treasury ink and paper and come up with something that can pass muster most of the time. Or maybe they're getting it from outside the country."

"You said the bills are turnin' up all over the South. That mean here, too?" Andrews asked.

Ewell poked out his lip and shook his head. "For some reason we haven't worked out, no. We find that especially interesting." Ewell pushed his hat back off his forehead and stared down at the body again. "This entire case is outside my experience. Most counterfeiters are small-time, passing the money a few bills at a time. But this time, we're finding it in significant amounts in banks insured by the Federal Deposit Insurance Corporation." He flicked a glance at Daggett. "What I'm telling you is in the nature of secret information. It can't leave this room."

"Okay," Daggett said. "We can keep our mouths shut but what about this woman? Why is she dead?"

Ewell shook his head. "I have no idea, but counterfeiters are among the most ruthless of criminals. This gang may have pumped tens of thousands into the economy already. When that kind of money is at stake, people have a funny way of turning up dead."

※

Later that afternoon, Wesley Farrell got out of a maroon 1940 Packard Victoria in front of a cocktail lounge called The Sunset Limited near the corner of Magazine and Washington Avenues. He found the lounge was dim and cool, a pleasant change from the late summer heat. He looked about until he saw a leathery sun-tanned man in red suspenders behind the bar.

"Hey, Wes. Long time, no see, man." He stuck out a hand and caught Farrell's in a firm grip.

"Damn, Sunset Breaux. You haven't aged a day in ten years. What've you been up to, old timer?"

"Mindin' my own business, what else? I ain't as spry as I used to be."

"Who is? So what's on your mind? You said you were trying to help somebody on the phone."

"Yeah. He's sittin' in that booth back there. Let's go over and jawbone with him a minute, let him tell you what he's up to."

Sunset led Farrell to where a frail-looking Negro sat in a leather-upholstered booth. As they drew nearer, Farrell recognized that he was dressed in the vestments of a Josephite priest. The man looked at them expectantly, but didn't get up from his seat. As he drew closer, Farrell saw that the priest's right leg was canted out at an angle beneath the table, bound in a heavy metal brace.

"Father Maldonar? This is Wes Farrell, the guy I told you about. Wes, this is Father James Maldonar."

"It's kind of you to come all this way. Please forgive me for not rising." Maldonar spoke in a high, precise voice, and appeared to be somewhere in his thirties. He squinted painfully at Farrell through a pair of steel-rimmed spectacles as he held out a hand to Farrell.

Farrell took it gently, noting when he did that there were irregular patches of pink skin on his wrist, and on his neck near the collar. "Pleased to meet you, Father." He and Sunset slid into the booth opposite Maldonar.

"Can I offer you a drink?" Maldonar asked. "I suspect you'd prefer something stronger than this." He gestured at a glass of milk in front of him.

Farrell smiled. "No thanks. It's a little early for me. What can I do for you?"

"Father Maldonar's tracking an old friend of ours, Wes," Sunset said. "I haven't seen him in years, but you were a lot closer to him than I was. Tell him, Father."

Maldonar took a sip of his milk. "I actually came to New Orleans to open a mission for the destitute. I named it St. Swithan's Mission and opened it at the river end of Joliet Street in the Uptown neighborhood. That has claimed most of my attention, but whenever I had a free moment, I've been looking for a man named Luis Martinez. I learned that many of his friends were gamblers and tavern keepers, so that is where I've concentrated my search." He paused to pat perspiration from his gleaming brown head, smiling apologetically. "I'm not used to the climate yet." Farrell noticed that lines of fatigue were sharply etched into the skin around his eyes.

Farrell scratched his head. "I haven't actually seen Luis in a while, Father. I don't even know where he is these days."

The frail priest sighed. "I've heard much the same from others of his friends. But nevertheless, it's important that I find him. You see, his mother is dying of lung cancer in El Paso, Texas, and is desperate to see him before she is gathered to God. She told one of my colleagues that New Orleans is the last place she had heard from him. Knowing that my mission is here, he contacted me and I began making inquiries."

Farrell nodded sympathetically. "That's tough. I can see why you're anxious to find him. There are some people I know who might be able to tell me things." Criminals, he was thinking. People a priest wouldn't know how to find. People like Luis. Like himself.

The priest's smile wiped some of the fatigue from his face. "That would be a great kindness, Mr. Farrell, a very great kindness. As you can see, I'm somewhat limited in my movements. I need most of my strength for the mission."

"Don't worry, Father James. If I can't find him myself, I'll find someone who knows how to reach him."

Maldonar placed a calling card on the table and pushed it to Farrell. "When you do, you can call that number, or you can visit the mission. I'd love to show it to you."

Farrell took the card and tucked it into his vest pocket. "I'd like that. Can I offer you a ride anywhere, Father?"

"Thank you, but no. Mr. Breaux promised to drive me uptown when his evening bartender comes in."

Farrell got up and offered his hand to the priest. "Take care of yourself, Father. I'll be back with you once I've heard something. Good seeing you, too, Sunset. I'll see you around."

"God bless you for your time and hospitality, Mr. Farrell. I hope we'll speak again soon." Maldonar took Farrell's hand and shook it lightly.

Sunset Breaux got up and saw him to the door. "I hope I did right by callin' you, Wes. The poor li'l guy was so beat down that I figured he needed some real help."

"Forget it, Sunset. Luis was like a brother to me once. I'm glad to do it. Keep your nose clean, okay?"

"I hear you, pardner. So long."

As Farrell returned to his car, he didn't remember Luis Martinez ever speaking about family, but then the Luis Martinez he'd known had been a crook, and an unsentimental one, at that. Farrell had met Martinez when the two of them worked for a rum-runner named Monk Radecker during the early 1920s. By then, Farrell knew his way around, but he'd recognized in Martinez a person to watch, and to emulate. Martinez wasn't a showy crook, but rather a patient, watchful, and cautious man, one who knew when to fight, when to avoid trouble, and when to back away from something he couldn't lick. He had the kind of brains that criminals rarely have, the kind that keep you alive, out of jail, and with enough money to last beyond the next week.

When the Radecker gang fell apart in the mid-'20s, Martinez had taken Farrell along to begin a new operation. Farrell supplied the muscle and Martinez the brains. Martinez treated Farrell like a younger brother, and a genuine affection grew between them. He often referred to Farrell as "kid," or "*chivato,*" Spanish for "kid" or more precisely, "young goat," which Farrell thought was as much a gibe at his womanizing as his youth. Martinez went about his work with a light heart, often singing Mexican love songs such as "Cielito Lindo."

Farrell had learned a lot from Martinez, eventually enough to split off and begin smuggling liquor on his own. He'd only seen his old partner a dozen times since 1927, and at each juncture, Martinez had had some kind of new racket, and had been doing well with it. Despite that diminishing contact, the affection between them remained firm.

Farrell looked at the clock in his dashboard. It was nearing 7:00. Savanna was still in Havana looking over some nightclubs they'd visited on their last trip. They were considering a semi-permanent move there, and had decided that a nightclub in Havana would add to their income while they resided there.

He drove with his left arm propped in the open window as he thought of her. Without her around, his evenings had been a bit empty, and he felt an old restlessness stirring his blood. He continued Downtown in the waning daylight, thinking how good it would be to see old Luis again.

❧

At that moment, Luis Martinez was in a Negro tavern on the highway just outside Gretna on the west bank of the Mississippi River. He was beat, having been on the move almost constantly for weeks in order to dodge anyone Compasso might send after him. He missed Linda. There were things he wanted to tell her, but he'd decided to keep them to himself for the meantime. There was no need in upsetting her until he needed to.

Martinez was almost fifty, a sturdily built man a couple of inches under six feet in height. He was a Texan by birth, a mixture of Mexican, Indian, and Negro that they called *mestizo* in old Mexico. His looks were exotic, but even in the Deep South, he managed to go unchallenged into most establishments on either side of the color line.

The tavern, called Handsome Alvin's, was no shabbier than most of the other juke joints in that part of the world. Leaving his dark green Mercury coupé out front, he'd come into the bar and ordered a double bourbon before asking for the phone. With the bourbon in his hand, he went into the booth, dropped his nickel, and asked the operator for Linda's number. A man answered.

"Who's this?" Martinez asked, perplexed. "Is Linda there?"

"Who's calling?" the man asked, ignoring both of Martinez's questions.

"Never mind who I am. Put Linda on the phone."

"Sorry. She can't come to the telephone. If you'll give me your name and number, I'll—"

Martinez hung up the telephone quickly as an icy ball began to form in the pit of his stomach. He drank the double shot in a single gulp, shivering as it hit bottom. When he had regained his composure, he fed another nickel into the telephone and asked for the number of a friend who owned a pawnshop on Rampart Street. Seconds later a man came on the line.

"Ozzy, it's Luis. Can you talk, man?"

Ozzy's voice was tense, fearful. "Where you at, Louie?"

"Listen, I just tried to call Linda a few minutes ago and a man answered. When I asked for her, he gave me a lot of who-struck-john. Do you know where she is?"

There was a tense moment of silence before Ozzy spoke. "Louie, you sittin' down? I kinda got some bad news."

"Bad news. Wait a minute—Linda, is she—is she—?"

"Get ready, Louie. It's bad. Somebody killed her last night. The old lady who keeps house for y'all knew I was a friend and called me. She didn't know how to reach you. Louie, you there?"

"Yeah—yeah. I—I'm here."

"Word is, Compasso set a hitter to lookin' for you, man. I don't know how he found out she was your woman, but I reckon he went there lookin' for you, and when he didn't find you, he tried to make her tell him."

Martinez's hand was aching from the grip he had around the telephone receiver, and tears had sprung to his eyes. My fault, he thought. All my fault. "Couldn't you of warned her, Ozzy? Jesus, we been friends for years. Why didn't you warn her, or warn me?"

Ozzy's voice was hurt. "By the time it came to me through the grapevine, it was too late."

Martinez wiped his damp eyes on the sleeve of his coat as he fought to regain his composure. "Jesus, Ozzy, Jesus."

"Look, you shoulda known he'd hit the roof when you copped the plates. You gotta give 'em back. Just send 'em to him by a messenger or somethin'. It's the only hope you got of stayin' alive."

"I—I dunno. I gotta think. I'm all broke inside."

"Don't talk foolish. This man's crazy—he'll kill you as soon as look at you."

Martinez blinked slowly. "No, I gotta think this through. All's I wanted was my fair share, and Compasso turned his back on me. I gotta think, then I'll call you back." Without waiting for Ozzy to reply, he hung the receiver back into the cradle. He sat there in a daze for several moments before he realized somebody was tapping at the glass door. He turned and pushed the door open.

"Hey, brutha, you all right in there? If you're tired, go on home, 'stead of fallin' asleep in my phone booth. Come on outa there, now." The bartender offered a hand and he took it, pulling himself out of the booth.

"Sell me a bottle, will ya? A quart of I. W. Harper, if ya got it." His voice sounded hollow and desperate in his ears, like it was crying out from a far distance.

The bartender looked at him skeptically. "Promise you'll go straight home?"

Martinez's face felt frozen, but he managed a tight smile. "Ain't got no home, but I'll find a room somewhere. Here's five for the bottle—you keep the change."

The Negro scratched his bristly scalp then he nodded, leading Martinez back to the bar. He handed an unopened bottle of bourbon across to Martinez. "I don't wanna hear 'bout you wrappin' your car around no light pole, you hear?"

"Yeah. Thanks, pal." Martinez took the bottle then walked back out to his car. Linda had been with him when he'd bought the Mercury. That had been a big day for them. Linda and Louie out on the town, raisin' hell, livin' big, makin' sweet love. Now all that was gone, and it was his fault. He should've known Compasso would send someone who'd do what it took to find him. There was nothing to do but stay alive long enough to make it right. He got into the new Mercury then drove toward the ferry slip in Algiers.

⊗⊗⊗

In a darkened room across the river, a man sat in the shadows as he stared out the window at the masthead lights of a freighter making its way downstream toward the mouth of the Mississippi. He had much on his mind today. He had put a very complicated plan into effect and had gradually watched it come to fruition. Now all was in jeopardy because of one man's arrogance.

As he stared at the lights passing in front of him, the telephone rang. He reached across the desk for the receiver. "Yes." His voice was deep, assured, the voice of a man who had control of things.

"It's Dixie Ray Chavez, sir."

"Good evening. Have you any news?"

"Nothing concrete. I found Martinez's woman. It took a bit of lookin'. He had her in a house leased under a phony name."

The man smiled. "I won't ask how you located her. I know you have your ways."

"Yes, sir. It was solid gold, but there's a hitch. Either she didn't know where Martinez and the plates are, or she was just too tough. She had the misfortune to die while I was conversing with her."

The man said nothing for a moment. "That's a bit of a setback, wouldn't you say?"

"Some, but not a big one. Martinez has three friends in New Orleans. I'm bettin' he'll go to one of 'em for help, sooner or later."

"I see. Who are the friends?"

"There's a fence named Theron Oswald who does some business with Compasso. He runs a pawnshop down on Rampart. He's a low-down, yellow, lyin' skunk, but he and Martinez been friends for years."

"That's one. Who's number two?"

"Ever hear of a fella named Wes Farrell? He's a gambler, owns a nightclub on Basin with a French name I can't never remember."

The man thought for a moment. "The Café Tristesse. It means the sad café. A peculiar name for a place of merriment. Yes, I have heard of him. He was involved in a rather spectacular fracas in St. Bernard last year."

"He's the one. If Martinez gets crowded too hard by the other people Compasso's got after him, my money says he'll go to Farrell."

"And number three?"

Dixie Ray laughed. "I'm backin' this one as a long shot. It's Miss Jelly Wilde, Compasso's li'l friend."

The man's eyes narrowed. "Why would she help Martinez?"

"You ever watched her with Compasso?"

"No, not really. Nor would I think you have. You're a man of the shadows, not cocktail parties."

"That's true, but a few times I've visited Spanish and watched her where she couldn't see me. She hates that boy's guts and he's too dumb to see it. I found out the other day that she was Martinez's li'l friend a few years back. Could be she might decide to lend him a hand. Women are funny, man. They'll love your ears off one day and slit your throat the next."

The man in the office cleared his throat. "I'll have to take your word for that. How will you watch these three people? There's only one of you."

"Have faith, pardner. I'll find a way." He hung up without waiting for a comment.

The man looked out the window and saw that the ship had passed. Time was also passing, and with each moment he felt opportunity slipping past. He needed a miracle. It seemed absurd that so much was riding on a person with the unlikely name of Dixie Ray Chavez.

Chapter 2

The bells at Holy Ghost Catholic Church were chiming midnight when Wesley Farrell crossed the threshold of a bordello two blocks off Louisiana Avenue on Annunciation. In the parlor, two teenaged brownskin whores were perched on the laps of two tipsy longshoremen, honey talking them, promising them a trip around the world in the cute little rooms upstairs.

A short, bespectacled Negro in a collarless shirt and vest stepped out from behind a partition and confronted Farrell. Farrell smiled at him. "Howdy, Oliver. Is Miss Carolina around?"

Oliver pretended to peer owlishly at Farrell. The thick lenses he wore were window glass. It was a trick to make rambunctious visitors take a poke at him. In reality, he was an ex-featherweight boxer who'd retired from the ring with only two technical knockouts against him. At forty-six, he still punched like a mule-kick, and when that wasn't enough, the sap and .38 Owl's Head revolver hidden in his vest always tipped the balance.

"Evenin', Mist' Farrell. Miss Carolina's in her private room. Follow me." He turned and led Farrell through a couple of big rooms to the one Carolina used as a combination office and sitting room. When Oliver announced him, Carolina was sitting beside her pride and joy, a deluxe console model RCA Victor radio. As she fiddled with the tuning knob, Farrell heard a crackle of static, then the voice of an announcer at KFFA in Helena, Arkansas announced a live number by Pinetop Perkins.

"Sit down, honey," Carolina said without looking up. "I wanna hear Pinetop sing his new song."

Farrell put his hat on the coffee table and sat down on the sofa. When the last notes of the blues singer's lament faded, Carolina turned her attention to Farrell.

"Baby, you ain't been by here in one hell of a long time. Where you been at?" She took a Chesterfield from Farrell's proffered case, tucked it between her cushiony red lips then leaned over to get his light.

"I'm looking for Luis Martinez, Carolina. You heard from him lately?" He took a cigarette for himself and settled back on the sofa.

Carolina squinted at him. "Funny you should mention that name. He was hooked up with a gal used to work for me—name of Linda Blanc. Somebody kilt her last night."

Farrell blinked, rubbed his thumb along the side of his chin. "Killed how?"

"Way I heard it, somebody burnt her with a hot iron 'til her heart give out." The woman took another drag, shaking her shiny black curls at such cruelty.

"Anybody know why?"

Carolina wrinkled her snub nose. "Not that I know of, but things from a past you already forgot can sneak up and lay you out, baby."

"Uh, huh. What about Luis? Does he know?"

She shrugged. "Dunno. Luis's been up to somethin' the past year or so. He's in and outa town all the time. People in Memphis, Montgomery, Miami, they tell me Luis comes and goes through them places. Never for very long, but people see him, then they don't see him no more."

"That have anything to do with the death of his girlfriend?"

Again Carolina shrugged. "I hope not. He's gonna be tore up enough as it is."

Farrell nodded. Twice Savanna had been hurt on his account, and he well remembered what that had done to him. "If he's in trouble, it might be he could use a friend. Do you know anybody in the city who's seen or talked to him in the recent past?"

Carolina sucked on her cigarette while her eyes rolled thoughtfully. "You know Theron Oswald?"

"He's a fence—hot jewelry, gold coins—"

"And any other damn thing you can bring him. He's runnin' that old pawnshop 'crost from the Metro Hotel on Rampart. Him and Luis are tight."

"Thanks, Carolina. I'll give him a try tomorrow."

She gave him an appraising look. "Luis is in bad trouble. You gonna get him out?"

"Ask me when I know what the trouble is."

⌘

At that moment, a fat man named Max Grossmann was midway through a late-night snack of sirloin steak, baked potato with sour cream and chives, and a mountain of mushrooms and onion rings lightly fried in butter. He ate with vigor, pausing his knife-and-fork work to gulp Lowenbrau beer from a large crystal tankard.

As he ate, he read the evening *States-Item*, studying all of the news from the war in Europe and in the Far East. Grossmann was vice-president in charge of international investments at the First National Bank of New Orleans and was passionately interested in anything affecting the dollar value of different currencies. He had finished his snack and was considering a slice of Black Forest chocolate cake when his houseboy entered his dining room.

"Pardon me, Mist' Grossmann. There's a man on the telephone askin' to speak to you."

"At this hour? Who is it?"

"He wouldn't say, sir. Said it was important, though."

Cocking an eyebrow, Grossmann silently left the table for his study. He moved with a grace unusual in such an ungainly body. He closed the door to the study then went to the desk to pick up the receiver. "Hello?"

"If you recognize my voice, don't speak my name," a voice said into his ear. "The line might be tapped."

"I do recognize your voice. Why all the secrecy?"

"Are you aware that Treasury men have been all over the bank in the past couple of days?"

Grossmann pursed his lips. "Well, even in a bank as discreet as ours, rumors will make their way through the corridors. What brought them to us?"

"Counterfeit money."

Grossmann's chins quivered. "Did they find any?"

"No, but there was no reason they should."

Grossmann raised an eyebrow. "So why did they come?"

"They're going everywhere. Every bank in the city got the treatment. According to them, they haven't found a single bill in the city."

Grossmann sat down and cupped his large chin in his fleshy palm. "Well, I would think we have nothing to worry about then. We run a clean bank and take every precaution."

The other man was silent for a long moment. "They won't leave us alone, I'm afraid. Now that they've found money in the banks to the east of us, they'll be watching everyone like a hawk."

Grossmann settled his rump in the chair. "I think you worry too much. No one can point a finger at us or say anything against us."

"Don't ever let yourself become too complacent, my friend," the voice said. "Things have been pretty grim in this country for the past eleven years—nearly twenty if you count Prohibition. Don't get the idea that because we haven't got Nazis smashing the windows of Jewish storekeepers that it's been roses and moonlight, Max. A lot of money was made and a lot of it has blood on it. And bankers haven't always had clean hands."

Grossmann's eyes narrowed at that grim pronouncement, but he kept his tone light. "My, but you're in a mood tonight. Sometimes you think too much. If the Treasury people had anything against us, they'd have shut the doors and locked them by now. Go home, take a sleeping draught, and get into bed."

"You go to sleep, Max. I'll have all the time I need to sleep when I'm dead. I think I'll stay awake and worry some more. Someone needs to." Grossmann heard a metallic click as the other man hung up his receiver. After a moment, Grossmann put his own back into the cradle.

He continued to sit there for several minutes, his face slack as he thought back over the conversation. Finally he yawned, stretched and walked into the hall, calling down to the houseboy that he was through for the night and could go to bed. Grossmann trudged wearily to his own room and climbed into bed. He lay there in the dark, his eyes shining for ten or fifteen minutes before he closed them and drifted immediately into sleep.

∞

Earlier that evening Marcel Aristide sat in his office at the back of a small, quiet bordello at the river end of Soraparu Street that he ran for his cousin, Wesley Farrell. For once, however, he wasn't working. He had his coat off and his sleeves rolled up, his feet propped comfortably on the edge of the desk. The radio was on, and Charlie Christian was soloing on "I'm Confessin'." Music was Marcel's passion, and not even his cousin knew that his unrealized ambition was to be the boy singer with a swing band. He knew the lyrics to hundreds of love songs.

The song had just concluded when the door opened and a stocky, dark-brown negro named Fred Gonzalvo stuck his head inside. "Hey, boss. You busy?"

"Do I look busy?"

Fred grinned. "Just because you don't look busy don't mean you ain't. Don't forget, I know how much goes on inside your skull when you're sittin' quiet."

Marcel sat up and put his feet on the floor. "For once, you've caught me loafing. What's up?"

Gonzalvo eased through the door and shut it behind him. For once, his broad face had a serious expression. "Got a young sistuh out here. Says her name is Marta Walker. She's as cute as lace pants, boss."

Marcel shrugged. "What does she want?"

Fred made a face and scratched his bristly scalp. "Well, she wouldn't say, 'zactly. She said she'd heard that you helped people in trouble, and she's got trouble she needs help with. She ain't no hustler. Nice girl with manners, and cute as—"

"Yeah, I know, as lace pants." Marcel was torn between a laugh and a sigh. He'd gradually gained a stature in the community that clashed oddly with his relative youth. People who knew of his association with Farrell were already talking about him in the same hushed tones they used for his cousin. More than once, Marcel had entered a Negro juke joint or a gambling hall and discovered that people had paused to watch for what he might do. It was a persona he hadn't wanted, but had gradually accepted, along with the trouble it sometimes brought.

"Bring her in, Fred. And hang around afterwards, okay?"

Gonzalvo grinned and nodded appreciatively. He opened the door and went out, giving Marcel time to turn off the radio and roll down his shirtsleeves. As he was straightening his tie, the door opened and a woman of about twenty-two came in ahead of Fred. She was tall, maybe five-seven, with a lean, high-breasted figure and velvety skin the color of dark honey. She wore her light-brown hair loose to her shoulders and looked at him with large, deep black eyes. As he took her in, he had the insane urge to race around the room on all fours while he barked the lyrics to "Jingle Bells."

"Boss, this is Miss Marta Walker. This here's Mr. Aristide, Miss Walker."

Marcel cleared his throat. "Have a seat, Miss Walker." He gestured to a chair and held it while she sat. He then pulled the swivel chair away from the desk and sat down facing her. "Fred said you had trouble. You care to tell me about it?"

"It's very nice of you to see me," she said in a hesitant voice. "I'm not from around here."

"Uh, huh. Your accent sounds like it might have a little Texas in it."

"Why—why, yes. Brownsville, Texas. A gentleman there said when I got here that I should look you up."

Marcel rubbed his chin reflectively. "The only man I know in that neck of the woods is a lawyer named Herbert Alexander."

She nodded eagerly. "Yes, that's the man. After I told him my story, he mentioned his acquaintance with you. He told me some of the things you've done for others."

Marcel tried not to frown. He'd lent Herbert Alexander the money he needed to set up a practice in Brownsville after getting him out of some trouble with a local loan shark. He hoped that this little Texas belle didn't have the same kind of trouble. There wasn't much profit to be had in scaring off loan sharks.

"What did Herb think I could help you with, Miss?"

She dropped her eyes and her complexion deepened as blood came into her face. "I know I'm going to look like an awful little fool but—but I had to know."

"Know what?"

She looked up at him again. "There was a man."

"Uh, huh."

"I had some feelings for him. I—I thought he was returning them. Then—"

Marcel laced his fingers together over his flat stomach. "Then he ducked out on you?"

"Y-yes." She sniffed a couple of times, but she managed not to cry. "We weren't engaged or anything. But I thought things were going in that direction."

"So what's his name?"

She looked back up at him, trying to keep her composure. "Albert Chenier. He told me he was from a New Orleans Creole family."

"Chenier's a fairly common name in these parts. What else did he tell you about his family?"

"He said his father died when he was seventeen, and his mother passed away before that. Being an orphan seemed to make him sad, because he didn't talk about them very much."

"I know how he feels." Marcel's mother had died when he was very young, and his grief-stricken father had drunk himself to death. "What will you do if you find him, Miss Walker? Did he make any promises to you? Did he take anything from you when he left?"

She looked at her clasped hands. "It would be a lot easier if he had." She looked back up at him with that same determined expression. "I just want to know why he ran off without saying anything. I want to know if it was something I said or did. I—I really thought he cared for me."

Marcel's business self urged him to tell her to go back to Brownsville, but the romantic in him wanted to dry her tears and help her forget the faithless Albert. "Ummm, what makes you think that Albert came here?"

"You'll think I'm a terrible snoop."

"No, really. If we're going to find him, we've got to know for sure where he went."

"Well, I went to the bus station and the railroad station in Brownsville and asked around. I found out that he'd bought a one-way train ticket to Houston with a connection on the Sunset Limited to New Orleans. I had a photograph of Albert and the ticket agent remembered selling him the ticket."

"That's not bad gumshoeing. How long ago was this?"

"About three weeks ago now. It took me a while to find out where he'd gone. After that, I had to do some soul-searching before

I made up my mind to come after him. A friend who knew Mr. Alexander was from New Orleans sent me to him, and he told me how to get in touch with you."

"He sent you to this address?" Marcel felt his mouth pucker with chagrin.

"Well, he told me you ran a boarding house for young women," she explained. "He described this as the headquarters for your other businesses."

A chuckle escaped Fred's throat, and he coughed loudly to keep it from growing into a full-blown guffaw. Marcel raised his left eyebrow threateningly at his associate.

"Well, let's forget that for now," he said. "Do you know anything else about Albert? You have any idea where he might've lived or worked before Brownsville?"

"No. Like I said, he didn't talk much about the past. All I've got that might be of any help is this pair of snapshots I took once." She reached into her purse and removed a white envelope. From the envelope she shook out two four-by-six photos, which she handed to Marcel.

Marcel saw a sturdily built, light-skinned young man who might've been any age between twenty-five and thirty, with smooth hair, sharp, handsome features, and what some might think was a charming grin. He put them on the desk. "What can you tell me about his appearance that doesn't show in these photos?"

"Well, he's six feet tall—maybe a teeny bit more. His hair is dark brown and he's got a mole on the back of his neck that's hidden in the hairline. He's terribly smart, too, Mr. Aristide. I've never known anyone who seemed to know so much about so many things."

Marcel stroked his chin as he looked at her. "I can't promise you anything, but we'll take a stab at it. Where are you staying?"

"Mr. Alexander arranged a room for me at the Metro."

"Okay, we'll drop you off. If you get tired of hanging around the Metro, just leave word with the deskman where you'll be."

Her face glowed with gratitude. "Oh, thank you, Mr. Aristide. Mr. Alexander was right. You're ever so kind."

Fred cleared his throat and walked to the window to escape Marcel's withering look.

"Just leave it to us, Miss Walker. If Albert's in New Orleans, we ought to be able to find him." He wondered whether that was really true or not, but he liked her smile, and for now, that was sufficient.

⚌

Jelly Wilde braked her '38 De Soto convertible across the street from Maxwell's Chicken Shack on Derbigny Street. In spite of the corn-pone name, Maxwell's was a rather luxurious place, almost on par with the Sassafrass Lounge across town. It had the tall snow-white columns of Tara and large windows that let vast quantities of light out into the darkening street. She got out of the car, crossed the street, and entered the restaurant.

The place was so packed with diners that the murmur of voices and the tinkle of china all but drowned out the pianist at the far end of the room. She drifted to the bar, enjoying the attention of the diners she passed. She was wearing a royal blue cocktail dress that left one shoulder bare. A heavily boned bodice with a deep *decolletage* invited hungry stares at her dark gold skin.

She reached the bar and eased herself up on an upholstered stool. When she was comfortable, she opened her bag and removed a cigarette case, took a Pall Mall from it, and held it, waiting. A millisecond later, a bartender held a light in front of her. She smiled, accepting it as she looked at the bartender from under her thick lashes. "You're so kind. What's your name, sugar?"

The bartender, a good-looking tan-colored youngster in his early twenties, returned her smile. "Ricardo, ma'am. Can I get you a drink?"

"Scotch and soda, Ricardo. Light on the soda, please."

"Yes, ma'am." Ricardo's hands moved in a blur and in about forty-five seconds he slid the drink in front of her on a paper napkin.

"Ummm." She made a pleased sound in her throat as she tasted it. "You have good hands, Ricardo. Tell me, have you worked here long?"

"Four years, about. It's a good place to work. You get to meet a lot of interesting people." As he spoke, he looked upon Jelly with unbridled admiration.

"A friend of mine—Luis Martinez—told me about it."

Ricardo nodded. "I've met him a few times. He's a friend of the boss, Mr. Maxwell."

Jelly knew this already, but pretended ignorance. "Well, let me tell you of a problem I have. I have something that belongs to Mr. Martinez that he forgot the last time I saw him. He must not have missed it yet, or perhaps thinks he lost it. I'd like to get in touch with him, that is if he's in town."

Ricardo's wistful expression told that he'd switch places with Luis Martinez in a second. "Well, ma'am, I haven't spoken to Mr. Martinez, but the boss may have."

"Why don't you ask him? I'll wait right here."

That suited Ricardo just fine. He nodded and disappeared down to the end of the bar and went through a door. He returned in about a minute and a half behind an older man with bold, hawkish features.

"I'm Jim Maxwell. I own this place."

Jelly reached out a hand and let Maxwell take it. "I'm pleased to meet you. This is a very nice place."

"Thank you, Miss—"

"Green. Ella Green. I'm an old friend of Luis's."

"Really. I don't remember ever hearing Louie mention you, but I know he gets around a lot."

"Well, I know him from Miami. This is my first time up here. I remembered him talking about your restaurant, and thought I might find him here."

"Well, I'm sorry to say he's not. I doubt if he'd be in on this particular night anyhow."

Jelly's pleasant smile didn't waver. "This night? I don't get you."

Maxwell's eyes burned in his dark brown face. "If you haven't seen him lately, you wouldn't know he's been with a woman named Linda Blanc for a while. I heard on the radio today that she was killed last night."

Jelly had been through a lot, and the hardness of those words wasn't quite enough to jar her pleasant expression loose. "I'm terribly sorry. Was she a friend of yours, too?"

"Yes, she was. You'll have to excuse me now. I've got work to do. He bowed his head in a quick gesture then turned on his heel to go.

Jelly inhaled on her cigarette and blew the smoke out in a long stream from between her pursed lips. She turned her head and saw Ricardo staring at her, and recognized the look. She had seen it enough times to be amused by it. "Well, I suppose I should be going. What do I owe you?"

"Nothing, ma'am. Nothing at all."

"You're very kind. Maybe I'll see you again one day."

Ricardo beamed at her. "I hope so, Miss Green."

She returned his smile as she slipped off the barstool and walked toward the entrance.

As she got into the De Soto, she thought about what she'd been told. Maxwell had said Linda Blanc had been killed. He didn't say it was an accident. She put the key into the ignition and started the car. She thought about that for a couple of minutes before she put the car into gear and drove away from the restaurant.

Chapter 3

Luis Martinez had been on the dodge for more than a month, visiting people in outlying parishes as he dodged Compasso's men. He'd known at the outset that so long as Compasso had a stockpile of counterfeit bills, there would be no parlay. But it had gone beyond a simple disagreement over money now. Compasso had found the only thing in the world that mattered to him, and had destroyed it. Ownership of the plates and splits held no meaning now.

He elected to go to a dumpy rooming house at Thalia and Magazine Streets because it was the last place anyone would think to look for him. He left the ferry at the foot of Canal, driving southwest toward the lower Garden District. He drove slowly, eyes sticky with fatigue as he fought off successive waves of grief.

It took him a half-hour to reach the neighborhood he sought. He was tempted to park his car at some distance, but he'd switched his Louisiana license plates with those from an Arkansas truck he'd found abandoned along U. S. 90. He decided to trust them a bit longer, leaving the Mercury on the street as he trudged wearily inside with his suitcase.

The atmosphere of the interior was redolent with the odors of cheap perfume, unwashed bodies, and defeat. The lobby furniture dated from Grant's second term, all of it sagging from the combined weight of too many shabby losers.

The front desk was surrounded by a wire cage. In the cage, under a single electric bulb, sat a reedy, sallow man. He looked up from an issue of *Ranch Romances* and eyed Martinez with contemptuous disregard.

Martinez put his suitcase on the floor. "Need a room."

"Five bucks—in advance."

Martinez knew he was being grossly overcharged, but he didn't care. He thumbed a five from his wallet and shoved it through the screen. The clerk took it and dropped it into a drawer. He opened the register and held up a pencil. "Name?"

"Palermo. Anselmo Palermo. Address, Hotel Ponce de Leon, St. Petersburg, Florida."

The clerk dutifully wrote down the information, then reached under the desk and came back out with a threadbare towel and washcloth, a piece of Ivory soap, and a room key. "Upstairs, fourth door on the left. We don't allow no cookin' in the rooms, no women in the rooms, and no drinkin' in the rooms."

"Is it okay if I sleep in it?"

The clerk snorted contemptuously, slapped the register shut, and went back to his pulp magazine. Martinez hefted his suitcase and trudged up the stairs.

Inside the room, he dumped the suitcase onto the bed, opened it, and removed the bottle of whiskey he'd bought in Gretna and a Colt .38 Super automatic pistol. He put the pistol on the nightstand before removing his coat, necktie, and shoes. Tearing the foil off the neck of the bottle with his teeth, he drew the cork and took a long pull at the bourbon. It felt good going down, but it couldn't dull the pain gnawing at him. That would be with him forever.

He lay down on the lumpy bed and put his forearm over his eyes. He wanted to sleep, but he was scared and angry and sick of running. *You brought all this on yourself, you stupid necio,* he thought.

He took another pull at the bottle, feeling the alcohol begin to numb his body. He wanted to weep for Linda, but he felt like a brittle husk left behind in an autumn field. Maybe it was better this way. If he started weeping, he might not be able to stop.

Goddamn. How was it possible for things to be such a fucking mess?

⁜

As midnight gave way to early morning, Farrell found himself on Rampart Street where the night sky was firmly held at bay by the flickering of countless neon signs. Music leaked from a hundred doors—maudlin blues laments, raucous Dixieland, sweet, hot jazz. The center of New Orleans was beating like a healthy heart, and the death of a Negro woman in Gentilly meant little or nothing to the teeming life of Rampart Street.

Farrell moved silently through the crowd, his eyes glowing in that peculiar way from the shadow of his hat brim. Occasionally someone felt the feral quality emanating from him and stepped to the side, hurriedly dragging a companion from Farrell's path. Some recognized him and furtively whispered his name to others.

He paused beneath a red and yellow neon sign in the shape of a top-hatted crawfish leaning negligently against a martini glass, then turned and stepped inside in a single fluid motion. It was late, but the juke joint known as the Happy Crawdad always had a crowd, some of which were dancing to the big Wurlitzer jukebox while others crowded the bar or made cow-eyes at their dates. It was a Negro joint, and always had been, but Farrell had been in there so many times that he'd become an accepted part of the background.

Farrell made his way across the crowded room to a table at the back where a dark-brown giant sat at a table with a chessboard. He was considering a move for the black knight when Farrell pulled out the chair opposite him and sat down.

"Brutha, you're out on the town kinda late tonight, ain't you?" said the man, still fingering his knight.

"I got restless," Farrell replied. "Who are you playing tonight, Little Head? Capablanca or one of those mad Russians?"

"American. William Ewart Napier."

"Never heard of him."

Little Head Lucas looked up with a grin. "You never heard of Capablanca neither, till I told you about him. It's too late for heavy drinkin'. How's about a couple of Mex beers?"

"As long as they give me a lime with it," Farrell said, making a face.

Little Head Lucas snapped his fingers, caught the attention of one of his waiters, and told him to bring two Dos Equis and a dish of lime wedges. He was back with a loaded tray about two minutes later. Farrell took a long drink, then bit into the lime.

"Ahhh. I'm feeling human again. Thanks, pardner."

"*Por nada* as they say south of the border. What's up, man?"

Farrell wiped beer foam from his lips with a napkin. "Heard about Linda Blanc?"

The big man nodded. "That kind of news travels fast. I bet even her man knows by now."

"I'm looking for Luis. You heard anything about him lately?"

Little Head drank about half his beer then sucked the pulp from a lime wedge. As he chewed the pulp, he nodded. "Ain't talked to him, only talked to other folks who talked to him. They say he's movin' 'round a lot, that he's up to his armpits in some racket."

"Anybody know what kind?"

"Nope." Little Head picked up the black knight and countered a white pawn that had crept within striking distance of the black king. "But he's mixed up with some ofays, so they say."

Farrell caught the note in his friend's voice and sat there quietly, listening, letting Little Head Lucas get to it in his own way.

"One of the ofays is Santiago Compasso."

Farrell nodded. "I've heard of him. He used to be in Miami."

"Was, but he killed one crooked politician too many and had to leave."

"So what would Luis Martinez be doing with Compasso? Compasso's a drug smuggler. Luis wouldn't touch that with a ten-foot pole. Besides, he's an organizer, a guy you go to when you've got something complicated you want done."

Little Head nodded solemnly. "I can't say what Luis was doin' with the man, but Linda could'a only been killed for two reasons."

Farrell drank some beer, bit into the lime while he thought that over. "To find out where Luis is, or send him a message."

"Maybe both. If Luis and Compasso done had a fallin' out, Compasso ain't the kind to kiss and make up. He won't stop 'til Luis is a corpse."

Farrell shook his head. "I can't see Luis getting jammed up like this. It's not like him. When he takes a risk, it's because he's holding good cards."

Little Head grunted. "Are you tellin' me you never lost a hand when you had good cards? Unless the hand's four aces, there's always somethin' can beat it." Little Head finished his beer in a single long draught, sucked the juice of another piece of lime, then snapped his fingers at the waiter and motioned for two more beers.

Farrell drummed his fingers lightly on the table. "Whoever Compasso sent after Luis must know quite a bit about him, about where he's likely to go. Linda Blanc was just the first stop."

"Uh, huh. And that means you, brutha. You and Luis was pretty close. That paints a target on your back."

Lucas stopped talking when the beer arrived, staring across the table at his friend.

Farrell grew sober as he watched Little Head grab a fresh bottle and drink from it. "I've been trying not to think about that."

"You're slippin', brutha. To stay alive, you got to hear the jive. Lotta the guys you and Martinez was friendly with in Prohibition days are dead or in jail. How many people could he turn to if somebody was hot on his trail?"

Farrell shook his head. "I heard that he was friends with Theron Oswald. But you're right, there aren't many left from the old days he could go to."

"I might know somebody that the killer might not know. Somebody who was close to Linda."

Farrell cocked an eyebrow, his attention riveted on the big man. "I'm listening."

"A woman named Wisteria Mullins. She runs a place across the river called Wisteria's Riverboat Lounge."

"Uh, huh."

"She's Linda's first cousin. Grew up together in St. Francisville. They was more like sisters than cousins. Wisteria'd know where Luis might hole up, if anybody would."

Farrell felt himself become restless. He took a drink from the fresh beer. "The longer Luis is out there, the sooner he's gonna run out of places to hide."

"You gonna drift across the river, maybe?"

Farrell got up from the table. "That's me you see on the boat. I'll check you later."

"Walk soft, my friend."

"Always." Farrell laid a hand on Little Head Lucas's broad shoulder, gave it a squeeze as he walked to the door.

◈◈◈

After they dropped Marta Walker at the Metro Hotel and asked manager Arthur Bordelon to look after her, Marcel and Fred began to make the rounds of places where information could be had. Eventually they made it across town to Mama Lester's Homestyle Bar and Grill. Although it was barely into the evening, there was a crowd inside, playing the games hustlers play when they don't have jobs. For once, bartender Harvey Prado was hard at work rather than jiving some chick.

"What's goin' on, Harvey?" Marcel asked.

Harvey looked up from his inventory sheet. "Evenin', Mr. Aristide, Fred. Get y'all a beer or somethin'?"

"Thanks anyway, Harvey. We're looking for somebody."

Harvey shrugged. "Only just got busy. Who y'all lookin' for?"

"Guy named Smoker Cauvin. He wears dark glasses."

"Yeah, he's here someplace—" Harvey quickly scanned the room. "There—over by the juke box."

"What's he drinkin'?"

"Four Roses with Pabst Blue Ribbon chasers."

"Let us get over there, then bring him another round. Anything for you, Fred?"

"Pabst sits right in my stomach."

"Two extra Pabsts, Harvey. Give us a minute." Marcel drifted from the bar, Fred shambling in his wake.

Smoker Cauvin might have seen them coming. It was hard to tell with the dark glasses. He was smoking, as usual, his expressionless face wreathed in blue smoke.

"Takin' the day off, Smoker?" Marcel asked.

"A person in my position never takes the day off, man. Even if I ain't workin', I'm thinkin' about work, thinkin' about what I gotta do to get more bread in my pocket. Time is money, you dig?"

"Uh, huh." Marcel pulled up a chair, and Fred pulled up another, turning it around and straddling it. He studied Smoker Cauvin, saying nothing.

The beers and shot of Four Roses suddenly arrived on a tray and there was no talk while Harvey doled out the drinks. After he left, Smoker raised the shot of whiskey to his mouth and downed it. "Mighty kind of you, brutha. Now what you want, anyhow?"

"You're related to the Cheniers, aren't you?"

Smoker picked up his beer and drank a swallow as he looked in Fred's direction. "You lookin' to turn this moose loose on some of my relatives, Marcel?"

"Uh-uh. No strong-arm stuff. Just want to talk. To a certain Chenier."

"They ain't but about two hundred of the fuckahs 'round here. Which certain one you have in mind?"

"Albert. He's been living in Texas, if that helps you."

Smoker drank some beer, his brow furrowed above the rims of the dark glasses. "Albert Chenier. Can't say that I've heard tell of him. Might be one or two I ain't met."

"Could you ask the ones you know if they've got a cousin or a brother by that name in from Texas?"

"Might be I could. Like I say, time is money, Marcel."

Marcel took out a roll of bills, peeled off a five, and slid it across the table. The man's hand captured and stowed it with remarkable economy of motion.

"I'll get started on it tonight. You still operatin' outa that cathouse on Soraparu Street?"

"Yeah, but if I'm not there, somebody'll take a message."

"I'll be back with you, brutha. And thanks for the drink. Liquor does wonders for my thought processes."

"Any time at all." Marcel got up and Fred followed.

They drifted through the crowd, nodding occasionally to a familiar face, taking note of newer ones they didn't recognize. Fred eased up to his elbow and spoke into his ear. "You think that spook's gonna do you any good?"

Marcel shrugged. "When you're lookin' for somebody, you just keep movin'. You buy a drink here, lay a finif down there. It's an investment. Sooner or later it pays off. If not directly, then sometime down the line."

They had nearly reached the door when a man they knew approached them.

"Hey, Aristide. They tellin' me you need a Chenier."

"That's right, Harley. One who calls himself Albert."

Harley's muddy eyes slid from side to side beneath his pulled-down hat, his thin lips drawn into a narrow line. "There was an Albert Chenier who was up in Angola 'til maybe ten years or so back."

Fred's eyes narrowed. "How would you be knowin' that?"

Harley's eyes did their side-to-side again. "Used to run with him. Did some bootleggin', some penny-ante shit."

Marcel studied Harley's narrow face intently. "How'd he end up in Angola? I don't recall you did any time."

Harley's thin lips cracked open and he licked them with a long, pale tongue. "Didn't. His luck was bad. We was runnin' a con out in the sticks. He got caught. I didn't."

"Didn't rat on you, huh?"

Harley shook his head. "They didn't come no squarer than Albert. He kept his lip buttoned and took the fall. They give him seven to ten up there at hard labor, too."

"So where is he now?"

"Dead." Harley's gaze was bleak and he shook his head with a weary chagrin. "He was out with a chain gang choppin' cane one day. Got into a beef with another con. Con cut his head damn near off, they tell me."

"Whew." Marcel shook his hand as though he'd touched something hot. "That's tough, man. I'm sorry as hell."

Harley blinked and shook his head. "Yeah, me, too."

Fred scratched his head. "Couldn't be our man."

Marcel's eyes were thoughtful, but he shook his head. "No, not at all. Thanks just the same, Harley."

"Forget it. See y'all around, hear?"

Fred and Marcel walked outside and stood on the gallery of the lounge as a cool evening breeze swept past them from the north. Fred pulled his hat down low over his eyes.

"Funny story Harley told. The only Albert Chenier we've heard about all day long, and he ain't got no more in common with the one we're lookin' for than I got with Pres'dent Roosevelt."

"Yeah," Marcel said. "Funny is the word."

⊗≋⊗

Daggett and Andrews were nearing the end of a frustrating day. Their canvas of Linda Blanc's neighborhood had been a bust, and Nick Delgado's sweep of the murder scene picked up nothing useful. They'd spent the afternoon questioning known associates of the dead woman with no more profit. It was now three hours past the end of their normal day watch, and their rumpled clothes were stuck to their sweaty skins.

"What's next on the list, boss?" Andrews asked as he skillfully took the Dodge through evening traffic.

"This is tougher than I expected. I figured an ex-prostitute with her associations might lead us to somebody who'd know more about her business."

"Somebody taught her somethin' about keeping her business to herself," the stocky man replied. "Nobody we talked to even knew she was hooked up with Luis Martinez."

Daggett had no comment to that. He continued to stare into the darkness while he tapped his fingers restlessly on the ledge of the open car window. Finally, he said, "I'm dead beat. Take us to the Fat Man Lounge. I'll call into the office and we can have a beer before we go home."

"I like your thinkin', boss." Andrews took Napoleon Avenue up as far as Saint Charles then headed in the direction of Lee Circle. He turned across the streetcar tracks at Clio Street to drive several blocks before bringing the car to a stop in front of the lounge. The two big brown men got out of the car and strolled through the door as they shook the wrinkles out of their pants. It was early yet, and the place contained only a handful of male customers and a couple of bored working girls.

The detectives approached the bar and gave a wave to the big black man busily polishing glasses with a bar towel.

"Evenin', Big Boy," Daggett said.

"Iz, Sam. Long time no see. What'll it be?"

"Two Dixies," Daggett said as he eased a hip over a barstool. He and Andrews both leaned their forearms on the bar as they waited for the beer.

As he served them, Big Boy saw the dullness of frustration in their eyes. He spoke to them in a low voice. "Who you guys lookin' for?"

"We don't know for sure," Daggett replied. "We're workin' the Linda Blanc murder."

Big Boy's eyes narrowed as he shot quick glances about to check for unwanted listeners. "I knew that gal. She was all right. You ain't got no idea who done it, huh?"

Daggett shook his head. "We don't know a hell of a lot of nothin'. We got some dope that she was hooked up with a guy named Luis Martinez. We think there's a connection."

Big Boy screwed up his mouth as he considered Daggett's words. He cut his eyes at Andrews, and saw the other detective watching him over the rim of his beer glass. "I told her a couple years ago that he was gonna bring her grief. She just patted my cheek, said she loved the guy and for me not to talk bad about him." He shook his head. "Crock of bullshit."

Andrews sipped his beer, paused to lick the foam from his lips. "We want to talk to Martinez some kinda bad, Big Boy. Any idea where he might be?"

Big Boy slowly wiped the bar in front of him as he flicked his eyes about the room. "Been hearin' some funny shit lately."

"About what?"

"Martinez is supposed to be connected to a heavy hitter—white man."

Daggett raised his eyes. "This white man got a name?"

"Santiago Compasso."

Daggett and Andrews exchanged a look and shrugged. "Never heard of him. What's he into?"

"Don't know. And nobody I talked to knows, neither."

Daggett considered this as he sipped some beer. "A racket nobody knows about. That's new."

Big Boy reached under the bar and brought out a dish of salted nuts and shoved them between the two detectives. "Supposed to be all out-of-town people that Martinez got for this Compasso. But that ain't the interestin' part."

Andrews dunked a meaty hand into the bowl of nuts, captured some and transferred them to his waiting mouth. "What is?" he said around the nuts.

"Martinez is in the soup with this Compasso. Word is there's a contract out on Luis. Nobody's seen the guy in a few weeks. Might be he's dead already."

Andrews swallowed audibly, chasing the nuts with some beer. "Maybe he took the hint and split town."

Big Boy shook his head. "Uh-uh, brutha. He wouldn't make a permanent disappearance without takin' Linda. They was two beats off the same drum. He had her in a place he thought was safe, but the contract has somebody hungry. He musta sniffed out the house and killed her to let Luis know they wasn't playin' no game."

Daggett had been silent through most of Big Boy's story, remembering what Paul Ewell had told them about the counterfeiting ring. The name Santiago Compasso was clearly something Ewell's people didn't know.

He picked up his glass and drained the rest of the beer down his throat. "Thanks, Big Boy. We owe you one."

Big Boy turned up a big pale palm and shook it. "Just do me a favor and don't go spreadin' nothin' with my name tacked on it, okay? I ain't interested in gettin' a reputation as no pigeon, you dig?"

"Okay, brutha," Andrews said. "We'll be silent as the grave."

"That ain't funny, Sam."

"No," Andrews replied. "It sure ain't."

Chapter 4

By the time Farrell reached the Algiers Point ferry it was nearing 3:00. His was almost the last car to board before deck hands raised the gangway and cast off lines.

Farrell remained in his car as the ferry rumbled and vibrated beneath him. He had been on the prowl at this hour many times, but he recognized an unfamiliar fatigue tonight. His life was so full that he tended to ignore the passage of time, but lately there had been little reminders—fine lines at the corners of his eyes, stray gray hairs among the reddish brown ones on the backs of his hands, an unreadiness to jump out of bed first thing in the morning. It made him think of his father, whose own red hair was graying noticeably these days.

Farrell wondered would he be so quick to venture into the night like this if he and Savanna were married and had children. He did not probe his motives as a rule but on this night, he recognized that he was putting himself in harm's way out of boredom. The priest's visit had set him in motion, but it was the murder of Luis's girlfriend that had heightened Farrell's resolve to find his old friend. He faintly recalled another priest reading from the Bible, "am I my brother's keeper?" but it was too late to ponder that question.

The ferry shuddered and groaned as they approached Algiers Point, slowing until the bow nudged the dock and bounced away. Deck hands hastily made the boat fast then let down the gangway with a clatter. A few minutes later, he drove across to dry land.

This side of the river was almost rural in comparison to the New Orleans side. Most buildings he passed were shuttered and dark, and few cars shared the road with him.

The village of Gretna's Huey P. Long Boulevard was empty of all but shadows. Farrell continued to the eastern edge of the village, driving north to the brink of a bayou.

There was a considerable Negro population on this side of the river, composed mainly of people who fished, crabbed, trapped, or did back-breaking labor in fish canneries, boat yards, or on farms. Roadhouses or juke joints along the rural roads outside Gretna offered such folks the only entertainments they could afford: white lightning, canned beer and the romantic laments of a lowdown bluesman.

However, Negroes who worked in town for white people or had small businesses of their own craved a more genteel kind of enjoyment, and for them there was nothing to equal the opulence of Wisteria's Riverboat Lounge. As Farrell came upon it, he saw the huge neon sign lighting up the area for a hundred yards around. The sign featured a Southern belle in layers of petticoats with an articulated coquette fan at each end. In between them a Mississippi sternwheeler huffed smoke from its stacks. Farrell had heard that even the white people on this side of the river viewed it with a mixture of envy and awe.

Farrell parked at the edge of the lot and got out into the late night air. The sounds of tree frogs seemed to vie with the Dixieland coming from inside the lounge. Something made him pause, and in response he faded into a shadow. He remained there, listening as his eyes made a circuit of the area. He sensed a presence, but it was no more than that. He moved softly, threading a path through the clutter of parked vehicles to the entrance.

He pushed through the doors, pausing just inside to let his eyes adjust to the soft lighting. A Negro in a white dinner jacket saw him enter and strolled unobtrusively toward him. Farrell made him for the bouncer by the width of his shoulders and his loose-limbed, flat-footed saunter. His right hand was clenched, no doubt hiding a roll of nickels, a weapon as effective as brass knuckles.

"Evenin', sir. Can we help you with somethin'? Maybe you're lost." At least he had a few brains. He was going to try being polite before he threw a punch.

"I came to see Wisteria Mullins," Farrell replied. "The name's Farrell."

The bouncer nodded with recognition, but his expression said it didn't bother him. "It's mighty late, sir, and we gonna be closin' up here in less than a half-hour."

"I won't need very much of her time. It's about her cousin, Linda, and Luis Martinez."

The man became rigid, and Farrell could sense him considering his next move. Just as suddenly he relaxed, his concern for his boss evident in his expression. "I'll tell her, but I don't know. She's had a real bad day."

Farrell nodded sympathetically. "I'm not here to cause her any extra grief. I'm just trying to find Luis."

He considered for a second. "I'll see what she says. Tell the barman I said to give you whatever you want."

"That's friendly of you. Thanks." Farrell took off his hat and went to the bar. The bartender came close enough to catch Farrell's order for a rye highball. Farrell had put about half of it away when the bouncer returned.

"She'll talk to you. Follow me." He led Farrell through a door and up a flight of stairs to the second floor. There was a door open up there, and through the door Farrell saw a willowy woman in a sea green evening gown. A cigarette burned in her right hand, and a tendril of blue smoke floated up past her handsome brown face. "Thanks, Terry. You can go on back to the floor now." Her voice was like honey seasoned with pepper.

Terry cut his eyes at Farrell. "You sure?"

She smiled indulgently at him. "Mr. Farrell only wants to talk. He don't have to beat women to get what he wants, do you, Mr. Farrell?"

"I never want that much," Farrell replied.

Wisteria's mouth flew open and a rich, full laugh escaped. Terry, seeing he was outclassed, turned and left.

"Don't mind Terry. He thinks he needs to protect me from people. Buy you a drink?"

"No thanks." Farrell sat down in an armchair and put his hat on the floor by his feet.

She sat down across from him and crossed her legs. "Terry said you'd come about Linda."

"I think Luis is in some kind of trouble and what happened to Linda is connected to that. I'm hoping you can tell me where he is so I can help."

She held her hands in her lap and looked down at them. "I like Luis—always did. But I knew he was trouble first time I looked at him. He's too slick for his own good." She was quiet for a long moment, and as she sat there, Farrell saw two tears escape from her eyes and flow soundlessly over the curve of her cheeks.

"I'm sorry," he said. "People said good things about Linda to me. Have you got any idea where Luis might be?"

Wisteria Mullins' eyes grew hard and her nostrils flared. "If I knew, I'd go after him myself. I want to slap his face and spit in it." Her mouth gaped suddenly and she began to weep, the sobs like groans of agony. "All his talk about how much he loved my sweet b-baby girl, and now she's lyin' dead over there." She swiped angrily at the tears blurring her eyes and looked up at him fiercely. "You ever look down on somebody you love 'at's been butchered like some hog?"

Farrell nodded gravely. "Yes."

She started at the single word then relaxed. "I don't know where he is. I thought he'd call, but maybe he's afraid to." She shook her head ruefully.

Farrell sat back in his chair and rubbed the bridge of his nose with a thumb and forefinger. He saw from his watch that it was now 4:00, and he was no closer to Luis Martinez than when he'd left the Café Tristesse. "If you hear from him, tell him to call me at my club. The number's on this card." He laid a business card on the table, then picked up his hat and turned to go.

"Mr. Farrell?"

He turned his head and saw her looking at him. "Yeah?"

"I don't know what it means, but it's somethin' I heard Luis say. It went 'luck is where you find it, and I always look for mine down by the river.' You know what that means?"

He shook his head. "I remember him saying it, but I thought it was just some trash he was talkin'."

She nodded. "Maybe so. Thanks—for what you said."

"Sure." He walked through the door and downstairs to the club. Except for Terry, everyone else was gone. The man turned as he heard Farrell's approach.

"How's she holdin' up?" he asked.

"She's hurt, but all hurts get dull with time. She just needs her friends to get her over the rough spots."

He nodded, his mouth stretched tight. "Yeah. Sorry if I acted impolite with you earlier."

"Forget it. I'll be on my way now."

Terry let him out into the warm, humid night. Without the neon sign, the brooding darkness of the bayou enveloped the place completely. As Farrell strode across the grassy parking lot to where he'd left his car, his eyes and ears continued to probe the darkness. That indefinable something he'd felt at his arrival was still there, but the surroundings were empty for as far as he could see. Casting a last look around, he got into the car, cranked the engine, and headed in the direction of home.

⊗⊗⊗

Terry locked the metal grate over the glass front doors before going through the club to turn off the remaining lights. When he reached the kitchen, he noted that the rear service door was slightly ajar, and he grimaced. He'd told the cooks and busboys to be careful about that door. He'd come back one night to find three raccoons there tearing the place apart. He cast a quick look around the kitchen, but detected nothing out of order.

He walked to the door, cursing under his breath. As he reached it, he pushed the door closed and set the deadbolt. It was then that the lights went out. He whirled around. "Who's there? What's the idea, Goddamnit?" He moved in the direction of the nearest light switch, but a noise checked him. His hand went instinctively to the revolver in his hip pocket. "Who's there? I got a gun, fool, so don't be messin' around." Drawing the gun, he sped to the light switch. As his hand closed over it, something hit him over the temple and he fell to the floor unconscious.

His attacker stood over him for a minute, prodding him with his shoe. Although Terry didn't move or make a sound, the attacker kicked him very precisely in the back of the head. Satisfied, the man made his way through the darkened kitchen, heading for the stairs.

He reached a hall, and saw an open door with light shining through it. "Terry?" a woman's voice called. "Terry, that you, honey?"

The man walked softly to the door, looked through it and saw Wisteria Mullins at a desk, thumbing through some receipts. He moved toward her in a smooth, soundless glide. He was grinning when she looked up, saw his face, and gave a single, ululating scream.

⋙⋘

A ray of daylight, filtered through the dusty, ragged curtain on the window, dropped across Martinez's face, bringing sweat out on his forehead. He squirmed out of it, turning on his side. The damage was done, however. The movement brought him out of the stupor he'd finally fallen into the night before.

As he gradually came awake, the memory of what had happened elbowed its way to the front of his consciousness, reminding him of the trouble he was in. He forced himself up on his elbows, and swung his legs over the edge of the bed. A flash of sharp pain shot through his temples and he grabbed his head, groaning.

A sour belch forced its way up his throat and out between his clenched teeth. He got up and walked unsteadily to the toilet, just making it before he vomited up a mess of bourbon and yellow bile. The retching almost tore the top of his head off, but eventually the pain subsided. He looked at himself in the mirror to see that the face staring back was that of a worn-out *mestizo*, not the sharp operator who had always known the right answer, always been standing somewhere else when the axe fell on someone less lucky.

With shaking fingers, he tore off his wrinkled, sweat-stained clothing then ran cold water in the basin as he stooped painfully over it. He cupped his hands and rubbed his face over and over with the cold water, drinking every other handful, swishing it around in his mouth to cut the scummy taste on his tongue.

He found his toothbrush and can of Pepsodent tooth powder, using them until the foul taste in his mouth diminished. That done, he turned on the hot-water tap until the sink was filled with scalding hot water. With the washcloth and soap he'd gotten from the deskman, he systematically washed himself from head to foot, rinsing with cool water. He found his razor and shaving soap, and very carefully shaved himself. His mustache needed trimming, but he let that go.

When he was clean, he went through his bag and chose a pale blue shirt with a soft collar, fresh underwear and socks and a light gray tropical wool suit.

The soiled clothing he wrapped into a bundle and dumped in the wastebasket. He had no time for laundry. He closed his valise, put on his hat then left the room. The desk wasn't occupied when he reached the lobby, so he dropped the room key on the counter before leaving the building.

He saw from his watch that it was a few minutes past 7:00. Magazine Street was quiet, only a few cars passing through at low speeds and a couple of pedestrians hurrying to work across the street from him. There was a feeling of peacefulness about the neighborhood that made him want to stay and enjoy it, but he knew better. He walked across the street to his Mercury and quickly drove away.

As he drove, he considered his options. If he went to the cops, he could make a deal for his cooperation, but would still serve time in a Federal pen. He'd never been in jail in his life, and knew he couldn't stand to be locked up for years. If he gave the plates back to Compasso, he'd be admitting defeat and submitting to execution. All that was left was to make war.

There were the plates to consider, too. Four blocks of chrome-plated nickel, each representing several months of work by a master engraver. He had them wrapped up and tucked under the spare tire in his trunk. Even if Compasso got to him, Martinez was determined to deny him the plates.

He drove into Downtown and parked in front of the railroad depot at South Rampart and Girod. Even at that early hour, there were enough people for him to comfortably blend in. He rummaged in his glove compartment until he found a small pad of paper and a pencil. He wrote one sentence in neat block letters:

Ozzy—keep safe until I come—Luis

He retrieved the cardboard package containing the plates and put the note on top before going inside to the Railroad Express Agency desk. A tired, gray-haired white man wearing steel-rimmed spectacles waited on him.

"Yes, sir. What can we do for you this morning?" he asked in a cigarette-coarsened voice.

"I need to send this to a party downtown." Martinez laid the box down and pushed it to the man.

The man got out some shipping labels and a pencil. "Where to?"

"Blue Note Pawn Shop, twelve-fifty North Rampart Street. To the attention of Theron Oswald."

The white man glanced up with a peculiar expression. "That's not too far from here, Mister."

Martinez grinned. "I'm leaving on a fishing trip and promised to get this to him today. When the fish are bitin', you can't keep 'em waitin', can you?"

The man gave him a tired smile. "Reckon not." He made out the label, fixed it to the box, then wrapped it securely in masking tape. He charged Martinez a dollar and ten cents, and promised it would be delivered that morning.

Martinez thanked the man and left the depot. Retrieving his Mercury, he backtracked, continuing all the way down Magazine, past Audubon Park, until he met the curve into Leake Avenue. He followed Leake until he reached the Carrollton area. He stopped at a diner and ate two orders of bacon, a stack of buttermilk pancakes with cane syrup, and a pot of hot coffee. He felt almost human afterward.

He gassed up the car at a Sinclair station, then got back on Leake and followed it until he reached the river road that led into Jefferson Parish. Ten miles later, he stopped at a general store and bought a box of food and a flashlight, a portable radio, and batteries for each.

The store's owner had a secondhand Ithaca Featherlight pump shotgun that he was persuaded to part with for fifteen dollars. For another five, the owner sold him two hundred rounds of 12-guage double-ought buckshot. A hacksaw was added to the pile for an extra twenty-five cents.

With his purchases stowed in the back of the car, Martinez got back on the river road and followed it for twenty-five miles until he came to a dirt road that led to a shanty sitting on pilings out in the river. Martinez could see that the boards he'd nailed across the windows and doors two years ago hadn't been disturbed.

With his tire iron, he removed all the boards, then went inside and threw open all the windows. While the place aired out, Martinez took all of his food and equipment inside and set up housekeeping. An hour later, he had created a headquarters for himself.

His last chore was to break out the hacksaw and shotgun. It took five minutes to cut the barrel off even with the magazine tube, and another three to clean the burrs off with a piece of emery cloth. With that done, he loaded the magazine with five cartridges and added a sixth to the chamber. He took it ashore and walked to within twenty feet of a dead tree trunk with a number of projecting branches. Bringing the shotgun to his hip, he fired all six rounds, snapping a branch with each shot. With the explosions still reverberating, he nodded, satisfied with his work.

He saw from his watch that it was nearly 11:00. There was nothing to do now but wait.

❈

Bank President A. J. McCandless's private plane landed at Shushan Field at 9:00 that morning. No one was waiting for him, which was how he'd planned it. He taxied the twin-engine Lockheed Vega to his private hangar at the western end of the field, steering it expertly through the open hangar doors. He cut the engines and made his way through the rear of the silver plane to the cabin door, where his personal mechanic waited. McCandless, a lithe, agile, dark-haired man, jumped nimbly to the concrete and walked past the mechanic with the barest of nods. His steps took him to a private office within the hangar where he closed and locked the door behind him.

Settling himself at the desk, he picked up the telephone receiver and gave the operator a number. It buzzed three times before a man answered.

"It's McCandless. I just flew in."

"What are you doing back in town already?" the other man asked.

"The Treasury Department is crawling all over my bank. Did you think I was going to remain in Atlanta while that was going on?"

"I suppose not. What now?"

"I'll tell you what now. I've got to be bloody careful. I can't afford for the wrong people to find out too much about me. It could cost me everything."

"It could cost me too, A. J. I've been backing you up all this time, you know." A wry tone had appeared in the other man's voice.

McCandless wasn't amused. "*I'm* the one with the most to lose if this thing blows up. See that you don't forget that."

The amusement left the other man's voice. "Now that you're here, what do you want to do?"

"Nothing. Keep your ears open. Be helpful but ignorant if anyone asks you anything."

"That should be easy. I made it a point to not know very much."

McCandless stroked his long bony jaw. "All right, then. I'll be in touch with you later." McCandless hung up the telephone without waiting for a reply, then he strode out into the hangar. The mechanic had just finished putting his bags into the trunk of a pale blue Lincoln Continental. McCandless grunted his thanks, got into the car, and left through the rear of the hanger.

∞∞∞

Farrell crawled out of his sheets about 9:30, grimacing as he saw the face of his bedroom clock. Coffee was the most immediate thing on his morning agenda.

The act of walking into the kitchen did something toward waking him up, and by the time he drained a pan of hot water over coffee grounds, he began to feel human again. He had transferred coffee and hot milk into a cup and was taking a bite out of a cold dinner roll he found in the refrigerator when the kitchen telephone began to ring. He slowly chewed the roll, hoping whoever it was would give up and let him wake up in peace.

By the time the instrument had emitted a half-dozen rings, it occurred to him that it might be important. He took a sizable gulp of the coffee, then reached up and snatched the receiver from the cradle. "Hello?"

"I knew you were home," Frank Casey's voice said.

"Hi, Dad. Yeah, I had kind of a late night, and woke up too early. Are you free for dinner tonight?"

"You were over in Gretna last night," his father said, ignoring his question.

Something in the tone of Casey's voice put Farrell on his guard. "Yeah, as a matter of fact. How'd you know?"

"I'll be there in about twenty minutes. Get yourself together so we can take a ride across the river."

Casey's words were casual, even polite, but Farrell noticed that he didn't make it a request. He was telling his son that they had to go, and now. "Okay, Dad. Pull into the parking space behind the club. If I'm not there waiting for you, just come on up, the kitchen door'll be open."

"Okay. See you soon."

"Right." Farrell hung up knowing that if Casey wanted to go to Gretna, it had to be about Wisteria Mullins.

❊❊❊

The early September sun was already growing hot when a gunmetal gray Chrysler sedan turned off Elysian Fields Avenue onto North Villere and parked in front of a neat white and green cottage. A neatly lettered sign hanging from a bracket read "Abraham T. Rodrigue, M.D."

A good-looking, well-dressed man got out of the car, carefully locked the door, then walked up on the porch and unlocked the door to the cottage. It was already stuffy in there, so he spent several minutes opening the windows and turning on oscillating table fans located in all the rooms. When he had finished, he took off his jacket and hat, and carefully placed them in the closet of the room he used as an office. He heard a noise behind him and twirled quickly.

"Goodness, Dr. Rodrigue, I'm sorry. I didn't mean to startle you." The speaker was a doe-eyed young brown woman.

Rodrigue put a hand to his heart as though to still the pounding there, and a relieved smile came to his face. "It's all right, Phyllis. I didn't hear you."

"Sorry I didn't get here on time. I planned to get the place cooled off before you arrived, but my little brother woke up with a fever this morning. I waited to see if he needed to come in for a visit."

"He's all right, then?"

"He's the baby and Mother still treats him that way."

Rodrigue laughed, nodding. "That's a common failing of older mothers. It passes when the babies grow up."

Their chat was interrupted by the telephone in the reception room. Phyllis went to get it. Seconds later, the telephone buzzed on Rodrigue's desk. "Yes, Phyllis?"

"A Mr. Huntsville calling. Shall I put him through?"

"Yes, please. He's a patient from my old practice." He waited for a moment, then the receiver clicked as the call was transferred. "Yes, Mr. Huntsville, how are you?"

"Poorly, Doc. I need some pills, and soon."

"Well, that's not a problem. Why don't you drop in later this afternoon, and we'll fix you right up."

"Lemme call you. I'm tied up with something and might not be able to get away. You still live on North Broad?"

"Why don't I drop them off with your friend downtown?" Rodrigue suggested. "You shouldn't wait any longer."

"Sure. You're *muy bueno*, Doc. See ya now, hear?"

"*Si, companiero. Vaya con Dios.*"

Huntsville laughed as he hung up the phone.

He looked up to see Phyllis watching. "Yes, Phyllis?"

"Was that Spanish I heard you speaking? You speak it beautifully." She looked at the handsome doctor with a glow of admiration in her eyes.

"Just something I picked up in Texas, Phyllis."

Chapter 5

It took about an hour for Casey and Farrell to make it to the site of the Riverboat Lounge on the outskirts of Gretna. When they arrived, there were five Jefferson Parish Sheriff's Department cars, a car from the Gretna police, and an ambulance parked outside the club.

Casey pulled up between two of the Sheriff's cars and cut the engine. He and Farrell walked toward the front door of the club where a muscular man dressed in the uniform of the Jefferson Parish Sheriff's Department waited. His gimlet eyes examined them with a decidedly unfriendly look.

"Thanks for bringing him over, Casey. I doubt he'd have come just because I asked."

"He didn't refuse to come, McGee. He admits he visited the club last night."

"That's swell. Let's go inside and show him what he left here." He turned on his heel with military precision and led them through the club and up the stairs to the office. As Farrell entered the office, he felt as though he'd been dealt a blow in the chest. What was left of Wisteria Mullins was bound hand and foot to a chair. Like Linda Blanc before her, she had been stripped naked. He saw that she'd been cut—precise cuts meant to cause a maximum amount of pain. On some of the more sensitive parts of her body, it looked as though skin had been flayed from her. Farrell fought the urge to get sick.

He turned to McGee, saw the man watching him in an appraising manner. "She was alive when I left. Her bouncer, Terry, let me out."

McGee made a clucking noise with his tongue. "Too bad Terry can't talk to us. He's in a coma from the beating he took. Doc's not sure he'll pull out of it." He hooked his thumbs inside his Sam Browne belt and moved a bit closer to Farrell. "The cleaning people found both of 'em this morning. When the Gretna police discovered your calling card on her desk, they called me. Seems your reputation ain't all that good in this parish."

Farrell felt his face growing hot. He and McGee knew each other well, but there was no friendship between them. "Go on, McGee, arrest me. But you'd better have something better than my business card, because even in this hick parish the D. A. won't indict on something that flimsy."

McGee smiled thinly. "Okay, hot-shot. Then start convincing me. Why were you over here last night?"

Farrell looked at his father and saw Casey nodding at him. "There's no charge against you, Wes, but you'd better tell what you know, and tell it straight."

Farrell took in a breath and let it out slowly. "I was over here looking for a man named Luis Martinez. His girlfriend was killed in New Orleans two days ago."

"I recognize the name," McGee said. "Martinez is a racketeer. Casey says the Feds are looking for him."

"The Feds?" Farrell looked at his father.

"That's right," Casey affirmed. "They think he's involved in a counterfeiting racket."

Light bloomed on in Farrell's mind. That explained the presence of Compasso and a gang of outsiders. "Do you know who Martinez is working for?"

McGee's lip curled. "What're you, Farrell, an apprentice G-Man? You're here to answer questions, not conduct a separate investigation. And while we're on the subject, why are you looking for this Martinez character?"

Farrell cut his eyes at his father and saw nothing there. It seemed clear that neither of them knew of Martinez's connection to Santiago Compasso. "It's a personal matter. I'm trying to get a message to him from a relative in Texas." He got out his cigarette case and offered it to McGee, who stared at him intently before taking one. Farrell put a cigarette in the corner of his mouth and took out his lighter. He used it on McGee's cigarette before lighting his own. "Here's something for you to think about, Lieutenant. I used to know Martinez pretty well. He's an organizer, a guy who puts things and people together, then sets a plan in motion. He's never the big boss, but he's the kind of guy every big boss wants, a ramrod who can recruit, plan, and execute."

McGee drew on the cigarette as he listened, not interrupting. It was obvious that Farrell's theory interested him. Casey, too, was listening.

"Wisteria Mullins was the cousin of Linda Blanc, Martinez's woman," Farrell continued. "This kind of torture is gangland stuff, probably to get information."

"Unless it's just some psycho," McGee said.

"Some psycho who deliberately tortured two women connected to Luis? I don't think so. Martinez is in hot water with somebody, and whoever killed these women is scouring the city for him, going to people who know Luis well and trying to force his whereabouts out of them."

Casey nodded, fingering his chin, and McGee frowned thoughtfully as he drew on the cigarette again, his eyes focused somewhere beyond Farrell. Casey finally spoke.

"Since you know him so well, that could mean you, Wes."

Farrell nodded slowly. "If it's true, the best thing I can do is keep looking for Martinez until I find him."

McGee crushed the butt of his cigarette in an ashtray and looked up at Farrell. "And we just sit around waiting for the killer to strike again? Nuts."

Farrell moved closer to McGee, looking him straight in the eye. "Listen, McGee, if I'm standing under the headsman's axe, too, there's no better man to find Martinez than me. If I find him, I'll give him to you. It may be the only way to keep him from getting killed."

McGee could not quite believe Farrell, but there was doubt in his eyes. He looked at Casey questioningly.

Casey tugged thoughtfully at his earlobe. "I think he's talking straight, McGee. He's never lied to me, and he's figured things out that the entire Detective Bureau couldn't see through. My suggestion is leave him free to move around. What have you got to lose?"

The deputy looked at Farrell again, his arms folded across his broad chest. "Okay, Farrell. Casey's word is good enough for me. I want the guy who did this, you understand? Her being a Negro, maybe it looks like something we'd shove into the wastebasket and forget, but that's not the way I do things. Anybody gets killed in my parish, white, black, or Indian, somebody pays for it."

Casey grinned. "Get in line. We want the guy, too."

"We'll dope that out when the time comes. You can go, Farrell, so long as Casey's responsible for you."

"Swell. I'll keep in touch." Farrell took off his hat and smoothed his hair under it. "Can you get me back across the river, Frank?"

"I brought you here, so I guess so. So long, McGee." He turned and Farrell followed him out of the club.

When they were back in Casey's squad car and on their way back to the Algiers Point Ferry, Casey glanced over at his son. "Okay, now that we're alone, why don't you tell me what you didn't tell McGee?"

Farrell tipped his hat onto the back of his head and leaned his elbow on the open window ledge. "All I've got is a rumor that Martinez is working for Santiago Compasso."

"Who's he?"

"He's from Argentina originally," Farrell replied. "He moved into Miami in 1927 and cut himself a slice of the booze racket there. In time he controlled about a third of what came in and went back out. They ran him out of south Florida a couple of years ago, and he operated mainly between Mobile and Pensacola for a while. His operation was mostly narcotics, illegal gambling, and prostitution. Last night I discovered he'd sneaked into New Orleans and set up shop with Martinez."

"So you think this counterfeiting ring is Compasso's?"

"The evidence leans that way, but what I know about Compasso makes me wonder. Compasso got everything he ever had with a gun. He's tough and he doesn't scare. But counterfeiting is a different game. It requires subtlety, planning and patience, all things Compasso's short on."

"But you said Martinez was the organizer, the man who puts the people together with the plan. Maybe Compasso's using him for the brains and subtlety."

Farrell frowned and shook his head. "I wonder. Successful counterfeiting requires a steady hand over a long haul. Luis could put the gang together and get it started, but he'd never hang around long enough to see it through. And Compasso wouldn't be able to run it by himself."

Casey grunted. "So who's the guiding hand? And why is he calling attention to himself with all this killing?"

Farrell shook his head again. "Something's off the rails. The killing has Compasso's name written all over it, but there's somebody above him. Somebody who's probably very worried about his operation falling apart."

"You going to tell the Treasury boys what you know?"

"Give me twenty-four hours, Dad. If I tell Ewell, the first thing he'll to do is put surveillance on Compasso and a tap on his phone. I want him free, because he's clumsy and impatient. He'll make a mistake soon."

Casey sighed. Farrell's way went against his instincts, but he trusted his son enough to go along with him. "What will you do in the meantime?"

Farrell shrugged. "I'll go around making a nuisance of myself. Sooner or later, somebody will get careless or reckless, and I'll be there. But Luis is the key. If I can find him, I'll find out what this is all about."

⁂

"Damn," Fred grumbled. "I reckon we drove a hundred miles and walked another fifty in the last two days."

"And talked to about a thousand Cheniers," Marcel added. "You'd think one of them would have a relative named Albert, even if he was dead."

It was late afternoon, and both men were tired and hungry. Fred got an idea.

"Ya know, we covered New Orleans, but it might be this Chenier's from out in the sticks 'round here. Maybe he only tells people he's from New Orleans, 'cause it's easier than sayin' he's from Jefferson Parish or St. Bernard Parish. Nobody outside the state ever heard a' them places, but everybody knows New Orleans, man. They know us in Siberia."

Marcel chucked softly. "Yeah, 'the city that care forgot.' I met a girl from up in Ohio once who was disappointed to find out we don't hold Mardi Gras every few weeks." Both men laughed aloud at that, then Marcel made a suggestion. "Let's head out to Avery's joint over in Jeff Parish. We're not too far from there now."

"Yeah, and he'll have some crab gumbo on the stove."

"Always thinking of your stomach. Yeah, I'm hungry, too. Let's go."

About twenty minutes later, they crossed the parish line on Jefferson Highway, and another ten minutes later, they were driving down a marl road that ran north of the highway. Soon they saw the low, squat building where Avery and his partner, an ex-bank robber named Ernie Le Doux, operated their honky-tonk. The hot sun was just beginning to fall, but already the French doors were folded back all along the gallery and people could be seen gathering around the openings. Fred parked his Chevrolet Straight-8 between a pair of aging jalopies, then the two young men walked through the grass to one of the open doors.

Inside, a bluesman who went by the name of Charlie Boy White lazed in a ladder-back chair plucking chords out of his battered Gibson while a few men and women idled nearby with their Mason jars of beer, some of them already snapping their fingers and rolling their hips to the music. Avery leaned against the wall behind the bar beside Ernie Le Doux, each of them watching the crowd for trouble. Every juke joint has its share of trouble, but they were both rough men. It was a rare visitor who was dumb enough to cut up in their place more than once.

"Evenin', fellas," Marcel said, touching two fingers to the brim of his Stetson.

"Hey, li'l brutha," Le Doux rumbled. "How's it hangin', Fred?"

"Ain't seen you fellas out here in a while," Avery said. "Makin' too much money to come out and spend any?"

"You know how it is. Every year I seem to have more business than the year before, and less time to kick up my heels. You got any crab gumbo for a couple of hungry men?"

"Pull up a stool," Avery said. "I'll dish some up. Give these boys a beer, Ernie."

Marcel and Fred each pulled up stool to the bar and eased a hip over it as Le Doux drew two beers. Marcel took off his hat, placed it on the bar beside him, and ran his fingers through his light brown curls. A moment later, Avery returned with a tray bearing two thick china bowls full of fragrant stew, a dish of soda crackers, and spoons.

"Lawd have mercy," Fred said. "Y'all sure make a fine gumbo. Let me at it."

As Fred tore into his food, Marcel tasted his in a more leisurely fashion. After a couple of bites, he said, "Tell me, you boys know any Cheniers?"

Le Doux laughed. "That's like askin' how many Smiths we know. Which one?"

"The one I'm looking for is Albert."

Both Le Doux and Avery scratched their chins as they looked quizzically at each other.

"I recollect an Alfred, but he's about seventy years old," Avery said.

"The fellow I'm after can't be more than thirty or thirty-five. Take a look at these." He reached inside his jacket for Marta's snapshots and laid them on the bar.

The two older men put their elbows on the bar as they intently studied the shapshots.

"Chenier, you said." Avery stepped back and rubbed the back of his neck with a meaty palm. "He don't even look like none of the Cheniers I know of."

Marcel shifted his gaze to Ernie Le Doux, who had straightened up, his left eyebrow raised dubiously. "It ain't a very good picture, but if it's who I think it is, his name ain't Albert nor Chenier."

Marcel felt a ripple of electricity dance its way up his spine. "Who is it, then?"

"When I was in the stir, back in 1926, there was a seventeen-year-old kid in there, shared the cell with a man I knew. Kid was in there for some kind of con—I forget which—but he looked like this fella one hell of a lot."

"What was his name?"

"They called him 'Keys'. Said he could look at you for the first time and know what it'd take to unlock your heart and your wallet. His right handle was Wilbur Lee Payne. He was a hell of a smart kid. Claimed to have studied in some Negro college for a coupla years. Read books all the time."

Marcel sat up straight, his hands flat on the bar. "What else do you remember about him?"

"Like I say, he was one hell of a smart kid. He had one a' them photographic memories. Once I let him look at a page of a magazine I was readin', and I'll be Goddamned if he didn't repeat it word-for-word without a single mistake."

Fred swallowed a mouthful of gumbo and soda crackers. "'Pears we been askin' after the wrong man all day, Marcel. This Wilbur's liable to be layin' up on Rampart or runnin' a con out in Gentilly somewhere."

Marcel rubbed the back of his neck. "Sounds like you knew this fellow pretty good, Ernie. What else do you remember about him?"

Le Doux squinted at the ceiling as he thought. "Kid was a talker, I remember that. Claimed his daddy was a white man and that he was born in Haiti. Told stories about travelin' by ship all over the Caribbean Sea, visitin' islands and such. Said he could cast voodoo spells, too." Ernie turned his gaze back to them, smiling. "He kept his nose clean, though, and they let him out at the end of '27. Ain't heard a word about him since."

"Marta said he worked in a pharmacy with her. That's a poor living for a guy as smart as you say he is."

Ernie shrugged. "He mighta just been layin' low over there, makin' enough to keep a roof over his head while he figured out a new con."

Fred shrugged. "Or he come here just to get away from Miss Marta."

Marcel nodded. "He wouldn't be the first to pull that trick."

"Who's this Marta y'all keep talkin' about?" Avery demanded.

Fred grinned. "She's this sweet young thing from Brownsville. She thought this Albert/Wilbur fella was gonna marry her, but he up and run off to New Orleans. Some good friend of Marcel's told her to come up and see him, that he'd work a miracle for her and find this fella."

A booming laugh escaped Ernie Le Doux's massive chest. "Boy's a reg'lar social worker, by Jesus." He laughed again, with everyone except Marcel joining in. He was already thinking ahead to the next step in the search.

"This is the first real lead we've had today, Ernie. It explains why nobody knows an Albert Chenier."

Fred scraped the last of the gumbo from his bowl and put it into his mouth, then pushed the bowl and spoon away from him. "What now, boss?"

Marcel, who had been eating as he listened, pushed his own bowl away and blotted his lips on a paper napkin. "Go back to town, I guess. Thanks fellas, for the food and the information. The day's not a total loss, after all."

Ernie held up his hand as he saw Marcel reach for his wallet. "The grub's on the house, li'l brutha. It's good seein' you boys again. Come on back and let us know what you find out. I wouldn't mind talkin' to ole Wilbur again. He was an entertainin' kid, even if I did think he was fulla shit most of the time."

Fred let loose a guffaw as he and Marcel crawled off their stools and departed as small knots of people entered the honky-tonk to hear Charley Boy White sing the blues.

∞∞∞

Marston Leake was still in his office at First National when the telephone rang. He picked up the receiver and heard the operator's voice.

"Mr. Leake, we've got your Atlanta party on the line."

"Put him on," the white-haired banker said.

"Hello, Marston. How are you, old timer?"

Leake's face betrayed no particular pleasure at the greeting. "I've had Treasury people crawling all over my bank, that's how I am."

"I heard. It's the same here. They're like a nest of angry bees. The governors at Federal Reserve, too."

Leake snorted. "Good. Anything that stirs up that pack of hidebound old goats is music to my ears."

"Still holding a grudge, eh, Marston?"

"Still. But that's not why I called. Do they know anything over there yet?"

"If they do," the other man replied, "they're keeping it damn close to the vest. They'd behave that way whether they knew anything or not, as you well know."

Leake grunted. "If there's any change, call me, day or night, you understand? We might have to move quickly."

"You're the boss, Marston. See you." The man hung up.

Leake placed his receiver carefully back in the cradle, then opened his desk drawer. He pushed a .380 Colt automatic aside in order to retrieve a small leather-bound notebook. He opened the book, made some quick notations, then put the notebook back. He took out the gun, placed it inside his jacket, then closed and locked the desk. He sat there thinking for a long moment before getting up and leaving the office for the day.

⊗⊗⊗

The woman called Jelly Wilde had lived several lifetimes in her thirty-one years. She had run away from home at the age of fourteen after she tired of fending off the unwanted advances of her brother and male cousins. By the time she ended up in New Orleans, she was five years older chronologically and about thirty in experience.

She'd embarked on a series of domestic jobs that had almost always included sleeping with the master of the house when the wife was away. The first had been a young-hearted fellow of forty who'd taught her every way to please a man that he could think of before his wife and sister caught them in the act one day. She got away with a couple hundred dollars and the realization that certain men would go to extraordinary lengths to have sex with a woman like her.

She went along that way for some time, doing well for herself until one day she allowed herself to be picked up by a good-looking, slick-talking young man who went by the name of Georgie Sam McGuire. Georgie Sam carried gold all over his body: stickpin, watch chain, cuff links, and even in his teeth. The overall impression was that of a man who knew where he was going and what he'd do when he got there.

Within a few weeks, she learned that all that glittered with Georgie Sam wasn't gold. His gold jewelry turned out to be mostly gold plated, and even the five-dollar gold piece on his watch chain was no more than a gold-plated "racketeer" nickel. Apparently the gold in his teeth was real, but that was as authentic as Georgie Sam got.

Worse yet, he was a drug addict. It was a rare night he didn't get tuned up on nose candy, and when he did, he was apt to do anything. She wanted to get away, but Georgie Sam had already gotten his hands on most of her money and spent it on heroin or cocaine.

Necessity is the mother of invention, and one day Georgie Sam hit upon a foolproof scheme to keep them in eating money and nose-candy. Jelly would go into a honkey-tonk and look for someone in the advanced stages of a good time. She would then insinuate herself into this gentleman's good graces, and proceed to get him blind drunk. When he was drunk enough to be pliant, she'd coax him outside with the promise of fucking his eyeballs out in the back seat of his car. Of course, when the love-starved drunk got outside the tavern, Georgie Sam would be waiting with a sap, and down would go the unlucky suitor.

They did pretty well with this con, and gradually Jelly made back all of the money Georgie Sam had squandered, with a nice little profit on top. It was her first experience at outsmarting a veteran con artist, and it was a wisdom she came to value.

However, no good thing continues forever. One night, after hitting the cocaine a little too hard, Georgie Sam got heavy-handed and beat the mark's brains out. As the crestfallen Georgie Sam looked down at the corpse he had by the collar, Jelly ducked into the nearest alley. She made her way quickly to the railroad station and got a ticket on the first train out. It took her from Jacksonville to New Orleans, where she changed her name and began a new life.

As a light-skinned Negro, Jelly found she had an added value in New Orleans, where white men had been making mistresses of such women for over two hundred years. With the right clothes and a few of the right friends, she found herself much in demand among the well heeled. With the help of some of those same men, she invested the money and gained an independence that she used to further her ambitions.

She had met Luis Martinez toward the end of Prohibition, and was charmed by his cock-sure way. Altogether she must've spent almost two years with Luis, on and off, and she'd gotten to know him pretty well. He was smarter than most of the crooks he worked for, and he knew it. He was also smart enough not to give away just how smart he really was, and got far more of the take than any of his bosses intended.

He was independent, too, and she was yet young enough to be irked by it, not understanding that it was the other side of the cockiness that had attracted her in the first place. She left him after a quarrel one day, knowing she was in the wrong. When good sense finally overcame her pride, it was too late. Martinez had moved on.

Santiago Compasso had much that Luis had lacked. He had charm, manners, and knew how to dress. He was a capable lover, if not a particularly inspired one. But gradually she learned things about him that troubled her. He was an unacknowledged misogynist, and she had heard him use the words "nigger" and "*indio*" and other slurs when talking about people. Jelly sometimes wondered if he used that language to describe her when she wasn't around.

Why are you doing this? she asked herself. Why help a man you dislike to find a man you've missed for years? The only answer she could identify was pride. She wanted to show Compasso, and Martinez, too, that she had value, that she was capable of accomplishment. But a question remained. How could she do that without hurting Martinez? She already knew she didn't want that to happen.

She thought back over the time she had lived with Martinez, trying to remember the things he had said, the topics that had interested him. Her self-absorption had caused her to ignore him at times, but some things she remembered. There was a saying he had—"luck is where you find it, but I always look for mine down by the river." What the hell did that mean?

Fishing. He had talked about fishing. Where did a person go to fish? She recollected seeing people fishing in the lagoons of Audubon and City Parks, but those were mostly old people, poor Negroes, and children. A man like Martinez would not be satisfied with such a sedentary occupation.

There was something else, now that she thought of it. Martinez had owned a rifle and a shotgun. What had he called them? They had the same name, and he spoke it like a man who understood such things. Web-something—no, not web. More like wind. And a man's name—Chris? Calvin? Chester. Yes, Wind-Chester. Winchester, that's it. She remembered the guns hanging from a rack under a pair of spreading antlers. He had often spoken of his life on the west Texas plains, and of the hunting and fishing he'd done there.

She drove to the street where Martinez had lived when she met him. It was a large house on Paris Avenue divided into three apartments. She hadn't been there in years, but she remembered the neighborhood well enough. It was largely residential, and perhaps somebody there would remember Martinez.

It took her three-quarters of an hour to reach the neighborhood, and to find the apartment house. She saw a man cutting the grass, so she pulled over and spoke to him.

"Pardon me, mister. Who owns that building yonder?" She pointed out the window, and the old man became immediately mesmerized by her long, golden arm and scarlet-tipped fingernails.

"Well," he said finally. "Reckon that'd be me." He had leaned over to get better look at the owner of the arm, and he was more mesmerized than ever.

"Did you own it when Mr. Martinez lived upstairs?"

The old man took off his sweat-stained fedora and wiped his shiny head with a tattered bandanna. "Well, let me think. This woulda been a few years back, right?"

"Right."

"Yeah, I b'lieve I remember him. Mex fella, kinda broad through the chest and shoulders, right?"

"Uh, huh. Did he ever talk to you about huntin' and fishin', sir?"

"Oh, golly, miss, that'd take a better memory than I got." He rubbed his neck, his face twisted with chagrin. It bothered him to disappoint such a fine looking female. Then he brightened. "Say, if he did, I'll bet he did some trade with Pelecano's hardware. It's two blocks down, then left, and three more blocks. Big white clapboard place. You can't miss it."

She favored the old man with a smile. "Thanks, mister. I'm sure sorry if I troubled you."

"Oh, miss. Please come back and trouble me any time," he said fervently.

She waggled her fingers at him playfully and pulled away from the curb. When she looked back into the rearview mirror, the old man still stared wistfully after her.

Chapter 6

After Casey dropped him at the Café Tristesse, Farrell got in his car and drove Uptown on St. Charles Avenue. He turned on to Freret Street near the bend in the river and continued to Joliet Street. He discovered that the mission the priest had opened was in an old church that had been abandoned by a fundamentalist Negro sect some years before. Although the building showed definite signs of age, the yard was clean, the fence had a fresh coat of whitewash, and a sign over the doorway proclaimed that it was "St. Swithan's Mission for the Destitute." Young children played on a set of swings while men and women of varying ages worked on the yard or were whitewashing the building.

Farrell parked his car near the entrance and went inside. He found a pair of young Negro girls in white dresses behind a hastily built information counter.

"How may we help you on this blessed day, sir?" the taller girl asked, her face wreathed in a beatific smile.

"I'm looking for Father Maldonar."

"Yes, the Reverend Father is in his sanctuary. Anita will show you."

The other young girl smiled, ducked under the counter, and led Farrell down the middle of the church to a door behind the altar. She knocked, then opened it and gestured for Farrell to enter.

Maldonar was sitting in his shirtsleeves at a battered oak desk that held a telephone, a blotter, and a few pencils. The irregular pale patches that Farrell had noticed on Maldonar's visit were apparent all the way up his arms, and down his neck. He sat under a sun lamp with a pair of sunglasses over his eyes. He started as Farrell entered.

"Sorry if I startled you, Father James," Farrell said as he removed his hat. "The young ladies said it was all right for me to come in."

Maldonar removed the sunglasses and turned awkwardly, his crippled leg dragging across the floor. "No, please don't apologize. I suffer from a condition known as vitiligo—it is another cross that God in his wisdom decided I must bear. I use the sunlamp to counteract the death of pigmentation in my skin."

Farrell nodded. He had a faint recollection of reading a magazine story about the disease, but Maldonar was the first person he'd met who suffered from it.

As Maldonar buttoned up his clerical collar and put on his black jacket, he gestured to a vacant seat. When he was dressed, he picked up the leg with the brace and moved it to a more comfortable position. "Have you information about Señor Martinez?"

"Not yet, but I'm learning things that might help me find him. I hope to locate him in the next day or so. I couldn't help but wonder how long his mother has before—"

Maldonar waved a hand. "One never knows how long one has here on earth, but God is merciful. I believe he will grant Señora Martinez's wish before she is gathered to Him."

"I hope you're right. I'm glad to see you putting some people to work, Father. The folks in this part of town are pretty hard up. I expect they're grateful to you and the Church."

"One does what one can, Mr. Farrell. I've found some splendidly generous people here, like those two young ladies out front, to help me. We've also got a magnificent cook who's making chicken and dumplings right now for those in the neighborhood who don't get to eat regularly."

"You've managed quite a bit here in a short time. How long have you been in the city, Father?"

"Oh, a month or two. But God was here before me. I only had to pick up the pieces and arrange them into a useful shape." He looked at Farrell and a shrewd look came into his eyes. "I sense that you did not come for a social call. What have you learned about your friend?"

"Only that he's in trouble with a gangster. Two people have been killed by someone who obviously wanted to know where Martinez was."

"Killed? You mean—murdered?"

Farrell nodded. "Uh, huh."

"Jesu!" The priest crossed himself, his eyes shocked.

Farrell studied the priest for a moment. "What do you know about Luis, Father?"

"Very little." He paused for a moment to blot perspiration from his forehead. "I have never met him, or his mother, so it would be truthful to say practically nothing. Why do you ask?"

"It's time for some frankness. You ought to know that Martinez is a criminal, Father James. I know because I worked with him during Prohibition. Afterwards, I got lucky and got to walk a straighter path. Luis stayed in the life. Lately he's been involved in a counterfeit ring, and he's in trouble with the leader over something I haven't learned yet."

"But you intend to keep looking."

Farrell got up and put his hat on. "He was like an older brother to me once. Yeah, I'm going to keep looking. I'll be back with you soon, Father James."

"Peace be with you, my son. I'll pray for your success." He shook hands with Farrell, then watched as he left the room. When he was alone again, he took off his coat, unbuttoned his collar, and turned the sunlamp back on.

❊❊❊

At his fish camp on the river, Luis Martinez changed into a pair of canvas trousers, a blue chambray work shirt, and a pair of work boots that laced up over his ankles. He strapped a holster containing his .38 around his shoulders, then put a light denim jacket on over it. Placing a battered gray fedora on his head, he picked up the sawed-off shotgun and went to the car.

Martinez stuck to back roads, entering New Orleans just north of City Park. After he passed through the park on Filmore, he drove north toward the lake and the amusement park at Pontchartrain Beach. The aromas of hot dogs and popcorn borne on a hot breeze released a flood of bitter-sweet memories that he ruthlessly pushed away.

He continued on Southline Drive, following it past the airport to Hayne Boulevard until he sighted a large airplane hangar about a mile distant. It had the name of a defunct regional airline painted on the roof, but, as Martinez was well aware, it now belonged to Santiago Compasso. It was also the hub of the counterfeiting gang, where the bills were printed, cut, and bundled for shipping.

He drove slowly around to the rear, finding three automobiles parked there—two Fords and an aging Jackson, its shiny brass radiator gleaming in the sun. He stopped short of them, leaving the motor of his car running. He picked up the shotgun, got out, and walked to the hangar doors. There was a smaller, man-sized door set into one of them. He went to it.

As he slipped inside, he heard the faint sound of a radio playing somewhere in the building. He saw light shining from a small interior office and moved stealthily toward it. He had nearly reached it when a sandy-haired man stepped suddenly from behind a stack of crates. It was Stevenson, the printing specialist from Atlanta. Stevenson stopped short, then snatched desperately at the butt of a revolver on his hip. Martinez let him free the gun before he squeezed the trigger. The shotgun blast swept Stevenson off his feet as the roar reverberated like summer thunder.

Martinez moved, knowing he had only a minute to get ready. He ducked behind another stack of crates, listening to the rattle of feet on concrete, the sound of men crying out in surprise. As they ran past him, he stepped from cover and fired twice at their backs. Both men staggered as a mist of blood flew from their contorted bodies.

Martinez racked the slide again, then stood there listening, holding his breath in order to hear. The ringing in his ears was fierce, and he trembled as he waited to see if a fourth man might jump from cover. When he heard nothing, he moved, checking the office, then the rest of the hangar. He kept the door to the outside in sight as best he could until he was satisfied he was alone.

He continued his search, tearing the lids off crates, cutting into bales with the blade of his knife. As Martinez had suspected, Compasso hadn't moved anything to another location, no doubt thinking Martinez lacked the gall to attack the counterfeiting headquarters in broad daylight. He found bags of bills, bound in phony bank bands, ready to be fed into the pipeline.

He went outside to his car, opening the trunk. He placed the shotgun inside, then removed two bottles of gasoline that he'd stuffed down inside a cardboard box full of paper. He took the bottles inside the hangar, where he lit the cloth wicks hanging from their necks. The first he threw into the office and the other into the printing press. The clash of breaking glass was swiftly followed by the whoosh of the gasoline catching fire. He didn't linger, turning on his heel and sprinting out. He was driving west before the smoke began to pour out of the half-open door. He was miles away when he heard the first siren.

He wanted to feel something. He'd just murdered three men, but he couldn't feel a thing. He thought about Linda being murdered, and he couldn't feel a thing.

⊗≋⊗

Daggett was waiting in Casey's outer office when he returned from Gretna. Casey greeted him and led the Negro detective into his private office.

"You look tired, Daggett. Long night?"

"Yes, sir, but profitable. We found a man who's heard some things."

"Tell it."

"Looks like Martinez has been in with a racketeer named Compasso. He's not from around here, but we looked him up and found out he's a big operator last known to operate in Pensacola. Martinez is supposed to've helped him put together a mob, all from outside the state. The informant doesn't know what the mob's racket is, but it makes sense it's got to be the counterfeiting ring."

"I agree. What else did you learn?"

"Martinez and Compasso have had some kind of falling out, about what, he didn't know. He believes Compasso brought in another outsider to track him down."

"I've had some of Snedegar's men checking murder reports for the past few weeks. There's nothing else like the Blanc murder. Except for the one in Gretna last night."

Daggett raised an eyebrow. "In Gretna? What happened?"

"Woman named Wisteria Mullins. She owned a joint over there called the Riverboat Lounge. Somebody knocked her manager unconscious, then went upstairs to her office. The M. O. is similar to the Blanc murder. She was stripped and tied to a chair. This time he used a knife on her. When he was finished torturing her he cut her jugular vein and let her bleed out."

"Christ on the Cross," Daggett exclaimed. "What's the connection between the two women?"

"Wisteria Mullins was Linda Blanc's first cousin. The killer probably thought she'd know where Martinez is." Casey paused for a moment as he pushed a paper clip around on his blotter. "The murder occurred right after Wes Farrell was there to see her. He's looking for Luis Martinez, too."

Daggett nodded. "What's his interest?"

"He didn't say, although he and Martinez have known each other since Prohibition."

"Mr. Farrell's a good man, but I wish he didn't turn up on the edge of things quite so often. He's stickin' his neck way out this time."

Casey gave a restrained grin. "The Compasso angle is a secret so far. I don't think the Treasury guys have made the connection yet. Which gives us something to work with. Paul Ewell wants a gang of counterfeiters, but we want a double murderer. Until I know more, we're gonna play our cards close to the vest."

"What do you want us to do, Captain?"

"These two murders are Negro Squad cases, and we'll continue to treat them that way. Assign teams of men to watch Compasso's house round the clock. Maybe we'll get lucky and his pet killer will come to call."

Daggett nodded. "Sounds like a plan. I'll get to it."

"Pick some lucky men, Daggett. We need some luck."

❈

Marcel Aristide had put the word out about Wilbur Lee Payne to a dozen people he knew in the Negro underworld before going to bed the night before. When he woke up it was past 8:00.

He got up and put through a call to the Metro Hotel, and asked for Marta's room. She was still there when the phone rang.

"Yes?" she said a bit timidly.

"Marta? Miss Walker? It's Marcel Aristide."

"Oh," she said, relief evident in her voice. "Forgive me. I couldn't imagine who could be calling me. I don't know another soul here."

"Well, I'm sorry if I upset you. I was wondering if you'd had breakfast yet."

"Well—no, I haven't."

"The Astoria Hotel not far from you has a swell restaurant. If I came by in about forty-five minutes, might you be ready?"

"Yes, of course. You're ever so kind, Mr. Aristide."

"Call me Marcel. I'll see you in a little while." Marcel hung up the phone, feeling the pleasant buzz of blood rushing through his veins.

When Marcel arrived to pick the young woman up, she was wearing a print sundress with a matching bolero jacket, and a small straw hat cocked to the side of her dark hair.

"Morning. You look great today," Marcel said.

Marta's complexion deepened at his compliment, and she looked down a bit shyly. "Thank you. I'm glad you called. I'm starved."

"Come on, then." Marcel led her out to his car, and a few minutes later he pulled up outside the Astoria, giving his keys to the bellhop. He led her inside the most luxurious Negro hotel in the city. He spoke to several people as they passed through the lobby to the dining room. Soon they were seated next to a window.

"This is so nice," she said, marveling at the draperies and table linen. "This won't be too expensive, will it?"

He smiled, and managed not to laugh. "No more than the law allows. Don't worry. Just enjoy the food."

After the waiter took their orders for scrambled eggs and bacon, Marta found the courage to ask about her missing boyfriend.

"I know you're doing all you can, but have you heard anything at all about Albert? Please don't think I'm being a nuisance." She stared across the table at him, her eyes luminous and full of questions.

Without thinking, he reached out and took one of her hands. "I've spoken to some people who recognized Albert's photo, Marta, but—"

Her mouth opened a bit. "But what? Please tell me."

"Well, Albert's real name is Wilbur Lee Payne."

"What?"

Marcel nodded. "You see, Wilbur had a—a kind of interesting life before he met you, Marta. I'm sure he'd changed and all—"

Her mouth dropped open as she sensed an unexpected revelation. "Changed? From what?"

Marcel tried not to grimace. He hadn't intended to progress quite so quickly to Albert's secret life, but he could see there was no backing out now. "I'm afraid he's a criminal. He served a term at Angola before you knew him."

Marta slumped in her chair, her complexion suddenly pasty and her eyes dull. She seemed incapable of speech.

"Marta. Marta? Are you all right? Marta?" Marcel anxiously patted the back of her hand. He'd heard that women sometimes fell prey to a malady called "the vapors," but he didn't know what a man was supposed to do about it.

Marta shook her head a bit, and her eyes refocused on his. "Oh my. Oh Dear Lord, Mr.—I mean, Marcel. I never knew—I never dreamed—"

Well, you've sure loused this up, Marcel thought. "No, of course. How could you? It was a surprise to me, really it was." He was babbling, thinking feverishly for something to rescue the two of them from this embarrassing tangle. Finally, it was Marta who rescued them. She began to laugh.

Marcel watched her, thinking she might be hysterical, but eventually he realized the laughter was genuine. He began to laugh, too, partly from relief. Others in the dining room looked at them curiously, but neither noticed, nor seemed to care if they did.

"Now I know you think I'm a foolish little goose," she said when she could speak again. She dabbed at the corners of her eyes with the edge of her napkin.

Marcel took a sip of water to clear his throat, feeling foolishly pleased. "Well, no. I was thinking what a good sport you are. I thought you'd be pretty cut up about it."

"Maybe I should be, but I'm not," the girl said in a more sober voice. "I thought it was something about me that made him leave, but I see now that he was lying to me the whole time about everything. If he had stayed, the Good Lord knows what might've happened to me."

Their food came, and they ate in a contented silence, occasionally smiling at each other. After a while, Marcel asked, "Do you still want to find him?"

She thought about it for a moment. "For some reason, I do. It would be good to just let him know that he can't come back and fool me again." She took a sip of coffee, still looking at Marcel. "It would be a way of cleaning the slate for me. Do you see what I mean?"

"Yes, I think I do."

"But do you still think you can find him in this big city? He could be anywhere."

Marcel smiled. "It's my town, Marta, and I've had a good teacher. I can find him."

⊗⊗⊗

It was early afternoon when the bell over the door announced a visitor at the Blue Note Pawnshop. The owner, Theron Oswald, looked up from the issue of *Spicy Love Stories* he was reading and recognized the visitor as an employee of the Railway Express Agency. He was a chubby white man in his mid-thirties, his skin shiny with sweat, dark circles under the arms of his uniform shirt.

"You Theron Oswald?" he asked as he approached.

"'At's me," Oswald replied. He was mildly curious about this occurrence, because he'd never had a visit from REA before. He wondered if the man wanted to pawn something until he saw the package under his arm.

The man put the package on the counter and held out a clipboard. "Sign here." He offered Oswald his pencil.

Hiding his curiosity behind a poker face, Oswald signed his name on the line with a package number, then handed the pencil back to the driver.

"Thanks," he said. "Have y'self a nice day, hear?"

"Yeah, sure," Oswald replied absently. He pulled the package to him and studied the handwriting on the label. There was no return address. He looked furtively around the shop, then pulled a knife from his pocket and used it to cut the tape. He lifted the lid carefully and saw the note. Just seeing Martinez's name made his blood run cold.

With a shaking hand, he took the four paper-wrapped objects from the box and carefully unwrapped them. When the finely engraved plates were laid bare on the counter, he began to tremble uncontrollably. A series of scenarios raced across his mind's eye like film in a movie projector. In one, he gave Santiago Compasso the plates. Instead of rewarding him, Compasso became suspicious and killed him. In the second, Oswald took the counterfeit plates to the police, who, knowing his underworld reputation, put him immediately in jail. In the third, Oswald buried them in the back yard, then got on a boat to Central America, where he changed his name and remained there for the rest of his life. Then he heard the bell ring as the door opened, and he had just enough time to shove the package under the display case, wondering if his stark terror could be seen in his face.

⚉

Special Agent Paul Ewell's conference in the office of A. J. McCandless was coming to a close, but he recognized that the tension in the room had not diminished in spite of his assurances. He found that interesting.

"Well, Agent Ewell. What happens now?" McCandless asked around his cigarette holder. It was made of yellow ivory and jutted upwards from the side of his mouth like a naval gun. Employees sometimes commented on the resemblance to President Roosevelt when he smoked, but none dared say so in his presence. He hated Roosevelt's guts.

"We wait. We keep our eyes open," Ewell replied. "You're clean, and so are the other banks in town. So far the epidemic of phony bills hasn't worked its way this far south."

"That's good news, I suppose," Leake said in a voice strangely devoid of emotion.

Max Grossmann held up a finger. "Tell me, Agent Ewell. What does your department make of the fact that so little money has been found in this city when you've found so much elsewhere? You have a theory, of course."

Ewell's weathered face was sober as he replied to the Jewish banker. "I'm afraid we don't, Mr. Grossmann. The general belief is that they just haven't gotten around to us yet. They may not be aware that we've begun to recognize the counterfeit bills. I consider it dumb luck that our inspectors spotted it in Atlanta. That tipped us off to the danger, and all our field offices went on the alert."

McCandless took the cigarette holder from his mouth. "It seems as though you're up against some pretty smooth customers. What are the chances of finding them?"

"Up until yesterday, I'd say they were pretty bad, but we've been able to identify a key man in the operation. His lover was brutally murdered two nights ago. We don't know why the murder was committed, but we think it's possible there's a connection with this case. We've got Federal and city police on the lookout for the man in question." Ewell watched the three men as he spoke. They seemed an uncomfortable bunch, their eyes everywhere but on him. Did the mere whisper of counterfeit bother bankers that much?

"What do you know about this man?" Leake asked.

"He's a career criminal with a pretty wide expertise. In the past twenty years he's participated in a half-dozen different kinds of crime that we know of. If he's been involved with counterfeiting before this, we haven't heard of it."

McCandless tapped his fingers restlessly on his spotless desk blotter. "You say he's a career criminal. Why isn't he in jail?"

"Because he's good. He's smart and doesn't make mistakes. But the murder of his woman might make him break cover. He's probably mad and isn't going to be as careful as he's been. We needed a break, and this might be it."

"Hummmp," McCandless said. "Well, is there anything we can do to assist you in the meantime?"

Ewell uncrossed his legs, recognizing that the interview was coming to a close. "No, sir, I don't think so. We've worked very closely with your head teller and your vault manager. My inspectors are satisfied that they'll be effective watchdogs. We've done the same with the other banks in the city, so New Orleans is as prepared as it can be to resist an onslaught of phony bills." He stood, picking up his hat from the chair beside him. "We'll keep in close touch with you, and men from my office will visit the vault from time to time. You can, of course, call my office whenever you wish."

McCandless stood up, as did Grossmann and Leake just a second behind. The bank president held out his hand and Ewell took it. "Thank you, Agent Ewell. Hopefully, we'll see the end of this soon."

Ewell shook hands with the other two men, exchanged goodbyes with all of them, then departed the room.

"That was certainly good news," Grossmann said. "I suppose we can devote ourselves to the bank's business instead of all this secret-service hugger-mugger."

McCandless laughed at the big Jewish banker. "Quite right, Max. It's the *bank's* job to make money, not the counterfeiters'. So let's get out there and make some for our customers."

Grossmann gave McCandless an ironic smile. "And for ourselves, A. J. Let's not forget ourselves." He flashed a grin at Leake, who looked away with a cold expression on his face.

⊗≋⊗

It took Jelly about ten minutes to find the hardware store the old man had described. It was a large clapboard building with two stories. There were curtains on the upstairs windows, indicating that the proprietor probably lived upstairs. A large sign proclaimed:

PELECANO'S FRIENDLY HARDWARE EMPORIUM

A smaller sign indicated that fishing and hunting licenses could be purchased there.

She parked the car, got out, and walked through the entrance, fanning herself with a perfumed handkerchief. The inside was dark and cool, and smelled pleasantly of cedar. A slender Greek with a bold hooked nose was ringing up some hardware purchases for a Negro dressed in paint-stained work clothes. As he accepted the man's money and bid him farewell, the Greek's gaze fell on Jelly, and his eyes got a pleasant gleam in them.

"Somethin' I can do for you, miss? If we ain't got it in stock, we can prob'ly get it for you by tomorra'." He spoke in a pleasant baritone with a confident lilt.

She favored him with a special smile, and walked to the counter. She was amused by his unabashed admiration. "Maybe. Would you know a gentleman named Martinez?"

The Greek put his thumbs in his vest as he thought about that. "If his front name is Louie, the answer is yeah. I ain't seen him for a while, though. He used to buy his fishin' and huntin' licenses from me, and we did some trade for fishin' line, shotgun shells, and like that."

Jelly leaned an indolent hip against the counter and pulled cigarettes from her bag. She offered one to the Greek, took one for herself, then leaned forward for him to light it with a kitchen match. She took in a lung full of smoke then luxuriously blew it back out. "I've been out of town, and was hopin' to find Luis. He seems to've moved away and nobody I've talked to knows where he went."

The Greek took the cigarette out of his mouth and tugged thoughtfully at his nose. "Yeah, that's true. Been a couple years, anyhow, since I seen him. He must be gettin' his huntin' and fishin' gear somewheres else now."

Jelly smoked in silence, nodding her head. Then she looked up with a gleam in her eyes. "Y'know, I was just remembering something Louie always said—'luck is where you find it, but I always look for mine down by the river.' Think he was talkin' about fishing?"

The Greek rubbed the edge of his jaw with a slender thumb. "Yeah, I used to hear him say that. Sometimes when we'd be playin' cards. Come to think of it, he had a fish camp upriver somewheres. I never could take enough time off from work to go up there with 'im, though."

"Aw, that's too bad," Jelly said solicitously. "He might be there on a day as nice as this. Louie never worked eight-to-five. Salesman or something, wasn't he?"

"Yeah—come to think of it, I never heard him talk about his work much." He looked at the sunlight falling through the entrance and sighed wistfully. "Today would sure be a swell day to lay up at a fish camp." He put the cigarette into his mouth and smoked as he rubbed his curly scalp. As he did so, an idea came to him and he turned back to her. "Y'know, I know somebody who used to go fishin' with Louie all the time. A colored bartender. Bet he could tell you."

She gave him a dazzling smile. "See, you had what I wanted and I didn't have to wait until tomorrow. That's service, Mr. Pelecano."

Chapter 7

It was nearly 2:30 when Farrell parked his convertible near Theron Oswald's pawnshop. The polished bells of trumpets, saxes, and trombones gleamed inside the display window like the gold in Sutter's millrace, in stark contrast to the hapless, out-of-work musicians who'd pawned them for eating money.

As he entered, a bell tinkled above his head. He saw a sharp-faced Negro with dark yellow skin staring at him from across the counter.

"Long time, no see, Ozzy," Farrell said.

"Mr. Farrell," Oswald said tonelessly. "Come to pawn your watch?" An insincere grin caused his droopy black mustache to twitch.

Farrell walked slowly to the glass counter, his hands loose at his sides. He stared into the other man's eyes, recognizing immediately that Oswald was scared. He enjoyed that possibility. "I'm looking for Luis Martinez."

"Ain't seen him."

"You're a liar. You and Martinez have been friends for fifteen years."

"So what? You think that means I keep the guy in my hip pocket? He's got his life and I got mine."

The planes of Farrell's face grew sharp and savage. "I never saw a man talk so hard and say so little. Maybe you haven't heard that Luis's friends are turning up dead."

Oswald stared at Farrell, his fear more pronounced than before. "I'm tellin' you the truth, man. I ain't seen Louie in a month of Sundays."

Farrell put his hands into his trouser pockets and expelled a gust of breath like a boiler letting off steam. He was sick and tired

of people lying to him or covering up. The urge to put his hands
on Oswald was almost overpowering, but he fought it. "You know
who Santiago Compasso is?"

Oswald decided to see what a little truth would buy him. "Yeah.
That's the spig Louie's workin' for."

"Why does Compasso want to kill him?"

Oswald licked his lips. "Louie and him fell out over a split.
Louie told me a few months back that Compasso was nickel-and-
dimin' him. Louie put together the experts for makin' phony
money and Compasso was gettin' all the gravy. You know Louie
ain't gonna lay down for no fancy-pants spig."

Farrell listened carefully, watching Oswald's eyes. The man was
shooting straight, but he was holding something back. "That's
not helping his friends, Ozzy. Linda Blanc and Wisteria Mullins
were tortured to death, a day apart."

Oswald rubbed his face, trying to stimulate his brain. He
couldn't be stupid with Farrell. "Christ!"

"Ozzy, Luis hasn't got many friends. With those two dead,
practically all that's left is you and me. I figure sooner or later,
he's got to contact one of us. That's if Compasso's killer doesn't
get to us first."

It took all of Oswald's will power to keep from looking at the
cardboard box at his feet.

"L-leave me alone, Farrell. I'm a fuckin' nobody. Why would
anybody wanna hurt me? Shit." He pasted a pathetic grin on his
face and tried to laugh, but the noise that came from his mouth
was more a strangled wheeze.

Farrell sneered cruelly. "You know too much, Ozzy. Until yesterday I didn't know anything about a counterfeiting ring operating
in the city—the Treasury Department doesn't even know. But *you*
know all about it."

"I—I—" Oswald couldn't get any words past his teeth. Farrell
bored in relentlessly.

"You know what I think, Ozzy? I think if Luis gets shoved
into a corner, he'll come straight to you because you know what
the game's all about." He walked around the counter and put his
face close to Oswald's. "If it happened to get out that you knew
all about the counterfeiting mob, where do you think that would
put you, Ozzy, old buddy?"

Oswald's vision was clouding from the pressure he was under. He needed to get Farrell out of there so he could hide the plates, then figure out what to do. "Man, you're scarin' me bad. Sure, I know what li'l bit Louie done told me, but not that much. I ain't botherin' nobody around here. Hell, I even do a li'l business with Mr. Compasso now and again, handlin' shit he wants to get rid of and such. Please—what've I gotta do for you man? Please tell me."

"Where's Luis?"

Oswald shook his head wearily. "I keep tellin' you, I don't know. I talked to him las' night—told him about Linda. He was close to crackin' up. Said he was gonna lay up somewhere. I been waitin' to hear from him again, but he ain't called."

Farrell felt no sympathy for Oswald. He was no better than an insect that left a trail of slime behind him. But he was terrified about something, something more than the things Farrell had said to him. Farrell decided to give him some slack. "All right. But if you hear from him, tell him to call me. Better yet, *you* call, and tell me where he is, understand? If you don't, I'll make you wish you'd never been born."

"Y-yeah, man. Yeah." Oswald hung his head wearily. He remained in that hangdog posture until he heard Farrell leave the shop.

When the door closed, Oswald bounded into action like a track star at the starting gun. He dragged the package from under the counter and hurriedly sealed the box with masking tape. Next, he pulled out the bottom drawer of his desk and shoved the package to the back of the opening. It was a hiding place Oswald had fashioned himself, shortening a drawer to leave a useful space behind. He quickly replaced the drawer, locked the desk, then wiped his sweating face on his sleeve.

He composed his features as the tinkle of the bell heralded the arrival of a customer. However, he turned to see a man locking the door to the shop, pulling down the shades over the glass door and the main window. When the man turned toward Oswald, the shop floor was in shadow. The man stood there, his features hidden in the gloom, but the distinctive shape of an automatic was visible in his gloved fist.

"What did Farrell want?" the apparition demanded.

"Huh?" Oswald said stupidly.

"Don't make me ask you again, fuckhead."

The pawnbroker was too scared to do anything but tell the truth. "He's lookin' for Martinez. He thought I might know where he is."

"Do you?"

"Naw, man. I talked to 'im las' night, but he wouldn't tell me where he was or where he was goin'. I tried to get him to give Mr. Compasso back his stuff, but he wouldn't do it. He wouldn't do it." Oswald's voice and composure cracked at once, and he broke into an anguished sob.

The man raised his gun and cocked the hammer. Oswald had never heard anything quite so loud. "Don't lie to me, boy. I get real steamed when people start lyin' to me. What did Farrell say to you? All of it, you Goddamned son of a whore." The man's teeth were bared and they gleamed like the fangs of a predatory beast in the dim light.

The pawnbroker began to tremble and he felt his legs about to collapse under him. "He—he knows about the counterfeit ring. He knows Compasso is the boss."

"What else?"

"Nothin', man. He don't know about the plates Louie stole. He don't know why you's tryin' to kill Louie, or why you done kilt those two women. He reckons you gonna work on Louie's friends 'til one of 'em gives Louie up."

The man with the gun nodded, his expression almost amiable. He walked toward Oswald with the gun leveled at his breast. Oswald fell to his knees, his hands clasped in front him like a religious supplicant. His mouth was contorted in a soundless scream and tears ran down his face.

The gunman's teeth shone brightly in the dim room as he slowly, lovingly, turned the barrel of his gun and eased it into Oswald's gaping mouth. "That's right, boy. Stay down there and suck on this for a minute, and listen to me." He nodded as the pawnbroker closed his lips around the barrel of the gun, whimpering. "That's good. See, I could work on you like I done the women. But you done give me an idea. See, way I got it figured, Martinez's gonna need a friend real soon. Since you the only one he's contacted, I think that's gonna be you. Yeah, and when he does that, you gonna set up a meet. You and him. 'Cept it's gonna be me who meets him, you understand? I'm gonna get the plates and take care of him at the same time."

Oswald's bladder and bowels had broken loose and he was choking on the gun barrel, near to vomiting. He nodded his head frantically, hoping the gunman would recognize his agreement. Finally, the gun barrel was slowly withdrawn, and Oswald felt a soft hand stroke his cheek.

"You're a good li'l boy, Ozzy," the gunman said amiably. "Do like you're told, and you might just live through this. Now go clean yourself up. Jesus Christ, that ain't no way for a man to be."

⊗⊗⊗

Frank Casey was rubbing his eyes after finishing with the day's incident reports, wondering if he was going to have to get some glasses when the intercom buzzed. His secretary, Officer Alan White, told him Nick Delgado was there with a report from the Mullins murder.

The door opened and a short, stocky man entered the office. Casey saw a look in his eyes that presaged some kind of development.

"Sit down, Nick. What have you got for me?"

Delgado's eyes gleamed behind his wire-rimmed spectacles. "A mystery, Captain. When the Jeff Parish lab men completed the identification of all the latent prints found at the Mullins homicide, they sent everything over here to compare with our files. I found something there that'll interest you, and the Treasury people, too."

"Let's hear it."

"Most of the prints found belonged to the Mullins woman, or her man Terry Buford. There were a few belonging to janitorial workers and a couple of other employees, but there was one that shouldn't have been there."

Casey felt the hairs on the back of his neck stand up. "Tell me."

"There was one print from a right-handed thumb on Wisteria Mullins' desk that matched no one else. I think the killer used gloves throughout the torture, but at some point he took his right glove off. Maybe he was looking for something and needed a hand free. The furniture polish on the desk held it bright and bold."

"Okay, that sounds positive to me. But I know that look, Nick. What's the punch-line?"

Nick raised his left eyebrow quizzically. "When I couldn't find a match in our files, I wired the print to a man at the FBI labs in Washington who owes me, and told him it was a rush. He did a more extensive search and discovered the print belongs to a dead man."

"Dead? How could that be?"

"I don't know, but the print belongs to a contract killer named Dixie Ray Chavez. He's operated mostly in Arkansas, Oklahoma, Louisiana and Texas. I checked up on him, then wired the State Police in Baton Rouge, and the Department of Public Safety in Texas. They sent back quite a bit about him." Delgado passed over a manila folder with a mug shot paper clipped to the front. It was of a round-faced white man with a sneer on his face. Casey opened the file and began to read.

"Dixie Ray Chavez. Born Plano, Texas, 1910. Height, five feet, eight inches, weight, one-forty. Hair brown, eyes brown, complexion sallow, no scars or marks. Three arrests for murder. No convictions due to lack of evidence or uncooperative witnesses. Five arrests for attempted murder, sixteen arrests for assault and battery. One conviction back in 1930 that got him a two-spot in Huntsville. Brief association with the Parker-Barrow gang, a rumor of association with the Dillinger gang." Casey read on in silence for a moment. "Here's the report of his death—supposedly killed in an explosion during a Treasury raid on an illegal distillery in southern Oklahoma in April of '34 but his file left open when no body found." He found a brief typed message from the commander of Company B of the Texas Rangers in Dallas that he read aloud.

"'I have spent years tracking the movements of Dixie Ray Chavez, and am not surprised to hear he's still alive. He's not just a clever killer, he's a vicious predator with the instincts of a coyote. He has the ability to blend in wherever he goes, and often has his prey in sight for some time before he finally moves in for the kill. He's been diagnosed as a psychopathic personality, and kills without compunction. If you get him in your sights, my advice would be to shoot him. If you give him half a chance, he'll sure shoot you.' Signed M. T. Gonzaulles, Captain, Company B."

Casey closed the file and put it back on the desk. "I guess we can safely assume he wasn't killed in that explosion, after all."

"No, sir," Delgado replied. "That print was as fresh as a daisy. Chavez is alive and well, and still killing people. The tortures are his trademark. According to his file, he likes hurting people."

"Just what we needed." Casey picked up his telephone and asked for Records and Identification.

"R and I, Sergeant Mulwray speaking."

"Mulwray, this is Casey. Nick Delgado has just discovered the identity of the killer in the Blanc and Mullins cases as Dixie Ray Chavez."

"Yes, sir, he shared that information with me. I've got a full description ready to call down to dispatch."

"Great. Go ahead and put it on the wire. Be sure to urge caution when attempting to apprehend."

"Can do, Chief." Mulwray hung up. Casey turned back to Delgado.

"Okay, Nick. Good work."

"It was luck, and we'll need more to find him."

Casey smiled as he tapped his fingers on the desk. "He just made a mistake. He may be about to make another one."

⊗⊗⊗

After Marcel took Marta back to her hotel, he had an inspiration. Remembering Wilbur Lee Payne had passed himself off as a pharmacist in Texas, Marcel decided to see if he was doing the same in New Orleans.

He left Downtown on Tulane Avenue, turning south on Jefferson Davis Parkway. Crossing the New Orleans Navigation Canal, he turned into the neighborhood on the other side and drove down Dixon Street until he reached the campus of Xavier University, a Negro college that was operated by the Catholic Sisters of the Blessed Sacrament. It was also the home of the only Negro school of pharmacy in the South. He turned south at Pine Street and parked near the corner of Palmetto.

It took him about five minutes to find the offices of the pharmacy school on the third floor of the west wing of the main building. A pebbled glass door with the legend "Dr. Malcolm Samson" proved to be his destination. He knocked lightly, opening the door as he heard a voice beckon him inside.

At a desk beside a window sat a distinguished-looking gray-haired Negro of about fifty dressed in a white lab coat. He looked up from the new issue of *The American Journal of Dermatology* and smiled. "Marcel Aristide? Come on in, boy. Have you finally decided to enroll in my program?"

Marcel grinned as he took off his hat. "No, sir, but I do have a pharmacy question, if you've got the time."

"Pharmacy is my business. I was just reading about promising new therapies for skin diseases. But you probably didn't come for a lecture. Sit down and take a load off. Could you use some coffee?"

"No thanks." Marcel caught a glimpse of some gruesome medical photos as he placed his hat on a corner of Samson's desk. He had met Malcolm Samson at the Fairgrounds Racetrack a year or so before, and had given him some horse racing tips that paid off for the scientist. Ever since, Samson had been trying to get Marcel to enroll at the university.

"Well, a pharmacy question, you said?"

"Yeah. I'm looking for a pharmacist from Brownsville Texas who is supposed to have come up here a few weeks ago."

Samson raised an eyebrow. "Supposed to have? Sounds like there might be a story in that."

"There might be. I was wondering if there was a way to find out if he was working here in the city. I'm helping a friend who's trying to reach him."

Samson fingered his chin. "What's his name?"

"Albert Chenier—at least that's the name he was using in Brownsville."

Samson leaned back in his chair and stared at Marcel. "You think that may not be his right name? Or do you think he's using an alias here?"

"Could be either one. I discovered from a friend of mine that ten years ago he was calling himself Wilbur Lee Payne, or perhaps used the name Keys."

"This man sounds like a criminal of some kind."

Marcel grinned. "Sounds that way to me, too. Can you help me at all?"

"Marcel, when this is settled, are you going to tell me the rest of the story attached to these questions?"

"Sure."

Samson consulted a desk directory, then picked up the telephone receiver and asked the operator for a number. Seconds later, he was speaking into the mouthpiece.

"This is Dr. Samson at Xavier University. I was wondering if you'd received any applications in the recent past for a state permit from a pharmacist by the name of Albert Chenier? No, eh? How about Wilbur Lee Payne? Nothing there either. How about a gentleman named Keys?" He looked at Marcel and shook his head.

"Ask if they've had any applications from pharmacists licensed in Texas," Marcel suggested in a low voice.

Samson relayed that to the person at the other end of the line, then picked up a pencil and wrote down two names. "Do you happen to know which pharmacies these men are working in? Yes, yes, thank you." He wrote some more information down on the pad, then thanked the other person and hung up.

"Well, we've got two transfers—Louisiana and Texas have a reciprocal agreement that enables pharmacists from each state to travel to the other and receive certification to work within a couple of days. The names he had were Orville Goff from Seguin, Texas and Milton Jasper from Austin. They're working at these addresses." He tore off the slip of paper and handed it to Marcel.

Marcel took it, glanced at it then slipped it into his coat pocket. "I remembered you saying that you worked with the Negro branch of state board of pharmacy. I figure these for long shots, but it's ground I have to cover."

"All right," Samson said, leaning back in his chair and folding his arms across his chest. "I answered your questions, so tell me what this is all about."

"Fair enough. A young woman came to town two days ago looking for a pharmacist named Albert Chenier, supposedly from New Orleans. He left Brownsville very suddenly without telling her goodbye, so she came looking for him. Last night I discovered the man is an ex-convict who went by the name of Wilbur Lee Payne."

"My God. An ex-convict posing as a reputable Negro pharmacist? That's a kind of publicity we don't need. What will you do if you find him?"

"Depending on what I find, I'll either hold him until his ex-girlfriend can give him a piece of her mind, or I'll hand him over to the police. Whatever brought this man to New Orleans, it's bound to be crooked."

Samson rubbed his forehead as he considered what the younger man had told him. "I'm not too experienced in this kind of conniving, but your story has my mind working."

"Go ahead, sir. I'm here to listen."

"Well, for one thing, I'm not sure that a man could get work in a big city pharmacy with fraudulent credentials. Even a small pharmacy would require a diploma from his school, a state certificate, and probably some references. A smaller town might not demand so much. Perhaps a letter of reference on some other pharmacy's letterhead addressed 'to whom it may concern.' Also, a phony diploma might more easily get by a small-town druggist, too."

Marcel's eyes narrowed and a smile grew on his lips. "Go on, sir."

"Well, it takes a considerable education to become a registered pharmacist. Much of what we study is identical to what is taught in a course of medical education."

Marcel folded his arms and cupped his chin in his left hand as he mulled this over. "One of the things I've been able to learn about this fellow is that he's got a remarkable ability to learn things—a photographic memory is how somebody described it. He must've learned all this medical and pharmaceutical knowledge on his own."

"Well," Samson continued, "this man might find it too risky to pose as another pharmacist here. He'd have too many hurdles to jump just to find work. Now I'm supposing the man you're looking for is a con artist of some kind."

"On the nose."

"Well, maybe I'm jumping to conclusions but an unscrupulous Negro looking to make a profit as a phony professional man would know that our people have a special feeling of respect for one of their own who has risen above his origins. This is particularly true for teachers, lawyers—and doctors. It would actually be easier for such a man to pass himself off as a doctor than as a pharmacist."

Marcel raised an eyebrow. "Why?"

"Well, if he set himself up in private practice, he wouldn't be answerable to anyone. He could hang out his shingle and gradually work his way into the community until he realized whatever goal he had. Plus, if he's played at being a pharmacist, he would know how to get various kinds of drugs and stock his own dispensary. With his own supplies, he wouldn't have to forge or fabricate prescription blanks that might be recognized as such."

"Wow," Marcel said. "He could operate indefinitely."

Samson nodded. "A skillful and lucky man would find many doors opened to him, including those of liberal-minded whites." Samson looked at Marcel appraisingly. "This thing you're doing, it seems like something the law should be handling, and yet you've taken it upon yourself. It sounds as though it could be dangerous."

Marcel nodded soberly. "Sometimes life has risks, and I guess you can say I'm a gambler in all things."

Samson rubbed the side of his face. "I'm beginning to believe a career as a pharmacist or a teacher would be a bit too tame for you, Marcel. I didn't realize until today that you're somewhat unconventional. Will you tell me how this turns out? For you as well as for the young woman?"

"If you're sure you want to hear about it. Some laws might get broken before this is all over."

"That'll make it a bit more interesting, won't it?"

"A bit."

⨯

Marston Leake gave the outward appearance of a fussy professorial type, but where it didn't show he was as tough as pig iron. Banking wasn't a business for the faint of heart under the best circumstances, but the boom-and-bust of the 1920s and '30s had been the crucible that dissolved some men and made steel of others. Leake had also worked for over twenty years with A. J. McCandless, a man with no more depth of feeling than an armored tank.

From the time he had first been approached by the Treasury Department, Leake had considered how quantities of counterfeit money could make it into the vaults of important banks and escape detection for so long a time. He had been in touch with colleagues in Atlanta and some of the other affected cities, and had interrogated them thoroughly as to what they had experienced. Gradually he developed a theory, but he was unsure as to what he could do with it.

He had been with McCandless a long time, and had long believed him to be obstinate and unimaginative. However, he knew the bank was McCandless's life. He had broached some of his concerns to the bank president, but had found him strangely preoccupied.

Leake read *The New York Times* and *The Washington Post* almost daily, and listened to the reports from Europe and Asia on his console radio each night, and what he learned made clear to him that the world was coming apart at the seams. It also seemed to him that this was no time for a banker, of all people, to get complacent about the very lifeblood of the United States.

Leake had his doubts about Max Grossmann, too. Part of it, he had to admit to himself, was due to the fact that Grossmann was a European Jew. Leake had been brought up in an environment prejudicial to Jews, and although he had taught himself to resist it, the prejudice remained. However, Grossmann was intelligent and insightful, if a bit fluttery in his temperament. With McCandless locked in some sort of self-imposed isolation, Leake decided to bounce some of his theories off Grossmann.

"Sorry to bother you," Leake said when he called at Grossmann's office.

"Not at all. Come in." Grossmann raised an eyebrow. "You have a look in your eye, Marston. Does it concern what we spoke about on the telephone earlier this week?"

Leake took a chair facing Grossmann's desk. "Yes. The size and scope of this counterfeiting scheme have my mind working overtime."

Grossmann put his pen down and clasped his hands on the blotter. "In what way?"

"What about the fact that they've *not* turned up any bills in *this* city? New Orleans is the biggest banking city between Dallas and Atlanta, and they've not found a single bill here."

"Why, indeed. But they've found no counterfeit in Texas thus far, either. Perhaps Agent Ewell is correct. Perhaps they simply haven't worked this far south as yet."

Leake's stern mouth was stretched tight. "I think there's a better reason, Max. New Orleans *is* the headquarters for the counterfeiting ring. What would make better sense? If no money is passed here, the police would never think of looking here for the criminals."

Grossmann put down the pen he had been toying with, his eyes wide. "I say, that is an interesting theory. That would make these crooks 'pretty slick,' as I think Humphrey Bogart said in a film I watched some time ago."

"Slick is the word," Leake replied. "I've been in banking all my adult life. Counterfeiting is something I've dealt with a few times before, and this gang is different than any other in my experience. I have a suspicion that the reason Treasury hasn't had any luck catching them is that they aren't thinking big enough."

"Surely you're wrong," the fat man said. "They've recognized that this gang has the resources to operate over a six-state region. Not many gangs could do that unless they were big and well-organized."

"It's more than that," Leake persisted. "Think about it, Max. American money is very difficult to copy. There are three different colors of ink, each a special formula. The intaglio printing process requires five separate steps to emboss the paper, then to print the three colors on the front and back of each bill. The paper is a special grade of linen and cotton with no wood pulp. It would require skilled chemists to come up with ink and paper that can fool the average bank employee. The time invested in analysis, production, and the engraving of the plates would be considerable, requiring resources to support the enterprise until profit began to roll in."

Grossmann tapped a broad finger against his fleshy chin. "Heavens, you really have made a study of all this. But I sense you have some point you're coming to. What is it?"

"Just this," Leake replied. "The world is in a condition of considerable upset, and nothing is more vulnerable right now than individual economies. Suppose, for example, one of the warring parties decided that the United States was particularly sympathetic to their opposition. That bloody conniver, Roosevelt, is doing everything but kissing Churchill on the cheek with all his lend-leasing and what-not. Suppose the Nazis decided to make a preemptive strike to cripple us."

Grossmann turned serious. "Whatever are you talking about, old boy?"

"Think about it, Max. This is a big operation with power and resource behind it. What if the German government decided to flood our currency market with counterfeit bills. Think what that would do. It would throw doubt on our currency and could cripple our efforts to climb out of this damn Depression."

Grossmann's eyes examined the ceiling while he thought Leake's words over. His fleshy jowls quivered occasionally before his face fell into an expression of calm deliberation. "Marston, that is a pretty extraordinary theory. It's rather like a plot from an E. Phillips Oppenheim thriller. Much as some of us might wish it, the United States has no war-like intentions toward the Nazis, nor have the Nazis any such intentions toward us so far as I can tell. I've certainly paid attention, believe me."

Leake snorted. "I seem to recall some other countries had no war-like intentions toward them, either, and now they're under Hitler's thumb. As a man driven out of Austria, I'd think you'd be a bit more suspicious of them, Max."

Grossmann made a deprecatory gesture and smiled nervously. "Well, it seems so melodramatic, after all. But say you're right. How is the money ending up in major banks over a six-state region?"

Leake leveled a finger at his corpulent colleague. "I've got a theory about that, too. I've been in touch with people in Atlanta. The Federal Reserve is the one point of contact with all the banks in this region. I haven't figured all the complexities out, but suppose, just suppose that someone at the Federal Reserve is somehow substituting counterfeit money for real currency? The criminals would realize thousands of dollars at one fell swoop. And what if the money is somehow being funneled to Germany?"

Grossmann wore a stunned expression. He put a hand to his forehead and rubbed it as though it were numb. "Tell me, have you spoken to A. J. about this?"

Leake snorted. "I tried, but he's too preoccupied with something else." Leake removed his glasses and polished the lenses with a handkerchief while he continued to squint at Grossmann. "A. J. has been behaving rather peculiarly over the last year. All these trips out of town he's been making. He's neglecting the very business he worked so hard to build up."

Grossmann nodded. "Yes, I have noticed that he is frequently away. Flies his own plane, I understand. Most of his trips are to Atlanta, are they not?"

"Yes, but he's never discussed with me the nature of his business there. I presume it has nothing to do with the bank."

"Yes, perhaps. Well, what do you propose to do with your suspicions, Marston? I mean, after all, you can't prove any of it, can you?"

Leake frowned. "No, but I have considered discussing the theory with the Treasury people. One of them might have enough imagination to recognize the merit in it. Then again, they might give me the big horse laugh."

Grossmann smiled indulgently. "My dear friend. You've been working much too hard lately. You tend to worry quite a bit. I'd advise caution before I said too much to the Treasury people. You know how A. J. is about drawing unwanted attention to the bank."

Leake nodded. "You may be right. I'll think about it." He got up from his chair and walked to Grossmann's office door. "I believe I'll just clear up a few things in my office and then go home."

"Yes. This kind of talk is rather dispiriting. I may follow your example."

Leake left Grossmann's office and strode wearily toward his office. As he walked, he noticed McCandless at the end of the hall, staring coldly in his direction. Without a wave, the bank president turned and disappeared into an adjoining hall.

Leake found letters waiting for his signature, along with some other paperwork he'd left undone when he went to Grossmann's office. As he finished, he sat at his desk thinking. He had rarely been as troubled as he was at this moment. Acting on an impulse he wrote a letter to Agent Paul Ewell. After sealing it in an envelope, he gave it to his secretary to post with the others.

It was close to 5:00 when he took the elevator to the first floor. As he neared the bank entrance, he saw Grossmann about to depart. "Max. Wait up."

The fat man turned, saw Leake. "Ah, you leaving, too? Splendid. Perhaps we can share a cab Uptown."

"Sure," Leake replied. "Why not?"

As they walked toward Canal Street, Grossmann glanced at his colleague. "You seem to be less distressed than earlier. Did talking about it set your mind at rest?"

"I needed to bounce my ideas off someone," Leake replied. "So I suppose it did. I decided to contact the Treasury Department after all and let them decide what to do."

Grossmann patted perspiration on his neck and forehead. "Marston, I'm dreadfully tired, but I'm hungry, too. What say we go to Kolb's German Tavern? I'm in the mood for some bratwurst, sauerkraut, and some of that dark Lowenbrau to wash it down."

"Better than eating my own cooking, I suppose." Leake's dry words evoked a laugh from Grossmann.

The sun had begun to wane, casting long shadows on the business district streets. The two were nearing a corner when a Negro in a dark green suit jumped from an alley into their path.

"Gimme your wallet," the man said, waving a large pistol in his gloved hand.

"Good Lord," Grossmann cried, stepping back instinctively. "Don't get excited, I'll give it to you. I'll give it to you." He reached into his pocket for his wallet with a trembling hand.

"Keep your hands where I can see 'em," the Negro hissed. "Gimme that." He snatched the wallet from Grossman's chubby hand. "You— gimme yours," the gunman said, waving his gun at Leake.

Leake's teeth were bared, his eyes narrowed. He was already angry about the counterfeiting, angry at the idea his bank could be assaulted. He had taken the gun from his desk and was in the mood to use it. "I'll give it to you all right." His hand dove inside his coat, his fingers clamping the butt of his Colt, but before his gun cleared the pocket, the gunman's pistol roared.

The shot was so close to Leake's chest that the fire leaping from the bore set his suit aflame. The white-haired banker fell to the pavement like a bag of sand.

"Help, police! Help, murder, help!" Grossmann shouted at the top of his lungs, waving his arms. "Help, for God's—"

The Negro's gun roared a second time, and Grossmann fell to the ground, wailing in pain and terror. The Negro reached into Leake's jacket, jerked the wallet out, then he ran back into the alley.

Grossmann's cries and the gunfire attracted some attention eventually, and several people, a police officer among them, ran from every direction to where the two men lay on the pavement. Grossmann, by this time, had raised himself up on one elbow, looking down at Leake's face.

"My friend. He's been shot. For God's sake, get a doctor. Get a doctor."

The police officer waded through the small crowd and got down on his knees beside Leake. He placed his fingers against the carotid artery, waited for a moment, then put his ear down by the man's mouth, listening for breath. His face took on a grim expression, and he looked over at Grossmann, shaking his head. "He's gone, mister. Did you see who did it?"

"A—a Negro gunman. Marston was trying to give him his wallet, and he fired. When—when I cried out, he fired at me, too. Dear God! What a catastrophe." Grossmann lowered his head, groaning.

The officer took a look at the wound in Grossmann's shoulder, determined he was in no immediate danger, then walked quickly to a police call box across the street. He quickly relayed information to the dispatcher, then came back to interrogate the crowd. Before too long, sirens sounded, seemingly from every direction. The ambulance arrived, followed by two radio cars and a squad car bearing Israel Daggett and Sam Andrews. They walked toward the ambulance as the attendants were loading Grossmann aboard.

"Hang on just a minute, fellas," Daggett said. He took out his badge and held it up so Grossmann could see it. "Sergeant Daggett of the Negro Squad, sir. Can you tell us who you are?"

Grossmann's face was pale, his mouth opening and closing as though he found it hard to draw breath. "Max Grossmann. I'm v-vice president for f-foreign investment—First National. My friend—Marston Leake. We were on our way to dinner when the bandit jumped out."

"Did you get a good look at him?"

"Y-yes. Medium sized—chocolate brown in color. Had a scar on his right cheek. Green jacket, gray cap l-like a newsboy wears. B-big pistol."

"A forty-five," the first uniformed officer supplied. "I found the shells over where they were shot."

Daggett, still looking down at Grossmann's pale face, nodded that he'd heard. "What did he say to you, Mr. Grossmann?"

"Demanded money. Marston—Marston was trying to give it to him. He—he shot my friend for no reason. No reason at all." Grossmann, his teeth clenched in pain, seemed grief-stricken.

"Okay." Daggett nodded to the ambulance men, who put the big banker inside. Seconds later they were tearing away in the direction of Charity Hospital. As the siren died in the distance, Daggett went over to look at the dead man. He saw the expended .45 shells lying nearby. He stooped down to pick each one up on the end of a pencil before transferring it into an evidence envelope.

"Western brand .45 auto. Nothing special there," Daggett said. "Looks like the killer surprised them at this alley."

Andrews entered the alley and began looking around. He saw something and moved toward it.

"Hey, Iz?"

"Yeah?"

"The shooter was here for a li'l bit. He smoked two cigarettes while he waited. One of 'em's still smoldering." He poked at them with his pencil. "Look like Lucky Strikes." He stood up and shined his light around the alley. "Must've gone back down that way."

Daggett picked up the cigarette butts one by one, making sure they were out before he transferred them to another envelope. "Let's see where the alley leads." He stood up and followed Andrews until they reached the next street. There were a few cars parked nearby, but no pedestrians in sight.

"He could be anywhere by now," Andrews said. "Even with the scar on his face, he looks like a hundred and twenty-five other colored men."

Daggett said nothing, thinking. Finally he jerked his chin at Andrews and they retreated back through the alley to where the shooting had occurred. A morgue wagon and one of Nick Delgado's assistants were there. Daggett gave the evidence envelopes to the lab man, then walked to the officer who'd been on the scene when they arrived.

"Officer, where were you when the shots were fired?"

"I was about three blocks away. When I heard the first one, I knew what it was. It was too flat to be a car backfiring. I ran like hell to get here, but by the time I made it, both victims were down and the gunman was gone. I've been questioning the civilians around here. None of 'em saw anything, just heard the noise and came to investigate."

"Okay, you did everything you could. We'll read your report later. What's your name?"

"Art Manion, out of headquarters division. You're Sergeant Daggett, ain't you?"

"Yeah. We'll get in touch if we get anything."

"Right. See you around." Manion turned and went back to help the patrol car officers control the crowd around the crime scene.

Andrews stared down the street. "Kinda funny, ain't it? This boy had him some balls."

"Uh, huh. A Negro stick-up artist all the way Downtown this time of the day. He'd stick out like a sore thumb. And then he's in the alley smoking cigarettes."

"Yeah, like he was waitin' for something."

"Or somebody. Let's call in the description to R and I, let them see if they've got any suspects that match the description. It didn't ring any bells with me."

"Me neither. I'd remember a guy with a scar who likes shootin' white businessmen in broad daylight with a .45. A man that stupid would sure be memorable."

"Let's go shake some trees, see what falls out."

"Right behind you, boss."

Chapter 8

Farrell paused at his car, glanced at his watch and saw that it was nearly 3:00 PM. He let his eyes travel up the street, then back to the front of Theron Oswald's pawnshop. A man entered the shop, but the sunlight was behind him, and all Farrell got was a glimpse as he went through the door. Something nagged at him. It reminded him of the feeling he'd had outside Wisteria's Riverboat Lounge, but he didn't know why.

Oswald had been telling the truth about what he knew of Martinez's movements, but Farrell doubted he would get a call from Oswald. Oswald had been terrified by something before Farrell even entered the room. Had the killer already been to see him? If so, why wasn't he dead, like the two women?

He got into his car and drove away. There was a lot on his mind, not least of which was his promise to hand his old friend over to the police. He'd been angry with McGee when he'd made that promise, and he didn't know how he could make good on it and still look himself in the face afterward. He knew his father had been forced to do this, not just once but several times. What part of him had he shut down in order to put a friend in jail? He shook his head irritably as he wrestled with the question.

Farrell drove in the direction of the Mississippi River, and when he reached it, he followed it down into the warehouse district. As he drew abreast of a huge brick building bearing a peculiar Oriental symbol, he pulled to the curb, cut the engine, and got out of the car. He walked around the corner, halting at a door set into a frame of granite blocks. His finger went unerringly to a hole that was centered waist-high in one of the bricks. He pushed the button set into it, then stood there waiting. A few moments later, the door opened and a large bald man stood there. He was dressed in a striped sailor's singlet and faded canvas trousers.

"I want to see Sparrow," Farrell said.

The bald man glared at him for a moment, and when Farrell didn't shrink from his gaze, he jerked his chin and stepped aside for Farrell to enter. The bald man led Farrell through a maze of corridors, occasionally passing open doors through which Farrell could see men gambling, others engaged in wrestling or bare-knuckled fighting, or dancing women dressed only in bracelets and nail polish. Sparrow's joint was known from Mississippi to Malaysia as a place where a man could get whatever he wanted, whenever he wanted, if he had the price.

Eventually they halted before a heavy door. The man opened the door and disappeared inside. Seconds later, he reopened the door, jerked his chin at Farrell again, then allowed him inside before departing and closing the door firmly behind him.

Sparrow sat, as usual, in a high-backed mahogany chair that might've been some primitive king's throne. Her black hair was cut short, in the Chinese style, and she wore the same kind of plain black silk dress with white piping favored by young Chinese women. Her sallow skin and bold, handsome features were those of a Jew or an Arab, Farrell had never known which. She was as likely to greet you with the Muslim *Inshalla* as with the Yiddish *shalom.*

Farrell removed his hat and walked toward her, trying not to wrinkle his nose at the aroma of incense that hung in the room like a flickering memory of some ancient time. "Good afternoon, Sparrow."

"Good afternoon, Farrell. I've not seen you in a while. Are you well?"

"Quite well, thanks."

"I've heard that you might leave us for Cuba. That would be a pity. You're as much a part of this strange city as the river."

Farrell didn't blink at her knowledge of his private life and plans. She knew a lot of things, and that was the reason he'd come to her. "If I leave, it'll be only for a few months out of the year. As you say, the city and I sort of belong to each other. I could never leave it entirely."

"Not for love nor money," she said, nodding wisely. "What brings you here so early in the day? You're more a creature of the night, Farrell."

"I'm trying to find a man before someone else does. He's in a lot of trouble."

"What is his name?"

"Luis Martinez."

She nodded. "I've heard some things about him. His woman was tortured to death. Another day passed and her cousin was also tortured to death. That's a heavy price to pay for a relationship." She paused and studied his face. "You and Martinez used to smuggle liquor together."

"That's right," Farrell replied. "We were as close as brothers once, but I haven't spoken to him in a year. I'm told he's gone underground."

A smiled traced itself across her thin lips for a brief second, then her face settled into its usual expression of unconcern. "Why are you such a boy scout, Farrell? Let Martinez take care of his own trouble. Whoever killed those women could just as easily kill you."

"Why isn't really the question anymore," Farrell said, settling into his chair. He had known Sparrow for a while, and he knew that part of getting her help sometimes meant enduring a philosophical sparring match. She was a woman of strange tastes. "He's mixed up with a counterfeiting ring run by a man named Compasso. If Compasso doesn't get him, the Feds might. Maybe I just don't like the odds."

She studied him as she fingered her delicately chiseled chin. "It's more than that with you. You don't know what it is, but it eats away at something in you, and you can't ignore it. It must be uncomfortable for you at times."

"Maybe. I never gave it much thought."

She laughed softly, the noise like a ghostly echo in the big room. "I don't believe you. What do you want?"

"I can't help Martinez if I can't find him. You've got eyes and ears in the city and in the surrounding parishes. Somebody has to have seen him."

She lowered her eyelashes and examined the rose-colored polish on her fingernails. "I'll put out the word, but I can't promise anything. What can you tell me about him?"

"He's about five-ten, stocky build, black hair, deep olive complexion. He's a Mexican, with Indians and Negroes in his family tree, but he looks more like a movie show *vaquero* than anything else. He wore a mustache the last time I saw him."

"How old is he?"

"He'd be in his late forties by now, maybe fifty."

"That's not much to go on. Why does Compasso want to kill him?"

"I'm told that Martinez felt Compasso was short-changing him. He wanted a bigger cut. Compasso wouldn't give it to him. Luis isn't the kind of fool to pick a fight he can't win. He looks for a subtle way to hurt an enemy. If I know him at all, I'm betting he's done something to gum up the works. Somehow prevented the phony money from getting into the pipeline."

She lowered her eyelashes and nodded. "That makes sense. And Compasso is fighting the only way he knows how, destroying everything his enemy holds dear until he buckles from the pain of it."

This revelation intrigued Farrell. "You know Compasso, then."

She nodded briefly. "Yes. When I heard he was in town, I told friends to listen to the whispers that I knew would rise around him. You are the first person to explain the existence of a counterfeiting ring to me. That is a far more complex crime than he is used to executing. He is a thief by trade, not a criminal mastermind. For example, there's been no real traffic in counterfeit money in this city. I find that significant."

Farrell squinted, as though he could force his mind to see into Sparrow's. "I didn't know that. What does it mean?"

"Think about it, Farrell. If you don't spread funny money around the town where you make it, the Treasury people won't look for you in that town, will they?"

Farrell's eyes widened as the implication struck home. "You're right. That's as slick as an onion. It would take a sharp bird to think of that angle."

"Yes, and you and I both know that Compasso is neither 'slick as an onion' nor a particularly 'sharp bird.' That can only mean one thing."

Farrell unconsciously leaned toward her, his ears straining to hear the sibilant texture of her words. "Tell me."

"It is rumored that Compasso might not be the true head of his own organization. He is used to bossing a criminal gang, yes, but he is not a subtle man. His role is strictly that of a figurehead. He draws attention away from the organization's true purpose by dealing in the things he understands, narcotics, women, illegal gambling."

Those words struck Farrell like a thunderbolt. "This is a lot more complicated than I realized. A gang made of outsiders, a crime that almost nobody realizes, and now a top man with no face."

"And likely Martinez is, but for Compasso and his boss, the only one who knows all. He is a threat to the gang on more than one level."

The words brought Farrell's attention back to Sparrow's face. "Luis had a saying—'luck is where you find it, but I always look for mine down by the river.' I have no idea what that means, if it means anything. Luis is a gambler, and all gamblers have a saying. It's like a trademark."

"More likely a mantra," Sparrow said.

"A what?" Farrell gave her a blank look.

She smiled enigmatically. "Forget it. It wouldn't mean a thing to you. I'll do what I can and get in touch if I learn anything." She paused as he got to his feet. "Your visit explains the significance of one other piece of gossip that came to me earlier today."

"What's that?"

"You're not the only person asking around for Martinez. Besides the police and the killer, there's a woman. She goes by the rather theatrical name of Jelly Wilde. Do you know her?"

Farrell blinked. "She and Luis were lovers once, a long time ago."

"Yes, but these days she's the mistress of Santiago Compasso."

Farrell felt a chill run down his spine, but he kept it from his face. "Compasso may be smarter than we think."

Sparrow shook her head negatively. "I think not. He is contemptuous of everyone but himself. I do not know this woman, but I'll venture she looks for Martinez for her own reasons, although that may not be to Martinez's advantage."

"Thank you, Sparrow. I'd better be on my way."

"Farrell, I normally expect some tribute from you at times like this, but for once I'll forgo that pleasure and simply tell you to be careful. The other side of the world is on fire now, but evil energy is in the air even here. This will test your luck, my friend."

Sparrow liked riddles, but she had never given him such an explicit warning. "I hear you."

"Go with God, Farrell. We'll speak again."

He touched two fingers to the brim of his hat, and left the room with her words ringing in his ears.

&xx;

Frank Casey parked his squad car about thirty yards from the burned-out airplane hangar and walked slowly toward a knot of men standing near the red hook-and-ladder truck. The stench of burning wood and heated metal was everywhere and the air was full of ash being blown about by winds off Lake Pontchartrain. Someone heard his approach and at a word, the knot of men turned to face him.

"It's an arson job, Skipper," a hefty white man in his shirtsleeves said. "Some of the firemen have found shards of broken glass with gasoline residue on them."

"Who does the building belong to, Grebb?" Casey asked.

"We're still checking on that," Inspector Grebb replied. "They've found the remains of three bodies inside—two of 'em burnt to a crisp, but there's enough to identify all three. There's also enough to see they're all dead from shotgun blasts to the body. Delgado's already found brass from several shotgun shells in there."

"So we've got a triple murder as well as arson," Casey said. "That makes it somebody a lot more serious than just a firebug. You find any witnesses yet?"

Grebb shook his head. "This place is a mile from the airfield, and there's nobody living close enough to've seen or heard anything. The killer had a free hand and all the time in the world to get his work done. It's gotta be a mob hit."

Casey looked past Grebb at the smoldering building. "Yeah, but what mob? Why would anybody burn down an old airplane hangar? If they wanted to cover the murders, you'd think they would've done a better job of burning up the evidence. I don't know." He shook his head and began walking closer to the hangar.

Firefighters knocked away loose flammable material while others dragged smoldering objects out of the hangar to wet them down. Casey loosened his tie and unbuttoned his shirt collar. Sweat was gathering on his brow and it trickled down his back while he made a slow circuit of the hangar, poking his toe at various objects he came across.

As he approached the far end of the structure, a gust of wind blew ashy flakes toward him. There was something about them that arrested him. He stared for a moment then reached out and caught one. He brought it to eye level. It took him only a second to realize it was the corner of a twenty-dollar bill. He looked down at the ground around him, and he saw other pieces of money.

His head snapped up. "Grebb! Grebb—over here." He removed his hat and waved it in the air. Grebb and two other plainclothesmen came at the double.

"What is it, chief?"

"Get some men to gathering up as many of these as you can find." He thrust the corner of the burned bill into the inspector's hand. "The ground's covered with them, and there may be more partially burned stuff inside. Get the firemen to help you. See if there's more in there that wasn't incinerated. Step on it, before the wind scatters it."

Grebb sent a man back to the fire captain at a run while he and the other shirt-sleeved detectives got down on their knees and began picking up every fragment they could find, transferring them to envelopes they pulled from their pockets. Casey jogged back to his squad car and got on the radio to headquarters. In about ten minutes, he had established a connection to Treasury Enforcement and had Paul Ewell on the line.

"Listen, Paul. I'm out a bit past Shushan Airfield where there's been an arson fire at an airplane hangar. There were three dead men inside, and we're finding bits of burned money. I think there's a possible connection to your case."

"Any identification on the dead men?" Ewell asked.

"Not yet, but we should be able to get some prints at the morgue."

"Give us a half-hour. We'll see you out there."

Casey signed off with headquarters then leaned against the fender of the car as he fanned himself with his hat. He thought about his son, and for some reason recalled Farrell's promise to turn Luis Martinez over to the police. Casey wondered how he'd tell Farrell that Martinez might have killed three men in cold blood.

Marcel left Xavier University and returned to the house on Soraparu Street with his mind buzzing. He recognized that what he and Dr. Samson had discussed was pure supposition, but the scenario had merit that Marcel couldn't deny. Marcel was well enough educated to recognize the power a title like "Doctor" had for less sophisticated people. He had heard a sufficient number of stories from the old days in which a snake oil salesman worked his way through the community by calling himself Doctor this or Doctor that. A well-dressed man with a slick line of jive could go a long way, even today.

Marcel reached his office and sat down at the desk, pondering his next move. More than anything else in the world, he wanted to talk to someone who'd actually known Wilbur Lee Payne— someone who could have observed him in a disinterested way. Ernie Le Doux's remark that Wilbur Payne had always 'had his nose in a book' gave him an idea. He had been involved in some things up in East Feliciana Parish a year before, and during that time he'd been thrown together with someone who might be able to help him.

He picked up his telephone receiver and got the long distance operator on the line, giving her the number for Angola State Penitentiary. After a few moments, he heard the line begin to buzz through the static in the line. After four buzzes, a man spoke.

"State Penitentiary. How can I direct your call?"

"I'd like to speak to the librarian, please." There was a series of clicks on the line before a woman spoke.

"Prison library. Mrs. Albertine speaking."

"Miss Roberta? It's Marcel Aristide in New Orleans."

"Marcel? My land, boy. What you doin' makin' a long distance call this time of the day? You made of money?"

"I'll write it off as a business expense, Miss Roberta. I need some help from you."

The old woman picked up the urgent note in his voice and replied to him crisply. "Tell me what kind."

"About twelve years or so back, there was a young Negro imprisoned up there by the name of Wilbur Lee Payne. You might know him by his underworld handle, Keys."

"Oh, yes. I recollect those names," she replied thoughtfully. "He spent about three years up here altogether."

"I've got some good reason to believe he might be here in New Orleans workin' a scam of some kind."

She snorted humorously. "That sounds like the boy I remember. He was a honey-talking thing, when he didn't have his nose buried in a book."

"A reader, eh?"

"Oh, yes. It seemed to be the only thing he cared about. Right after he came, he behaved himself and managed to get assigned to me in the library, and did he ever take advantage of that."

"Is that so? In what way?"

"Well," she began, "he seemed bent on improving himself. He read books on English grammar. Got to talking like a city man after a while. But then he got interested in science. He read all the books on biology and chemistry."

Marcel found himself smiling. "How about medical books?"

"Well, we didn't have too many of them, but I was able to get some for him. Read those books from cover to cover. He would even talk over with me things he'd learned, and a lot of it was over my head, I can tell you faithfully. By the time they released him, I realized what a remarkable mind he had. He could literally have been anything, Marcel." She paused for a moment as though remembering Wilbur Payne's wasted genius. "You think he's in N'Awlins?"

"Yes, ma'am, I'm afraid so. Let's keep that between us, okay? How are the kids?"

"Oh, surely. Betsy's in the tenth grade now, and Robert's hoping to go to Tuskeegee next summer. They're both doing fine. I'll tell 'em you asked. I think Betsy's still in love with you, even though I told her you were nothing but a disreputable vagabond. You can't tell young gals anything."

"Young fellas, neither," he said. "Thank you for the information, Miss Roberta. Let me know what I can do to return the favor, you hear?"

"I can do ten years of favors for you and still not pay you back for what you did for us last year. 'Bye, now."

"Goodbye." Marcel hung up the telephone and sat back in the chair. Well, he thought, you won't get any better confirmation than that. Now, how to find a phony Negro doctor in a city with a half-million people? Then he remembered having done a favor for a young Negro police officer. It was time to call the favor in.

∞∞∞

It was still daylight when Luis Martinez returned to his fishing shack. The rush of adrenaline that had sustained him after the fight had worn off during the long ride, and he felt an almost overpowering need to sleep the clock around. He recognized, however, that he'd only fought one battle in what might be a protracted conflict.

When he arrived at the shack, he dumped a can of Van Camp's pork and beans into a saucepan with a can of Armour Star Vienna sausage, and heated them on the wood stove in the shack. The smell of the heating food turned him ravenous, and as soon as it was warm, he crumbled some soda crackers into the pan and ate it all with a spoon.

Still dead tired, he found a cheap tin alarm clock he'd left there years before, set it to go off in three hours, then fell into an exhausted slumber on the rock-hard army cot. When the clock jangled him awake three hours later, he sat up, rubbing his eyes. It took him a moment to remember where he was, but he got up refreshed.

While he made coffee, he got the shotgun from the car, cleaned the bore and breech, then reloaded it. He drank the coffee black, savoring the bitterness of it. By now, Compasso surely knew of the fire and the dead men. He'd be screaming for Martinez's blood, and his people would be alert to trouble. Martinez knew his next raid would have to be a lot subtler. There was no way he could get to Compasso himself, so the next best thing was to hurt his ability to make money every way possible.

He got out a map of the city and unfolded it onto the scarred wooden table. Compasso owned other criminal enterprises besides the counterfeiting ring. There was, for example, a sixty-foot fishing trawler that made periodic trips to Mexico for marijuana, morphine and cocaine. He recalled that Compasso had made almost a hundred thousand dollars on the drugs he'd imported during 1939. Martinez smiled. Compasso was so focused on the funny money grift that it might not occur to him to guard the boat very heavily. *That'll be one more for you, Linda,* he thought.

It occurred to Martinez that he needed to contact Theron Oswald. He was certain the plates had gotten there, but he just wanted to hear a friendly voice. He walked out to the small fishing deck at the back of the shack and relieved himself into the Mississippi River. Watching the river roll past him, he thought of the days he'd come here from time to time to fish, and to find his luck. That was why he'd come here in the first place. The fishing shack had always been the place he'd come when his luck had gone sour.

As the darkness fell, he filled two more bottles with gasoline and stoppered them with cloth. He took them and the shotgun out to the car, and a few minutes later, he was back on the river road. Eventually he came to the country store and gasoline station, now closed down for the night. There was a telephone booth situated on the porch, so he drove over to it and cut the engine.

Inside, he gave the operator the number to Oswald's phone in the apartment upstairs from the pawnshop, fed in the correct number of coins, then waited as the phone buzzed. On the fourth buzz, he heard the receiver pick up. There was a silence, then a low, nervous voice said, "Yeah?"

"Ozzy? That you?"

"Man, are you crazy? Why the hell you send that package to me?"

"I had to get it somewhere safe, Oz. You were the only person I could trust."

"Trust? Shit. You got any idea the grief you done let loose on the world? First Linda then Wisteria. Ain't no friend of yours safe now, man, nobody." Oswald's voice had a tremor that Martinez could feel in the receiver.

"Wisteria? What about Wisteria? You ain't tellin' me—"

"Yeah. Her, too. He musta thought she'd know where you was, so he—he done—awful things, Louie. Just awful." Oswald was silent for a moment, but again his fear seemed to travel through the line into Martinez's ear. "Louie, I'm scared of dyin', man. Can you come on in here? You can stay at my place 'til you figure things out."

"*Madre de Dios,*" Martinez murmured as he slumped against the wall of the booth. For the first time in many years, he made the sign of the cross and murmured the prayers he had been taught as a boy. He forgot he was in a phone booth. He forgot he was talking to anyone else but God. He didn't know how much time went by until Oswald's voice brought him back to the present.

"Man—hey, Luis. Talk to me, man, please, talk to me."

"Yeah. I'm here."

"Look, man. You're in a real bad place right now. This man Compasso brought in, he means to put you in the fuckin' ground. Please don't leave me here with these plates. Come on in and lay low. We can get the plates back to Compasso, and he'll let you off the hook, I know he will."

The rapid rattle of words spilling from Oswald's mouth forced Martinez to reply just to shut him up. He had to be calm, and he needed Oswald to be calm, too. "Shhhh, listen, Ozzy. Just be cool, *amigo.* Things are bad, but they ain't hopeless. I'll come and get the plates when I've finished a few things. Compasso's either gonna deal with me, or one of us will die. There's no way around it now. It's gone too far. Just keep your head, and keep your mouth shut, *entiende?*"

"Man, please, I'm twistin' in the wind here. Don't you get it? This man Compasso's got on you—he's makin' the rounds of your friends, tryin' to find one who'll tell him where you at. Louie, talk to me, man."

Without making a reply, Martinez placed the receiver onto the hook. He leaned there, nearly exhausted. He realized now that he couldn't trust Oswald with his whereabouts. The man was so frightened that he might turn Martinez in the moment he thought he was in danger.

He had one friend left in the world that he might trust. Farrell. But Farrell had friends on the cops these days. Could Martinez call a man friend when he helped the cops? At that moment, Martinez felt more alone than he ever had. Action was his only solace now. He got into his car, then headed back into the city.

Chapter 9

The afternoon was nearly gone when Farrell departed Sparrow's, but the time had been well spent. He had insights into the gang that hadn't occurred to him before. That, and her promise to help find Martinez, put him into a more optimistic mood, although he felt an itch between his shoulder blades every time he thought about the killer stalking Martinez's friends. He wasn't carrying a gun, and he realized it was past time to get one.

He drove three blocks until he saw a telephone booth. He parked the car, went into the booth, then put in a call to Harry at the Café Tristesse. Harry told him that Casey had left a message to call him immediately. With a sense of foreboding, Farrell put a second nickel into the slot, then asked the operator for police headquarters. The desk sergeant handed him off to Casey's secretary and there was a brief wait before Farrell's father spoke to him.

"Are you someplace where you can talk freely?" Casey asked.

"Sure, Dad. What's happening?"

"I could almost laugh at that question if things weren't such a mess. I've just come from the lakefront where a defunct airline hangar was burned to the ground today. Three men were found dead inside from gunshot wounds along with a wrecked printing press. There's also a ton of half-burned counterfeit bills floating all over hell's half acre."

Farrell gripped the phone tightly as the words hit him. "Martinez's work?"

"Well, there are no witnesses, but given what you and I have put together, I don't know who else to blame. We haven't determined if Compasso is the owner of the hangar, but I'll bet we discover that it was at least in the name of someone in his employ, maybe one of the dead men. Compasso sure as hell didn't burn up a stockpile of his own counterfeit bills, so Martinez is the prime suspect." Casey paused to catch his breath before speaking to Farrell soberly. "This is as bad as can be, Wes. Your friend was just a suspect in a counterfeiting operation before. Now he's suspected of triple murder. Can you still stand behind that promise you made about turning him in?"

Farrell felt the muscles in his face sagging. "I made it to *you*. That's a promise I can't break."

"Sure you can. You can back away from this, now, and pretend you never heard of it. Somebody will bring Martinez in, but it doesn't have to be you."

"No. There was a time he was like family to me. The way things are going he's liable to end up dead, if not from Compasso's guns, then yours. I might be able to bring him in alive." Farrell paused, almost afraid to hear the answer to the question he was about to ask. "Tell me, Dad, if Luis comes in of his own accord and testifies against Compasso, what can the judge give him?"

Casey was silent for a moment. "Well, it's a complicated case. The counterfeiting charges are all Federal, but they don't take precedence over a murder beef. Maybe I could get Ewell to go with me to District Attorney Crockett and get him a break for turning state's evidence. If the D. A. went along, then he'd probably serve between ten to fifteen years on the Federal charges."

"That's a pretty tough sentence."

"Listen, son. I know he's your friend, and I know you go way back with him. But you've gotta remember something. Everything he's doing is a conscious choice he's made to break the law. He could've come in before now and made any deal he wanted. He made another choice."

Farrell braced his arm against the side of the booth and leaned on it as his father's logic battered at him. Everything in him wanted to rebel against it, but his relationship with Casey made that impossible. They had a trust between them he would not violate. He let out a sigh and relaxed his grip on the phone. "Okay, Dad. Okay. I'm still looking for him, and I've got some other people looking, too. We'll turn him up."

"I hope so. Every crime he commits makes it that much harder to get him a break."

"I understand. Look, I learned something you might find interesting."

"What is it?"

"It's possible Compasso isn't the real boss of the counterfeiting ring."

"You got any idea who is?"

"No, but it makes sense. Compasso's a thief who got everything he ever wanted from the barrel of a gun. A big operation like this that's spread over several states requires a finesse that Compasso doesn't have. Maybe Martinez can tell us who that man is."

"That would be one more point on his side of the score sheet. Remind him of that when you find him."

"Yeah. Yeah, I will, Dad. I'd better get going."

"Okay. Be careful, son."

"Yeah. See you later." Farrell hung up. He got ready to leave the booth, but had another idea. He dropped in his last nickel and gave the operator a French Quarter exchange. It rang three times.

"Broussard Detective Agency. Broussard talkin'."

"Jake, it's Farrell."

"Well, you ole hoss thief. Where the hell you been lately?"

"Havana, but I'm here now and got a problem."

"Spill it, young'un."

"You know who Luis Martinez is?"

"Crossed his path a few times. He's another ex-legger buddy of yours, ain't he?"

"Right. He's up to his neck in trouble with the cops and a hood named Compasso. I'm trying to find him before somebody puts the skids under him."

"Jesus," the private eye said. "Do yourself a favor and go home, boy. A man can get hurt mixin' into a mess like that."

"How many colored operatives have you got on your payroll?" Farrell asked, ignoring the advice.

"I can get six out on the street in twenty minutes. You want them to look for Martinez?"

"That's covered already. I'm playing a hunch. It might be all wet, but I want to give it a try. Years ago, Martinez was involved with a gal who goes by the name of Jelly Wilde. She's a real dish—

short and curvy, black hair, dark gold skin. I heard she was looking for Luis. I presume for Compasso's sake. She'll be hitting every colored dive in the city asking about Martinez. I want to talk to her."

"What, you think you can charm her into changin' sides? That chicken's a first-class gold-digger."

"Just find her, if you can. I'll be out on the street myself, but I'll call you every hour. Tell your men there's a hundred bucks extra for the man who turns her up."

"Hell, I'll go out and look myself for that."

"Just stick by your phone. I'll call you in an hour."

"Go ahead, man. Your money spends at my office just like everybody else's."

"Lucky me." Farrell hung up and went back to his car. He felt somehow that he had made some progress. With Sparrow's people alerted and Broussard's Negro gumshoes prowling, he felt that the odds had shifted somehow. The only thing that bothered him now was the fact that he could well be saving Martinez's neck for the executioner's noose. He pushed that from his mind as he fired up his engine and drove deeper into the riverfront warehouse district.

⚛

Compasso paced the floor of his study with worry twisting his gut. His face reflected no worry, only anger. A dumpy little guy peered at him through wire-framed spectacles as a droopy-eyed blonde man stood quietly beside him. "Mr. Compasso, we can get another printing press tomorrow, and Appleyard here can produce more ink within a few days. Our source can probably get us paper in about another week. We could go into overtime production if we had the plates, but we don't. And we can't produce brand-new engravings overnight. It took me six months of work to make the original plates. I can make you some more, but it'll take time. I only got started ten days ago. I thought we had more time."

"That was when we had a backlog of over five million dollars, Hardesty. We're down to less than two million now. We'll run through that before the month is up. We need new plates in another week, do you understand?"

Hardesty suppressed the urge to sigh. He had taken this job from Luis Martinez, not this Argentine wild man. He'd been trying for a half-hour to make the ignorant sonofabitch understand that engraving was an art, not something that could be rushed. He shook his head wearily. "Mr. Compasso, what I'm tryin' to tell you—"

Compasso came around the desk with the speed of a fast freight, grabbed the diminutive engraver by the collar and jerked him off his feet. "No, fool. *I* tell you. Give me new plates by the end of next week, or I'll kill you, *comprende?*"

Hardesty swallowed audibly, then nodded vigorously. There was nothing else to say. He could feel Appleyard silently trembling beside him.

Compasso pushed the engraver away from him and turned his back, giving Hardesty and Appleyard time to scuttle through the door and down the stairs. Compasso ignored his flight, caught up in his own problems.

He had been a criminal since the age of sixteen when he slit his first throat in Buenos Aires. Murder and intimidation were tools he had perfected, and he had never lost his willingness to commit them with his own hands. It was how he created respect and fear in friend and enemy alike. This skulking in an office while others did the work was not to his liking.

Not for the first time, he wondered why he had allowed his friends back in Argentina to talk him into this venture. His hands itched for something concrete to do.

The telephone on his desk rang, but he ignored it, letting one of his men downstairs get it. A man in Compasso's position did not answer telephones. The phone went silent and several moments passed before a brief knock sounded, followed by the opening of the door. A heavy-shouldered man with iron gray hair stood there.

"What is it, Tink?"

"That cop, Paret. He's askin' for you," Tink replied in a gruffly respectful tone.

For Paret to call was a sign something significant had happened. Willing himself to move slowly in front of his henchman, Compasso walked to the desk and picked up the telephone. "This is Compasso."

"Sorry to bother you, Mr. Compasso. Somethin' come up that you want to know." Detective Matty Paret's voice was pitched low, suggesting he might be calling from headquarters.

"What do you mean?"

"This afternoon there was a fire at that old aircraft hangar of yours out near the lake. When they got the fire put out, they found three bodies inside. Shotgun wounds in all of 'em.

"Maldito sea!" Compasso said in a harsh whisper.

"That ain't the worst of it. The Treasury boys been out there all afternoon sweepin' up bits and pieces of counterfeit bills. Treasury already done their tests, and they know it's the same stuff they've been finding in the banks east of here. I heard one of the brass say they're startin' to suspect the operation must be headquartered here. That ain't good."

Compasso felt a tremor run though his body. "Martinez again." Compasso spoke with a quiet, outraged dignity that made Tink wince as he stood by. He had seen his boss like this before, and somebody always got hurt afterwards. Tink was tempted to back out into the hall.

"So far as I know, nobody here knows nothin' about Martinez," Paret said. "His name ain't come up."

Compasso spoke to Paret in a quietly savage tone. "I am paying you a lot of money, Paret. You are a detective, so detect. Find this man for me. I will pay any price you ask, but find him."

The offer stunned Paret. "Consider it done."

"Bueno." Compasso put the telephone back in the cradle and stood there looking at it, a thick vein throbbing in his temple. After a moment he looked up at Tink, who remained patiently waiting for an order. "Tink, tell the men at the other operations to stay on guard all night. Tell them to kill anything that they see, even if it is only a rat."

Tink half-turned to go, but a sudden sharp command from Compasso stayed him. "Yeah, boss?"

"Jelly—has there been any word on her?"

"I got two men on her, just like you ordered. Last thing I heard, she was trollin' nigger dives askin' questions. Nothin' definite yet."

"I want to know, the minute you hear from them. Go now, and do what I said. Do not waste any time."

Tink turned without a word and left the room.

Compasso felt weak and sick. It was all coming to pieces in front of him, and he would take the full blame for it. They would not mention his name in Buenos Aires because it would turn their stomachs. He opened his desk drawer and removed from it a nine-millimeter Astra automatic. He put it in the middle of his blotter and sat down at the chair. Something would happen tonight, for good or for ill.

⚬⚬⚬

The bartender recalled by the Greek at the hardware store proved harder to find than Pelecano had indicated. Jelly found the man had left the bar known by Pelecano, and gone to another across town. Jelly arrived there only to discover that he'd quit that job the week before and gone to one at the river end of Jackson Avenue. Once again she got into her De Soto and headed out into the deepening darkness.

It was nearing 8:00 when she pulled up across the street from a place called the B-Sharp Club. As she entered, she heard a female vocalist scat-singing with remarkable dexterity as a saxophone and piano fought to keep up with her. The musicians were holding forth on a small stage and most of the customers were grouped around them, dancing, whistling, and yelling their approval. She grinned at their intensity as she sauntered past them.

A big, broad-shouldered bartender with glistening black skin slid soundlessly down the bar to her, his large dark eyes sparkling with good-natured hell.

"'Lo, baby," he purred. The sound carried to her in spite of the racket at the stage, and she responded to it with an appreciative smile.

"'Lo, yourself, you handsome chunk of meat. Got a bottle of Pernod back there?"

He showed all of his teeth, which glistened like pearls against the background of his glossy skin. "Savin' it just for you, baby. On the rocks?"

She fanned herself lightly with a glove. "It is warmish in here. On the rocks with a li'l water, sweetheart."

The bartender preened like a big jungle cat as he poured the green liqueur into a tall glass full of ice. He served it to her with a flourish on a paper napkin. "That be all, miss?" His smile became even more provocative.

She returned his smile with interest. "Your name wouldn't happen to be Otis McKelvey, would it?"

He could not quite hide his pleasure that this fine-looking female knew him by name. "Reckon it is, mama. You lookin' for me?"

"Matter of fact, I am. Friend of mine mentioned you to me—Luis Martinez?"

Otis's face lit up. "How is ole Luis? Ain't seen him in a dog's age."

"Well," Jelly said, seeming to melt a bit, leaning forward in such a way that her bosom strained the fabric of her dress. "It happens I haven't seen him in a while, either. I was kinda hopin' you might know where he's at."

"Damn, ain't no tellin' where that man's got to. We used to go all kinda places. I miss them days somethin' awful."

"What kinds of places did you go to?"

The negro rubbed his shiny bald head and grinned. "Lemme tell ya, that man liked bein' outdoors. That suited me fine, 'cause I was brought up on a farm myself. I liked to hunt, and so did Louie."

"Do tell."

"That man's a dead shot with a rifle. Seen him kill a six-point buck up near Opelousas, few years back. Drilled him through the neck and he dropped like a rock. Afterwards, we skinned out that buck, cut us a haunch, and be damned if Louie didn't make a first class roast outa that meat. He ever cook for you?"

"No, can't say that he ever did. I always thought Louie was a city boy."

"Shoot. That man was raised out in west Texas where the cowboys are. He can ride, shoot, and run a camp like somebody from the olden days. Always liked goin' out into the country with ole Louie. Used to entertain me singin' Mexican love songs, too."

She said nothing, but smiled and nodded, and let Otis go. He liked the sound of his own voice, and proved to be an avid storyteller. She discovered much about her old lover that night that she hadn't known, but she realized, she had never given him much of a chance to teach it to her. It came to her how arrogant and demanding she had been to him, how she had used that as a defense against that sense he projected that he was the master of all around him.

She realized now that it wasn't arrogance. It was self-confidence, a thing that Santiago didn't have, a lack he tried to keep hidden. She had a sudden recognition of what she had lost in walking away from Luis. Had she remained with Santiago all these years to punish herself?

"Tell you what," the bartender said midway through the evening. "Get that man outa the city, and you couldn't play cards with him very long. He'd clean you out in no time at all. Lucky? I reckon."

This tidbit of information resonated with Jelly, and she leaned forward, fixing the bartender's eyes with her own. "Tell me, is that why Luis always said when he lost his luck, he'd go find it down by the river?"

The bartender's grin was as wide and white as a piano keyboard. "I lost count of the number o'times that man said that to me. Just like I lost count of the times he cleaned me out playin' poker in that shack of his."

"Shack?"

"Yeah. Man had him a real nice fishin' camp up the river a ways."

"Really? I didn't know."

"Yeah. Real nice place. Don't reckon he ever took women there. It weren't that kinda nice. Sort of a rough place where some fellas could lay up, fish, do some drinkin', sleep late. You know, just take it easy for a while."

"You wouldn't happen to know where it is, would you? I'm kind of an outdoor gal, myself."

"Naw, not you." He guffawed at the idea.

She took one of his big hands in her small pale one and rubbed her thumb tenderly over his knuckles. "You got no idea, big boy. No idea at all."

❧

Max Grossmann required no surgery, as the gunman's bullet had done no more than carve a nice clean groove through the flesh of his bicep. Once the doctor had given him something for pain, he was able to calm down and regain his urbanity and good humor. His wound had been dressed and the arm placed in a sling, and he was waiting to be discharged when A. J. McCandless arrived. The man's face was grim, and his ever-present cigarette holder was clamped brutally in his teeth. He pushed into the room with an impatient gesture.

"Leake's dead?" he demanded.

Grossmann turned his sleepy eyes on the weathered bank president and gestured aimlessly with his good hand. "The gunman was right on top of us. He killed Marston with a single shot. A tragic loss to the bank. And we lost a good friend today."

"Yes, tragic." He eyed Grossmann with a flinty look. "How badly hurt are you?"

Grossmann gently touched the bandage on his upper arm and winced slightly. "I was lucky. The Negro got off another shot, but somehow he missed my vitals."

McCandless puffed on his cigarette as he walked around Grossmann's bed. "What happened, Max? I want to know."

Grossmann shifted his bulk as he tried to find a more comfortable position. He winced again, and a small grunt of pain escaped him. He didn't look at McCandless as he spoke. "Well, it was late afternoon. Marston had discussed some bank business with me and an hour later we happened to be leaving at the same time."

McCandless removed the ivory cigarette holder from his teeth. "What time was this?"

Grossmann made a vague gesture with his good hand. "About five. I had just talked him into joining me for dinner when we were waylaid. The gunman had taken my wallet already. He demanded Marston's then shot him as Marston tried to pull a gun. I cried out in terror, then the fellow shot *me*." Grossmann's voice held a note of mild irritation that he should have been so poorly used.

McCandless turned away from Grossmann as he removed the butt of his cigarette from his holder and pitched it into a metal wastebasket. He took a fresh cigarette from a silver case, inserted it in the holder and lit it. "Marston had been working too hard lately. A pity he didn't live to see retirement."

Again Grossmann made the vague gesture with his free hand. "Yes, I often worried about him. A very intense man, Marston."

McCandless looked at him sharply. "What do you mean by that?"

"Well, he was rather wound up about this counterfeiting business. I think it worried him quite a bit." Grossmann paused then shook his head. "I tell you, A. J., I feel just dreadful about this. What a loss to the bank and to us..." His voice trailed away to silence.

McCandless puffed silently on his fresh cigarette. "Yes. He'd been with me a long time. I'll miss him and his loyalty to the bank." He said this in a flat, unemotional tone. "Are you ready to go? I brought a car."

Grossmann tested his arm gingerly. "Well, the doctor says I can leave immediately if I feel up to it."

"Good, then let's get the hell out of here. I hate the smell of these places. Here, let me give you a hand." McCandless moved to Grossmann's elbow, and with a remarkable display of physical strength, hoisted the fat man from the bed and set him on his feet.

"Thank you, A. J. I think they have some papers for me to sign at the desk."

"I've already taken care of that," McCandless said brusquely. "My car is waiting to take you home."

"That's uncommonly decent of you."

"Nonsense," the president said in a gruff tone. He easily supported the other man out of the emergency room door to the ramp. He put two fingers to his lips and blew a piercing whistle, and almost instantly a dark blue Cadillac limousine pulled up beside them. McCandless helped the Jewish banker inside, then went around and got in on the other side. He rapped on the privacy window, and the chauffeur pulled smoothly away from the hospital.

"Tell me," McCandless said in a confidential tone after a moment or two of silence. "Had Marston anything else on his mind that he'd mentioned to you?"

Grossmann shifted his buttocks into a more comfortable position on the leather upholstery and cleared his throat. "Well, he spoke of many things, but I think he felt the strain of your continued absence."

McCandless stiffened, seemed to bite down on the cigarette holder. "I have other commitments besides the bank. Marston should have understood that."

"Yes, well, perhaps I shouldn't have mentioned it."

McCandless uttered a sardonic grunt. "Yes, perhaps. Tell me, do you need a nurse to take care of you tonight?"

"No," Grossmann replied. "I think not. My houseboy should be sufficient to meet my needs. I have some tablets for the pain, and I'm feeling all right. Some food would set me right as rain, I think."

McCandless eased his weathered face into a grim smile. "You sound like your old self already, but take tomorrow off if you need it."

"Perhaps, A. J. But I think I shall need work to distract me from poor Marston's death. It was a pitiable thing to see such a kind man put to death that way. It was like watching the martyrdom of an innocent."

Further conversation was cut short by their arrival at Grossmann's house. Without being told, the chauffeur got out and rang the doorbell, waiting until the houseboy answered. A few brief words were sufficient to bring the young Negro to the car, and with the efforts of the three men, Grossmann's bulk was ejected from the car as painlessly as possible. When Grossmann was safely at the door, McCandless gave a curt nod and salute of farewell, then he and the chauffeur got into the car and disappeared into the gathering darkness.

Grossmann went to his bedroom, and with the houseboy's help, undressed and put on some comfortable pajamas and a light silk robe. When he was comfortable, Grossmann gave the young man instructions for an evening meal. Once the houseboy retired, Grossmann reclined on a chaise. He rested his good forearm over his eyes and remained in that posture, his eyes gleaming in the shadow.

Chapter 10

If there had existed in Detective Matty Paret even a scintilla of honesty, he might well have become an outstanding detective. He was intelligent, thoughtful, and even possessed of a certain shrewd insight into the foibles of his fellow men. Had he liked money a bit less and hard work more, he'd have been a sergeant already.

There, had, however, been compensations. For example, he had a safe deposit box in the Hibernia National Bank that contained almost $200,000, a fortune he had accumulated by helping one big-time criminal after another. There were, too, the deluxe Buick sedan, the closet full of expensive clothing, and the string of available women, all things that a Third Grade detective's salary could never buy.

Having listened to all the reports from the arson/murder at the lakefront, particularly the manner in which the crimes were believed to have been committed, Paret came to some conclusions. The first was that Martinez had declared open war on Compasso, and that this was but the opening skirmish. Second, Martinez wouldn't wait long to strike again. Third, since Martinez had effectively put the counterfeiting operation out of business, he'd next hurt Compasso in some other area.

Paret had an encyclopedic knowledge of Compasso's various holdings about the city. He understood implicitly that the most important places were manned and ready after the hangar fire. There remained a handful of places very lightly guarded or not guarded at all. They weren't as important as the hangar had been, but their loss would still significantly impact Compasso's income.

These included a couple of small commercial buildings that housed gambling or prostitution enterprises and a fishing trawler used to bring narcotics from Mexico. After careful consideration, Paret put all of his chips on the boat.

The captain of the boat lived on Tchopitoulas Street near the Third District Ferry, and Compasso had arranged for the boat to tie up at The Governor Nicholls Street Wharf near the ferry slip. The ferry stopped running at 10:00 so Paret planned his arrival in the neighborhood for approximately fifteen minutes ahead of that time.

The detective left his car two blocks down Barracks Street, and walked through the dense summer heat to the wharf. Minutes later, the lights at the ferry slip were extinguished, and not long after, the voices of the ferry crew died as they went their separate ways. Paret had a clear view of the boat thanks to a three-quarter moon bathing the river in a pale silver light.

A half-hour passed, then a full hour. Paret wanted to give it up and go home to bed, but thoughts of the money Compasso would pay for Martinez's scalp lay in the back of his mind like a dull hunger. At half past eleven, Paret heard a noise and it took him a few moments of fierce listening to understand that the sounds were coming off the water. He moved from his hiding place near the warehouse to a tall piling from which he had an unobstructed view. The noises ultimately proved to be the movement of oars in the water, followed by the dull thud of the rowboat bumping the trawler's hull. The dark figure of a man crawled up a rope hanging from the stern, wriggling agilely over the edge when he reached the top.

Paret smiled. He drew his .38 Detective Special from under his arm and crept to the gangplank. He tested it with his weight then crossed as silently as a cat. He heard noises beneath him, and realized that Martinez had gone below decks. He positioned himself where he could see his prey emerge from the hatch, leveling his gun at the dark square in front of him.

He heard glass break down below, then the unmistakable whoosh of gasoline catching fire. Paret thought it too bad about the boat, but with Martinez out of the way and the plates recovered, Compasso would make up the loss in no time. When he saw the figure of a man in the hatch, he grinned with anticipation.

"Martinez! C'mon out with your hands in the air."

"Who's out there?" Martinez demanded.

"New Orleans Police. Haul your ass outa there or I'll ventilate it." Martinez's thick upper body became visible, his dark face indistinct in the shadows. He took his time, even with the flames growing in intensity behind him.

"Move faster, Martinez, unless you want your ass barbecued like them guys at the hangar."

"What do you want? Money?" Martinez was playing for time, and Paret didn't like that.

"I want the plates, spig. Gimme the plates and I'll let you go." Paret realized he'd just said the wrong thing. The cops wouldn't know anything about the missing plates, but it was too late to worry about it. "C'mon, spig. It's hot up here, but it's hotter where you are. Let's go ashore, get in my car, and we'll talk turkey. Whaddaya say?" He had the front sight of his gun centered on Martinez's chest.

"Okay, man," Martinez said. "I'm comin'." But he faded back into the shadow of the hatch. Without warning, a flaming bottle flew out of the hatch and smashed on the deck, fire spreading like it had life of its own.

Paret threw up a protective arm, cursing as the flames blinded him. He leveled his .38 and fired twice. He heard another gun explode then something hard struck him in the body. He lurched, grabbing for support. Martinez appeared in front of Paret, his face grim, his hand full of gun. Paret fought to get his own gun up, but Martinez fired again and Paret felt his right shoulder go numb as he fell forward.

The glare of flames was glinting up from cracks in the deck, and Martinez felt the boat settle and creak as the fire bit ruthlessly into the aging wood. He grimaced, holding his side where the cop's bullet had pierced it. He set the safety on the .38 Super and shoved it back under his left arm.

He started to the gangplank, then turned and looked back at the fallen man. Groaning with the effort, he grabbed Paret by the collar and dragged him to the dock. He dropped him to the ground then shoved his fingers into the side of Paret's neck. The pulse was weak but he wouldn't die just yet.

Martinez hobbled painfully down the dock and then crept out to the street. He knew that once the fire alarm was turned in he had only minutes to get away from the area before cops and firemen arrived. He'd just begun to fuck Compasso up, so he couldn't be caught yet. Not yet.

By the time he reached his Mercury, his side was on fire. He knew he had to have help soon, or he'd pass out from shock and blood loss. Grunting, he heaved himself inside under the wheel, fumbled the key into the ignition switch, and cranked the motor. He let the clutch in too quickly and the engine flooded and died. Behind him, he heard the sounds of sirens in the distance.

He cursed in a steady, monotonous voice as he carefully pumped the accelerator. As the sirens grew louder, he hit the ignition again. This time the Mercury started. With painstaking care, Martinez let in the clutch, and the coupé moved out into the street. Hugging his hurt side with his elbow, he accelerated slowly until he was up to twenty-five miles an hour.

As he drove away from Tchopitoulas Street, he considered his options. He couldn't go to Theron Oswald. Ozzy was so scared already he could barely breathe. Whoever was hunting him had killed Wisteria Mullins, too, so going to her nightclub was out. The nightclub made him think of Wes Farrell. Farrell was a good man to have in a fight, but his cozy relations with the cops made him a question mark.

As the pain in his side flared, he realized his only hope was to risk going to Doc Poe. Poe, who'd lost his license to practice, still made a substantial living stitching up wounded criminals and performing abortions on prostitutes. Martinez was banking that enough money in Poe's pocket would get him medical help and keep his mouth shut. Poe would, of course, know about his trouble with Compasso, but Poe was independent enough that he might take Martinez's money and keep his mouth shut.

Poe owned what had been a storefront on Prytania Street. He had bricked up the original entrance so that one could only reach his residence through a narrow alley between buildings. Martinez headed in that direction, fighting to stay conscious.

He reached Magazine and continued northeast until he reached Seventh. He turned left at Seventh and crept through the neighborhood until he reached Prytania. He parked at the corner, cut the engine, and dragged his failing body out of the car. He peered through the darkness, discovered there were lights on in the upper story of Poe's building. He staggered across the street, somehow made it without falling. He leaned on the doorbell button with his entire weight. After a while, he heard cursing and the fall of heavy feet coming toward him.

"What in the particular hell do you think you're doin', you Goddamned drunk?" Poe demanded.

"Not drunk, Doc. Hurt. Need help."

"Who...? Jesus Christ on the cross. Martinez, you must be nuts. Get outa here before—"

Martinez poked the muzzle of his automatic through the bars and cocked the hammer. "Let me in, Doc, or I swear I'll splatter your guts all over the alley. Don't think I won't do it."

Poe's face went through a transformation that began at shock, continued through fear, outrage, and finally, acceptance. "You Goddamned fool. Here, lemme open the gate." He turned a latch and pushed the gate open so Martinez could lurch inside. He nearly fell, but Poe grabbed him and began to help him down the alley. "You're gonna pay through the nose, Luis. Askin' me to stick my neck out like this."

"Sure, Doc, sure. Patch me up and I'll get out of here. I'll pay you plenty." He gasped as pain washed over him, and his legs turned to rubber.

Grumbling and griping, Poe dragged him down the alley and into the room he used for a surgery. He eased Martinez down on the operating table then cut his bloody shirt and jacket from his body. He unstrapped the holster from around Martinez's shoulders, then plucked the cocked automatic from his fingers and set them aside. Martinez passed out during this part of the operation, allowing Poe the leisure to paint the wound area with iodine, probe for the bullet and bits of cloth that had been carried into the wound, then stitch up the hole, all without having to administer anesthesia. He gave Martinez a shot of morphine, then got some coffee to keep himself awake until Martinez returned to consciousness.

Martinez awakened at 4:00, finding his torso wrapped in layers of white bandage. Poe sat on a stool nearby still sipping coffee.

"So, you've come back to the land of the living," Poe said. "Well, it wasn't such a bad wound as all that."

"You take a slug in the guts and tell me it ain't bad," Martinez said bitterly. "I feel like I been kicked by a *burro*."

"I'll bet you do at that. But the man who's lookin' for you will do worse if he finds you, Luis. Much worse. Rumor has it you give somebody a thumb in the eye."

"He'll get more than that before I'm through. I burned up his boat tonight. That's how I took the slug. Some guy claimed he was a cop, but he knew things a cop shouldn't."

Poe put both of his hands in the air. "Don't tell me, okay? I can still plead ignorance at this stage." He paused to sip more of his coffee. "Y'know, he's tearin' the town up lookin' for you. And so are some other people."

Martinez stared stupidly. "Who?"

"Lotta people. That chick you useta run with—Jelly Some-thingerother—I forget her right name. Then there's Farrell."

"Farrell? What the hell's he want me for?"

Poe shrugged again. "Word is, he's lookin' to give you a hand."

Martinez rubbed his face in the hope of making his brains work. "I don't get it. I ain't talked to Farrell in a year or more. Why'd he wanna help me?"

Poe gave him a bored look. "I'm a doctor, not a fortune teller. I'll tell you this much. Farrell might be the best hope you got. You can't scare him, and he's got some kinda in with the cops. If I was layin' on that cot with holes shot all through me, I'd get on the phone to him. You ain't got a lotta other people cheerin' for you today, Louie."

Martinez stared at Poe with a lop-sided grin. "I get it, Doc, I'm fucked. You ain't got to write a song about it." He closed his eyes as a wave of pain cut through the morphine, and he took a deep breath. "Jesus. What a fuckin' mess."

Poe laughed mirthlessly. "You're gettin' too old for this stuff, pally. If you had any sense, you'd of taken some of that money you made and retired a long time ago."

"Yeah." Martinez's voice was strained. "I could use some morphine, Doc. Gimme a shot, will ya?"

"Sure, kid. Sure."

⁂

It was nearing midnight when Farrell called into Jake Broussard's office for the fourth time. He felt his eyelids drooping, and a worse fatigue than he could ever remember. He braced his arm on the wall of the telephone booth as he listened to the line ringing.

"Broussard Agency."

"It's Farrell."

"Got some news, boy. One of my men has her spotted in a colored joint called the B-Sharp Club near the river end of Jackson Avenue. She's been gabbing with the bartender for a few hours now, and according to my man they've been talking about Martinez. The bartender claims to know him real well. 'Course, he could be bullshittin' her, too, hopin' to pitch her the high hard one when he gets off work."

"I'm about fifteen minutes from there. I could use your help if you can get away."

"I can make it there in about twenty minutes. My operative is Manny Favorite. Dark brown guy about six-two, one-ninety-five. He likes pinstripe suits and derby hats."

"I remember him. Ex-prizefighter, right?"

"He's the one, and he knows you, in case I don't get there in time. I'm leaving now."

"See you." Farrell hung up and left the booth for his car. The adrenaline was humming through his veins again and his fatigue was momentarily forgotten. He wanted a cigarette, but his throat was already raw from smoking, and he doubted another one would make him feel any better.

He left the edge of the Downtown district and traveled south until he bisected Tchopitoulas Street, then continued southeast until he neared Jackson Avenue. He turned off Tchopitoulas and slowed to a crawl. The neon sign of the B-Sharp Club was visible in the darkness, and just beyond it a car flashed its headlamps twice, and then once more. It was a signal he and Broussard had used in the old days, and he recognized it. He replied with a flash of his own as he cut his wheels into the curbing and killed his engine.

As he got out and walked across the street, he saw the private detective approach him from the opposite direction. Broussard's Panama hat was tipped over his left ear, and his tie was predictably loose at his neck. He was about forty-five years old, a pleasant-looking man with a prizefighter's body beginning to go to seed.

"Man, is this like old times or what?" Broussard greeted him.

"It's like old times, all right. We're sticking out our necks with no money at the end of it. Favorite still inside?"

"Yep. How you want to play it?"

Farrell took off his Borsalino and smoothed his hair before resettling it on his head. "We need to do this with a little finesse. I don't want to touch off a barroom brawl and lose her in the confusion. The smart thing would be to catch her as she leaves and pick her up."

Broussard nodded. "Manny'll follow her out when she comes and we can catch her between us. Unless she's packing a bigger weapon than what's in her dress, the three of us oughta be enough." He leered at Farrell.

"You knucklehead. Will you ever grow up?"

Broussard laughed. "Never. Let's take a load off." He gestured toward his sedan and they went to sit down.

They'd reminisced about scams they'd pulled back in the late '20s and early '30s for nearly an hour when Farrell stretched out a hand. "That's her." They were out of the car in less time than it takes to breathe.

Jelly paused to fish her keys from her bag, and as she found them she felt their approach. Farrell she recognized, but not the white man with him. She turned to reenter the bar and walked right into the arms of a big brown man wearing a derby hat.

"Don't kick up a fuss, Margaret," Farrell said. "I'll tie and gag you if you make me."

She turned to face Farrell, her features blurred with outrage. "If you want a date, call me on the phone. I don't care much for the hard pass."

"I'm looking for Luis, Margaret. So are you."

"So? It's a free country." She worked the keys between her fingers, planning to mark them up if they touched her.

"I'm trying to keep him alive. Compasso wants him killed."

She snorted. "Says who?"

Farrell shook his head. "Margaret, you're a smart woman, so I won't mince words with you. Everybody knows that Luis pulled some kind of fast one on Compasso and that he brought in a hitter from somewhere. The hitter's been visiting Luis's friends and so far two women close to him have been tortured to death."

She blinked. "What? What are you talking about?"

"That's right. Luis lived with a woman named Linda Blanc. Somebody tortured her with a hot iron to find out where Luis was. She died of heart failure. Later the killer discovered Wisteria Mullins was Linda's cousin. He went over there and cut slices out of her until he realized she didn't know anything, then he severed her jugular vein and let her bleed out."

Jelly had gone looking for Martinez for reasons she'd only half-understood at the beginning, but tonight she knew she'd been looking for something of herself, too. It came to her that she'd walked out on a man she couldn't bend, and in penance had bound herself to a man without pity, without feelings of any kind. A wave of sadness washed over Jelly for the woman who had taken her place and died for Luis Martinez. She felt soiled, foolish, and a bit unnecessary.

"What about it, Margaret? You want to let it go until Compasso remembers what good friends you and Luis were? There aren't very many of us left."

She looked around at the three men, examining their faces. She felt no threat from any of them. Farrell looked tired, but his pale-eyed gaze was steady. "What will you do if you find Luis?" she asked.

"That's up to him," Farrell replied. "He's in trouble with the cops up to his neck, but he can deal with that when the time comes. The main thing is to make sure he lives long enough to make the decision. Compasso wouldn't kill Luis's friends if he didn't mean to kill Luis, too."

Once again she examined each man's face for subterfuge. She had confidence in her knowledge of men, and something in her relaxed. "All right. I'll help you."

"Did the bartender tell you where Luis's hideout is?"

Jelly raised an eyebrow. Like many, she had often wondered if Farrell's reputation was justified, and she began to recognize that it just might be. "He claims to know. Claims to have been there with him lots of times." She offered Farrell a knowing grin. "Of course, he could've been feeding me a line. It's been known to happen."

A wisp of a smile fluttered briefly across Farrell's stern mouth. "Can you take me there?"

"Now?"

"The sooner the better. We don't know whether or not Compasso's men have been tipped off by anyone else. If I can get Luis somewhere safe, then I can deal with Compasso."

She nodded. "It's a long drive. You up to it?"

He nodded. "Jake, tell your men I said thanks. I'll settle up with you before the week's out."

"You don't want us to come with you?" Broussard asked.

Farrell shook his head. "I'd like you along, but Luis is trigger happy. If I show up with a carload, he might shoot first and ask questions later." He turned to the big Negro. "Good work, Favorite. I'll see you around."

"Anytime, boss."

"C'mon, Margaret. We can take my car." He clapped Broussard on the shoulder, then took Jelly by the elbow and steered her across the street to his Packard. Seconds later, they headed Uptown on Jackson Avenue.

Favorite rubbed his neck as he stared after them. "Is he as good as they say? He's bitin' off a mighty big chew."

Broussard laughed. "Yeah, he's almost as good as *he* thinks he is. Let's roll. I'm missing my beauty sleep."

❦

It was nearing 1:00 AM when a telephone began to ring in a darkened bedroom. It was a private, unlisted number known only to a handful of people. A man sleeping beside the telephone snapped to consciousness, the way a trained soldier awakens at the first note of reveille, the way he always did when that particular phone sounded. His eyes glittered in the pale moonlight that seeped between the slats of the Venetian blinds over the bedroom window. His hand went unerringly to the receiver, plucking it from its cradle during the second ring.

"Yes, what is it?" His voice was clear and bold, as though he'd been awake the entire night.

"It's Compasso."

"What is it?"

"Martinez. He's destroyed the hangar and most of the stockpile of counterfeit money. I'm told the police found scraps of it in the ashes and alerted the Treasury people. To keep Martinez from destroying all of it, I have sent the rest of the bills to our contact in Atlanta using the Railway Express Agency, as usual."

The man was silent, his eyes blinking as he considered the situation. "I see. All our efforts to mask our base of operations have been undermined, haven't they? And we haven't recovered the plates yet."

"No. But we may be able to get them without your *asesino*." There was a haughty satisfaction in his voice. He resented Chavez, and resented even more the fact that the hired killer wasn't reporting to him, personally.

The man ignored Compasso's resentment. "How?"

"My woman. She used to be with Martinez. She told me she could find him. Naturally, I did not trust her. Women are rarely trustworthy in my experience."

The man in the bed almost smiled. He trusted few men, either. "Get to the point, man."

"I had two men follow her. To see where she went and who she talked to. They followed her tonight to a bar on Jackson Avenue. She talked for a long time to a Negro bartender who is a friend of Martinez's. The bartender gave her instructions on how to find a camp Martinez has upriver in Saint Charles Parish."

"So that's where he's been hiding. No wonder none of your people could find him in the city. She has communicated the information to you, then?"

"Outside the bar she met Wesley Farrell and some other men. My men did not hear their conversation, but she and Farrell went off together."

"I see," the man said, rubbing the bridge of his nose. "You were right not to trust her. Where are they now?"

"My men also spoke to the bartender. He did not want to repeat his directions, but he was—convinced—to be helpful. Farrell and the woman are being followed upriver now. With luck, Martinez will be at his hideout, and they can bring him—and the woman—to me."

"What about Farrell? I'm told he's a dangerous man."

"He is only *one* man. And I made it clear to my men that they dare not fail me."

The man in the bed suppressed a sigh. Compasso's great drawback as a leader was his belief that men could be scared into doing anything, even committing suicide, in order to escape Compasso's wrath. "I hope you're right. One more setback and I'm pulling out of here."

Compasso's voice was silky. "In my country, one does not desert his *companieros* in time of trouble, *amigo*. If we pull out, we pull out together, *entiende?*"

The man continued to rub the bridge of his nose, and when he made no reply, Compasso gently broke the connection, leaving the man to stare up into the darkness above his bed.

Chapter 11

Frank Casey had been routed out of bed in the small hours of the morning with the news that Detective Matt Paret had been taken to Charity Hospital with two bullets in him. Another man might've grumbled at being awakened, but the shooting of a cop was something he moved on. He reached the emergency room at 3:00 and was met by Sergeant Ray Snedegar.

"Tell me what you got, Ray." The two had worked together for fifteen years, and enjoyed an easy informality.

"Arson near the Third District Ferry slip, boss," the hatchet-faced detective said. "Fishing trawler set on fire. Nobody knows why Paret was there."

"He regained consciousness yet?"

"No, but he ought to soon. The wounds weren't serious enough to put him in a coma. They dug two jacketed slugs out of him, either .38 auto or 9 millimeter. Paret must've either crawled off the boat or was carried off by the man who shot him. There's a blood trail leading from the gangplank to the dock."

Casey nodded. "What was Paret working on?"

Snedegar shook his head. "Nothing that would've taken him to the commercial wharves. He's part of the pawnshop detail, which is about as complicated an investigation as he could handle, his squad commander said." He shook his head again. "Paret's not a deep thinker, skipper. I can't think of a major case he's cracked."

Casey frowned. "You've heard the same rumors I have."

Snedegar's face grew a worried look. "The clothes he wears, you can't help thinkin' it, but nobody's ever caught him with his hands dirty."

"Which means he must be a lot smarter than we've given him credit for. Who's the owner of the boat?"

"The Captain of the Port says Pete McMasters."

Casey's head snapped up. "You recognize that name?"

"No."

"McMasters was one of Big Tony Romero's men. He went underground after the Feds sent Romero to Leavenworth. That boat's been used for something besides hauling fish. Get McMasters and turn the wrecking crew loose on him. Paret wasn't shot over a pawnshop item or a load of codfish."

"On my way, boss. You gonna stick it out here?"

"I'll be the first face Paret sees when he wakes up. I'll be at the station once I've talked to him."

"See you there." Snedegar departed, leaving Casey to walk to the nursing station.

An attractive nurse with prematurely gray hair looked up at Casey with a tired smile. "Hi, Frank."

"Hello, Julie. Still working the graveyard shift, eh?"

Her smile brightened. "One good thing about it, when I ask for a vacation, they give it to me, no questions asked. You here about the wounded detective?"

"Yeah. What can you tell me? Can I see him?"

She checked a clipboard. "Post-op report is pretty encouraging. A bullet broke two ribs and punctured his right lung, and a second bullet smashed his right shoulder. He's hurt, but he'll recover."

"Can I see him?"

She cocked a skeptical eyebrow. "I don't know what good he'll be, but c'mon. I'll take you to him."

She got up from her desk and led Casey down a hall and into a small room. Paret lay on a bed with an oxygen tent over his head and upper body. Whole blood was being fed into his left arm and saline solution was going into his right. His face looked flaccid and pale. Casey winked at Julie, then pulled up a chair and drew it close to Paret's bed. He took a cold pipe from his coat pocket, placed the stem between his teeth, then sat back to wait.

Forty minutes had gone by when a low moan reached Casey's waiting ears. He sat up, his attention glued to Paret's face as the man returned to consciousness, licking his dry lips, grimacing as the pain hit him.

"Paret. Matt Paret. Can you hear me?"

Paret groaned again, and with an effort, he raised his eyelids. "Cap—Captain Casey? Where'm I?"

"You're at Charity Hospital. Who shot you, Paret?"

"Wha—?"

"You heard me, Paret. Who shot you?"

"Dunno. Dark. Hard to see."

Casey was on his feet now, watching the wounded man's face. "What took you to the docks last night?"

Paret was almost completely awake now, and his face froze as the import of the question hit him. "What?"

"Why were you there, Paret? You're on the pawnshop detail. Since when does that take you to the waterfront?"

"Can't think. Pain—real bad pain in—"

"Don't try to bullshit me, Detective. I know just how badly hurt you are, and you're actually in pretty good shape. You're going to live, and if you don't answer my questions, I'll let Internal Affairs put you through the meat grinder. There are too many questions about you, Detective Paret. There have been ever since Joe Dante was the big noise in this town. If you want to help yourself, you'd better open up, get me?"

Paret was already pale, but as Casey spoke, his flesh blanched to the color of milk. "I—I got a tip."

"A tip about what?"

"About Luis Martinez." Paret's eyes were sunken in his face, but Casey could see the fear in them.

Casey looked down at the wounded detective, fixing the man's eyes with a cold stare. "You got a tip about Martinez, but you didn't contact your squad commander, or Inspector Grebb? You made a decision to go somewhere in the middle of the night, with no backup, to try to arrest a known armed felon?" Casey's teeth were bared under his red mustache. "Your boss thinks you're pretty dumb, Paret, but I believe you've got more brains than that."

Paret licked his dry lips. His left hand lay exposed on the sheet, twitching nervously. "I—I wanted to make a major case. Sure, it was stupid, but—"

"Cut it out, Paret. Let me tell you my theory. Luis Martinez has declared war on Santiago Compasso. Yesterday he burned up a building full of counterfeit money and killed three men. Now if I'm to believe you at all, Martinez burned that boat and he burned it for one reason—it belonged to Compasso, too. The skipper is an ex-rum runner named McMasters. Right now they're frying him under a hot light at headquarters. I've got ten bucks that says he'll name Compasso as the real owner of the boat."

"I dunno what you're talkin' about."

"Sure you do. Nobody else on this case knows the boat belongs to Compasso. The only reason you'd have been there is that you already knew it was Compasso's boat, and you doped it out that Martinez would strike there next." Casey laughed bitterly. "You've had everybody thinking you were dead weight all these years, Paret. It was a good act. Too bad you're nothing but a cheap crook."

"You got no right to say that. I got shot tryin' to make an arrest and you're givin' me the third degree."

Casey shook his head, his eyes gleaming malevolently. "You know what happens to cops when they get to Angola, Paret? I sent Murphy Culloz there five years ago and they had to put him in solitary to keep him alive. He got out last May, but they tell me he's still lookin' over his shoulder. Culloz was a saint compared to you. You'll be up there until you've got a gray beard hanging to your knees, if somebody doesn't shank you first."

Paret's eyes were large and sick, his mouth working as though he was about to vomit. "*Awright, awright!* Stop it awready. I worked for Compasso. I gave him information, did favors for him. Nothin' big, Captain, I swear."

"Nothing big. Tell me that when they send you upstate to work in the cane fields. Now what about Martinez?"

"Like you said. I made a guess he'd hit the boat. I tried to take him alive so I could get the plates back. Thought he'd play ball, but he threw a gasoline bomb at me. I fired. Hit him, I think, but he fired back, got me. I don't know nothin' after that until I wake up here."

"Plates? What are you talking about?"

Paret looked even more diminished than before. He shook his head. "Martinez and Compasso fell out over a split. Martinez got his hands on the engravings and took off. We been tearin' the town apart tryin' to find him."

"So that's why the two women were killed? Martinez stole the plates and shut the operation down? What's the killer's name, Paret?"

"I dunno, Captain. Compasso brought him from outa town last month. I never seen him. Don't even know his name."

"I'll bet." Casey turned away from the wounded man. There was nothing about discovering a dirty cop to make a man feel good. "All right, Paret. You can consider yourself under arrest. I'll have some men put on the door for your own protection and I'll have a stenographer come in later to take your statement. I suspect it'll take quite a while." He left the room without looking back.

He asked a uniformed officer in the hall to take up a position at Paret's door, then he went to find a pay phone. It was going to be a long day, but some arrests would make him feel better about it.

☕

Farrell took Jackson Avenue north until he reached Claiborne Avenue, then turned west on U. S. 90. Jelly, resting her long bare arm on the open window ledge, was silent as they slipped through the dark streets, occasionally casting a quick glance at Farrell's expressionless face. It made her feel strange to be with him this way. He had been gracious to her when she and Luis had been together, something that clashed wildly with the reputation he had. A different woman might have been afraid.

"You wouldn't have a cigarette, would you?" she asked. "I ran out at the bar and forgot to buy more."

Farrell brought out his hammered silver cigarette case and popped the lid open. "Light one for me, too, will you?"

Without thinking, she put two in her mouth and set fire to them. It was only after she took one from her mouth to hand to him that she realized she'd presumed an intimacy with him that she wouldn't even have dared with Compasso.

He took the cigarette from her and stuck it in the corner of his mouth without hesitation. "Thanks." He drew on it, letting the smoke feather out of his nose.

She smoked in silence for a mile or two, then words rose to her lips. "You're a funny kind of guy, Farrell."

"Yeah. I'm taking over *The Pepsodent Hour* the next time Bob Hope takes a vacation."

"Don't treat me like I'm just some dumb twist, okay? You're sticking your neck out with the cops for a Negro. I don't get why you're doing it. What's your angle? Some of the rake-off from the scam Spanish is running? Or do you just want to stick a thumb in his eye, too?"

He cut his pale eyes at her and she felt the chill as they fell on her. "I'm trying to help Luis stay alive, and you, too. Compasso won't like you going against him."

That bothered her, and she sat back quickly, blinking to keep fearful tears back. It was only now that she began to feel frightened. Farrell must have felt the spike of fear rising in her, for he spoke in a soothing voice.

"Don't worry, Margaret. Compasso will be out of business this time tomorrow. The cops are wise to him and pretty soon they'll have enough to put him away for a hundred years. He won't be around to bother you."

His quiet assurance calmed her, and her boldness returned. "That's what I don't get. Why should you care what a colored woman thinks, or whether or not a colored man lives or dies?" She waved a dismissive hand in the air between them. "Oh, I know all about the stories they tell about the great white hope, Wes Farrell, who reaches down to help all the poor, helpless niggers in distress." She paused, inhaled an impatient drag of smoke, using it to keep the quaver out of her voice. "White people don't help us unless there's an angle, so what's yours, Farrell?"

Her frankness surprised him, as tired as he was. Men never asked him why he did the things he did. It was always the women who tried to understand, who wanted an explanation for why he behaved in ways that were inexplicable in a white man.

"I could ask you that, Margaret. You've got it made with Compasso. You've been with him a couple of years now, but you're blowing all that up to help Luis. I was always Luis's friend, but you walked out on him a long time ago."

She deliberately ignored his question. "You're probably the only man in town who still calls me Margaret. That's what I'm talking about. I hate being called 'Jelly,' and for some reason you bothered to know that without me saying a word. That's what I don't get. A white man caring about a colored girl's Goddamned little feelings without wanting something back for it."

Farrell laughed softly. "Jelly's a pretty dumb nickname. Maybe I just feel sorry for you."

She gave him a hard stare, but decided to finally answer his question. "The reason I'm helping Luis is that I gave him a raw deal once. I hooked up with Santiago because—well, I guess it was because I knew from the beginning he was no good. When you're with somebody like that, you can ignore almost everything he says or does because you know he doesn't care and you don't care either. So when the day comes, you can walk away and not feel two cents worth of regret about it."

"And that's what you're doing tonight."

"Yeah."

"But you're doing it for Luis, too. You still care about something, Margaret."

She turned her head, tried to think of something to say in reply. When she couldn't, she turned her eyes back to the road and remained silent.

Jelly had told Farrell enough of the bartender's directions that he was able to figure a shorter route. Traveling west, he reached the village of Harahan, turning south to intersect the river road. Before long, they began to see the landmarks—the general store belonging to a man named Joe LaGrange, the burnt remains of an antebellum plantation house, and finally the two ancient oaks whose giant limbs swayed just inches from the ground around it.

"Otis said it was less than a mile from here," Jelly said. "Somewhere on the left."

Farrell switched on the movable spotlight attached to the door hinge and played it along the scrub across the road from them. A bit more than a half-mile beyond the oaks, he saw a pair of ruts heading off toward the river. Farrell cut his lights and eased the Packard off the road.

"Keep still," he said softly. "Louie might just take a shot at us, and I happen to know he's a good shot. If I tell you to get on the floor, just do it—quick."

The brightness of the moon provided enough light to keep them on the rutted path, and a few moments later, the shack came into sight.

"Doesn't look like anyone's home," he breathed.

"What now?" Jelly whispered.

"Keep still. I'm going to drive as far as I can, then get out and hail him. We'll play it by ear from there."

"You mean *you'll* play it by ear. What if he shoots?"

"Then you'll have to help him. I'll be past caring."

He got out of the car, taking a flashlight from the door pocket. He walked to within twenty feet of the shack, switched on the flashlight, and called out. "Luis—Luis Martinez. It's Wes Farrell. Luis—I'm here to help."

He waited for a moment then advanced slowly on the rude cabin, letting the flashlight beam light his path. When he reached the door, he stepped to the side, rapped on the door, and called out again. When nothing happened, he pushed the door open and flashed the light around inside. "Come on up. It's empty," he called.

Jelly left the car and tottered over the rough ground to the cabin door on her high heels. "Damn. These shoes are worthless out here," she hissed. She went in behind him and waited for him to light a kerosene lamp. It bathed the interior in an anemic yellow glow that wasn't quite sufficient to light the gloomy corners. "Jesus wept," she said. "What a dump." She wrinkled her nose at the musty smell. "It smells like an animal pen in here."

"Baby, you've lived one hell of a sheltered life. I know Negro families back in town who'd think this was a palace." He poked around the room until he found the saucepan with the remains of Martinez's hasty supper. He sniffed it, touched the bottom and then rubbed his fingers together. "He's been here, and not long ago, either. Not more than a few hours."

"There's his suitcase." Jelly pointed at the foot of the cot. "It's got his initials on it."

Farrell slapped his leg impatiently. "Where the hell are you, Louie? This is a rotten time to go missing."

"He's bound to come back," Jelly said. "Probably everything he's got is under this roof."

"If he's able. If he went back to town to give Compasso another hotfoot, he may not be able to come back. Each time he goes into the city he takes a bigger risk."

She folded her arms beneath her breasts and poked around the room, thinking. She took a breath, then looked back at him. "Then you should go back to town and keep looking for him. I'll wait here, and if he shows up, I'll convince him to come in to you."

Farrell regarded her solemnly as he rubbed the stubble growing on his chin. "I don't like it. This is no game, Margaret. Don't forget, somebody's already killed two women to get to Luis. It's too big a risk."

She shook her head stubbornly. "I don't expect you to understand this, but I owe Luis. I was a spoiled, rotten little bitch when I walked out on him. Maybe if I'd stayed with him, he wouldn't be in this mess now."

"You don't know that. When a man and a woman split up, there's usually blame on both sides. He wouldn't want you to risk your life."

She was exhausted and didn't have the strength to talk much more. "I'm staying. Just go and find him, if you can. Come back and get me later today. It's a way to cover all the bases, Farrell. It makes sense and you know it."

He opened his mouth to speak, but he was tired, too. He stalked out of the house without another word. He was back in a couple of minutes with something in his hand. "Here. Take this and keep it with you." He opened his hand and a small black .32 Colt revolver lay in it. "If somebody besides Luis comes in, get your back to a wall and squeeze the trigger until it's empty, you understand?"

Reluctantly, she took the gun, looking at it as though it were an unexpected bill. "I'm not crazy about this."

Farrell snorted. "We're even. I'm not crazy about leaving you here. Be safe, Margaret. Don't take any chances. I'll be back before nightfall." He turned and walked out of the shack, and a moment later, she heard the Packard roar into life, and gradually fade away.

She looked down at the gun, and for the first time, felt terribly afraid. She sat on the cot with the pistol in her lap, her eyes moving from one dark corner to another, until, exhausted, she lay down and fell into a deep sleep.

⚭

The news that the Treasury Department had recognized New Orleans as the probable distribution point for the counterfeit money put Compasso into an unusually introspective mood. Even if Dixie Ray Chavez or his own men found Martinez and retrieved the plates, the operation in this part of the country was pretty well finished. His silent partner was aware of that, too, or he wouldn't be talking about leaving. There was the chance, too, that the police might get their hands on Martinez before anyone else.

He went to Tink's room and woke him. The bruiser sat up, rubbing his eyes. "What's up, boss?"

"We're getting out of here. Get the others up and get everything of value into the Lincoln. Do it quietly but as quickly as you can."

The thug moved to obey, and Compasso returned to his study. The most expedient way out was by water. McMasters could take them to Mexico, where Compasso had friends.

It was nearing dawn when he picked up his telephone and gave the operator McMasters' number. The phone rang at least eight times before a woman answered.

"What the hell is it now?" she shouted.

Compasso's lip curled with contempt. "Put McMasters on the phone. Tell him it's Compasso."

"Oh," she said, "it's Compasso, is it? Well, get a load of this, you spig sonofabitch. Pete's down at headquarters being taken apart right now and it's because of you and that stinkin' boat of yours. Pete won't turn rat, and they'll pitch his ass into the jug. But I'll go down and tell 'em what they want to know. Pete ain't goin' back to the pen because of you nor nobody like you, see?"

"Why have the cops got Pete?" he shouted.

She laughed. "'Cause somebody burnt your friggin' boat to the waterline, and shot a cop, that's why. So start runnin', Big Shot, 'cause when I'm through, they'll have chains all over your stinkin' carcass." She slammed the telephone down in his ear before he could respond.

With a shaking hand, he dropped the receiver into the cradle. Martinez again. And the cop he shot was probably Paret. Paret would talk, too. He'd have to, before it was all over. He slid the big Astra automatic into the holster under his arm and was putting on the jacket to his dark brown tropical wool suit when Tink came into the office.

"We got it all loaded, boss, but Rojo says there's a car watchin' the front. What do we do?"

"You and Rojo make sure they don't follow. No guns."

Tink turned and disappeared. He and Rojo had removed inconvenient people before, so there was no need for elaborate instructions. Twelve minutes from Compasso's order the two men met him and a third man named Gil Davenport at the garage. Rojo indicated the completion of his instructions with a brief nod of his shaggy head.

The pale light of dawn was faintly glowing in the east as the heavily laden Lincoln slid quietly into City Park Avenue. Rojo, the red-haired ex-*gaucho* Compasso had brought with him from Buenos Aires, was at the wheel. He was a good, steady man who didn't need a lot explanation. He drove as though they were part of a funeral.

"Rojo," Compasso said.

"Si, patron?"

Compasso slipped easily into the gutter Spanish that he used with the red-haired man. "We are going to have to hide from the police until we can leave the city."

"But the boat—"

"Was burned last night. I just spoke to *la Señora McMasters por el telephono.* The police picked Pete up."

"Basta," the old gaucho muttered darkly.

"So we need a place to lay low until we can get some clean license plates. After that we head south to Mexico."

The red-haired man drove in thoughtful silence for a moment. *"Patron—la estancia por el puente grande."*

Compasso almost smiled. To Rojo, any house with more than one floor was an *estancia,* or estate, but he was right. The property not far from the foot of the Huey P. Long Bridge in Jefferson Parish was distant enough from New Orleans that they could not easily be located. *"Muy bien, muchacho. Andele."* For the benefit of Tink and Davenport, Compasso said, "We are going to the house near the bridge. If we can acquire some new license plates, we can be halfway to Mexico by tomorrow evening."

"Sounds good, boss. I know a guy who can help us out."

"Good. A helpful man would be a pleasant change."

Tink knew when to shut up. He folded his arms and settled back in the seat.

Chapter 12

Somehow, Casey wasn't surprised to discover that Santiago Compasso had flown the coop by the time five police cars converged on his house at 5:30 that morning. Inspector Grebb and his men found the doors unlocked and everything incriminating gone from the yawning file cabinets and desk drawers. "They've skipped, Chief," Grebb reported. "Both men in the surveillance car were knocked cold. We just sent 'em to the hospital."

Casey's mouth was stretched tight with chagrin, but he realized that if Compasso had flown, he was running scared. He also knew Compasso was too wily to try to drive out of the city limits just when he figured the cops might be looking for him. "My money says he's lying low until he thinks the heat's off. I'll notify the Jeff Parish and St. Bernard Sheriff's Departments, too. There are a couple hundred places they could hide to the west and south of us."

"What do you want us to do, Chief?"

"Come back in and get your men on the phones. I want every stool pigeon you can find listening at keyholes and peeping over transoms until we get a lead."

"Right, skipper. I'll leave two men and bring everybody else back home."

"Good." Casey hung up his telephone and rubbed his reddening eyes. Getting too old for this, he thought. He looked at the clock and saw that it was about the normal time he arrived at the office. He keyed his intercom. "White, go across the street and get me two fried egg and bacon sandwiches on rye toast and a gallon of black coffee."

The officer responded and Casey heard him leave the office. He found himself rereading the report of the Leake shooting. There was something about that case that bothered him. Why had the gunman so precisely drilled Marston Leake, but left the other man alive?

He picked up his phone and dialed the three-digit extension for Daggett's office. It rang only once.

"Negro Squad, Sergeant Daggett."

"This is Casey. Were you able to nail anything down about the shooting of those two bankers yesterday?"

"Sam and I both believe something stinks, sir."

"Uh, huh. Tell me more."

"Well, for one thing, this Negro gunman's out of his patch. You know that a colored stick-up artist isn't gonna ply his trade Downtown when the sun's still shining. Too much chance of having your face remembered."

"That crossed my mind, too."

"The next thing," Daggett said, "is that the guy's packin' a lot of gun for a stick-up man. Most of those characters carry Owl's Head .32s or some relic from the Spanish American War. This guy has a Colt .45 automatic, in A-one condition according to the forensics report."

"Anything strike you as funny about how the shooting went down?" Casey asked.

"I was getting to that. The shooter was right on top of both men. He kills one and leaves the other one alive."

"That bothered me, too."

"The last thing, though, is the item Sam and I both chewed over all last night. There's evidence that the shooter was waiting in that alley for somebody. He was there long enough to smoke a cigarette all the way through, then start another. The second one was still smoldering when Sam and I investigated the alley he came from."

"It adds up to murder," Casey said. "But if that's what went down, what made Marston Leake so dangerous that someone had to kill him for it?"

"That one kept me awake, Captain, but I don't have even a faint glimmer of an idea this morning."

"Have you got anything on the killer?"

"We got a fairly good description from the survivor and we found some men who were a close match. Trouble is, they've all got believable alibis. This guy may be new in town, but if so, he's several notches up from our local talent. He's clever, ruthless, and you might even say reckless for a simple holdup man."

"Yeah," Casey said thoughtfully. "I tell you what, let's go on the assumption that this wasn't simply a garden-variety stick-up. See if your men can pick up any gossip about a Negro hit man, somebody new in town. I've got another angle I'm going to follow, so check back with me later."

"Will do, Captain." Daggett broke the connection.

Casey tapped the button in his cradle until he got the operator. He asked her for the office of Treasury Enforcement in the Customs House. Within a few minutes he was on the line with Agent Paul Ewell.

"Paul, it's Frank. Have you got a few minutes?"

"Sure, Frank. What's on your mind?"

"Did you get a report of a shooting yesterday afternoon involving a pair of vice presidents from First National?"

"Why no." Surprise was evident in Ewell's voice. "What happened?"

"The short answer is that Marston Leake and Max Grossmann were confronted by a Negro stick-up man. When it was over, Leake was dead and Grossmann was wounded, although not badly."

"Jesus. I was just talking to them in A. J. McCandless's office a couple of days ago. We'd just given them a clean bill of health after inspecting them for counterfeit. You say it was a stick-up man?"

"That's what it looks like, but we think there's more to it. The killer was waiting in a very convenient alley not far from the bank. The shooting happened in broad daylight. I just got through talking it over with my Negro Squad sergeant, and he found plenty wrong with the entire picture. I thought I'd run it in front of you."

"Leake struck me as the brains of that bank, a very watchful, cautious man. The others seemed—I don't know—nervous or shaky about something. I just chalked it up to jitters over a possible scandal. But when a banker gets killed in the midst of a currency investigation, it's like a red flag waving. How badly was Grossmann wounded?"

"Barely. His arm was grazed and they released him after treatment. He might be back at work today."

"Hmmmm," Ewell said. "Have you got time to visit the bank president with me later today?"

"Let me know when and I'll meet you there," Casey said.

"Good. I've never given a bank president the third degree. It might be handy to have a New Orleans cop there to give me a few pointers."

Casey laughed. "I'll wait for your call."

"Right." Ewell hung up the telephone.

Casey put his own receiver back into the cradle and was rubbing his face as Officer White came in with a bag full of breakfast for him. Casey allowed himself to briefly imagine what circumstances could bring together a counterfeit ring, a murdered banker, and a lone Negro gunman with more nerve than sense as he bit into his first sandwich.

∞∞∞

Farrell made it back to the Café Tristesse at about 4:00 AM feeling utterly worn out. He stumbled up to his rooms, took four aspirins with a big glass of water, then stripped and fell across his bed. He was deep into sleep within seconds of his head hitting the pillow.

He saw himself walking down a dark city street with grotesque shadows playing all about him. Ahead somewhere, he could hear a voice singing a song that was oddly familiar. Farrell quickened his pace.

Soon he saw a man ahead of him. He was at some distance, but his posture, the cocky way he wore his hat, identified him to Farrell as Luis. "Luis—Luis—It's Farrell," he called. He was rewarded by a jaunty wave from his old friend, and he once again quickened his pace. Then Margaret Wilde appeared in front of him. She was on all fours, naked but for a collar around her neck attached to a long length of rope staked to the ground. He made to set her loose, but a noise stopped him. His father appeared with a pair of handcuffs that he dangled from his finger. He wore a stern look on his face and shook his head negatively.

Farrell backed up a step, and his father and Margaret vanished. Blinking with surprise, he ran toward Luis, calling out to him. However, as he got closer, he saw that Luis was blind, his red, empty eye sockets bleeding down into his smiling mouth. Farrell reached out to touch him, but a pale gray wisp came between them, a thing that was both shadow and specter. Farrell fought it, found it insubstantial and entangling all at once. He was yelling, cursing with frustration, tearing at the shadow.

The telephone woke him. It rang steadily and insistently on his nightstand, and he had to untangle himself from the sheets before he could grab it. "Farrell," he said breathlessly.

"It's Sparrow. You sound tired, Farrell."

"Yeah, I guess so. You have news for me?"

"Yes, and it seems reasonably good. A source tells me that Doc Poe has a new patient that checked in last night."

"Tell me the rest."

"Somebody—it's believed it was Martinez—set fire to a boat operated by a seaman in Compasso's employ last night. During the fire, a cop named Paret intervened and there was shooting. Paret was injured, but there's some evidence the other man was wounded, too."

"What makes you think the man at Poe's is Martinez?"

"I happen to know from another source that Martinez owns a new dark green Mercury coupé. A car like that is parked within a block of Poe's building. It has Arkansas plates, but the first thing a man on the run will do is steal some new license plates."

"That would explain why Luis wasn't at his hideout last night. Margaret Wilde found out where it was and we drove out there, but it was deserted."

"She's supposed to be an intelligent woman, in spite of that ridiculous nickname she uses."

"It was pasted on her, Sparrow. She hates it. Call her Margaret and she'll be your friend for life."

"I'll remember that if I ever invite her for tea. You'd better get moving, Farrell. Martinez may try to leave Poe's, or Compasso's man may discover his whereabouts."

"Thanks, Sparrow. I'm once again in your debt."

"Just stay alive, Farrell. That negative energy I mentioned is still there, and you're in the middle of it. Good luck, my friend." She hung up before he could reply.

Farrell looked at the bedside clock and saw it was 9:00. He wanted to go back to sleep, but he knew that was out of the question. He walked to the bathroom, turned on the hot water full blast, and stepped into it. The heat soaked into his bones and brought him the rest of the way to wakefulness. He soaped himself, then lathered and shaved his face in the metal mirror bolted to the tile wall. When he was finished, he stood under a stinging blast of cold water for a full minute before climbing out and drying off. It took him another ten minutes to dress in fresh clothing, and two more minutes to get his German steel razor and .38 Colt automatic from his desk. He wanted coffee and food, but that would have to wait.

It took about twenty minutes to make it to Poe's neighborhood in the early morning traffic. As he rolled to a stop across the street from Poe's, he saw the new green Mercury coupé parked nearby. He passed it on his way to Poe's locked gate to ring the doorbell.

He recognized Poe's bulky shape as he appeared at the end of the alley. He approached cautiously, and Farrell noticed his right hand was held a bit behind his hip, no doubt holding a gun. Farrell reached up with both hands and grabbed the bars to show he was empty-handed.

Poe eyed him skeptically. "Well, well, well. What's the matter, Farrell? Infected hangnail, or perhaps you cut your finger on a sharp playing card?"

"Let me in, Doc. I want to see Luis."

"I tried to get the dumb bastard to call you last night. He knows you're looking for him. Before I let you in, I've gotta know you're not gonna try to harm him. I can't afford that here."

"I'm here to help, Doc, not make things worse. Let me in and he can make up his mind what he wants to do."

"Come in, then." Poe shoved his pistol into his hip pocket, then unlocked the gate so Farrell could squeeze into the alley. He led him back through the courtyard and into the infirmary where Luis lay. His body was swathed in bandages and his face was pale. He offered Farrell a wan smile as he entered.

"Hey, *chivato*. Talk about a coincidence. You been lookin' for me, eh?"

Farrell tipped his hat up off his forehead and looked at Doc. "Nobody's called me *chivato* in years. You got any coffee, Doc? I haven't eaten today."

"Or yesterday from the look of you. I'll get something for the two of you." Poe turned and left them alone.

Farrell dragged up a chair and straddled it, leaning on the back with his arms. "Boy, you're really in it now."

Martinez affected an air of nonchalance. "Nothin' big, just takin' care of a li'l business."

"Save the applesauce, Luis. The cops want you for murder and arson, the Feds want you for counterfeiting, and Compasso's men just want to kill you. Your life isn't worth a plugged nickel right now."

"Man, you're a grouchy bastard when you don't get your morning coffee, ain't you?"

"Okay, tough guy. I get it. You can handle it all by yourself."

"Sure, just like I did in the old days before you started taggin' along." He moved his arm a bit thoughtlessly, and a grimace of pain swept across his face.

"Luis, Compasso's pretty much finished. If you're smart, you'll go to the Treasury Department and make a clean breast. It may be enough to get you out from under the murder charges. A smart lawyer can play the jury in such a way that you'll get off with a few years at Leavenworth."

Martinez's eyes flattened and his mouth tightened. "Well, well. My old *compadre*, my partner in crime. You've turned into a real *ciudadano sólido*, ain't you? *Gracias,* but I'll take my chances with Compasso."

Farrell shook his head. "No matter how much you hurt him, you can't bring Linda back. Play it smart and own up to your part in it. It's the only way to live with it."

The words came out harder than Farrell meant, and he saw the muscles in Martinez's jaw ripple. He turned his face from Farrell and sucked his breath in. Farrell saw his mouth stretch and crumple.

"I'm sorry, Louie. I didn't mean it to sound like that. Or maybe what I meant to say is that what's happened to you has happened to me. When you play with fire, sometimes the people you care about get burned. It's part of the price we pay for being the kind of people we are. I came to get you out from under before Compasso's killer does what he was paid to do."

Martinez coughed a couple of times to clear the lump in his throat. "I can't just quit, Wes. I can't leave Compasso standin' there after what he did." He turned his anguished face back to Farrell's, his eyes beseeching. "Don't you see? I gotta finish it."

"You damned dumbbell. You've already hammered Compasso into the ground. Last night while you were burning Compasso's boat, you shot Detective Matty Paret. He's been in Compasso's pocket ever since he came to town. The cops are gonna ask him some hard questions about what he was doing down on that particular dock on that particular night, and he'll sing his lungs out, if he hasn't already. That's all the police will need to peel Compasso like an onion. If you go forward now and tell what you know, there's a chance for you to come out of this with something. I'll stick by you. I'll get you the best lawyer in town. Sure, you'll serve some time, but you've lived through worse."

Martinez stared at him bleakly. A greasy sweat lay on his pale skin and his eyes were like those of a dying animal. He reached up with his good hand and rubbed his face, closing his eyes with his fingers and thumbs, strangely like a man closing the eyes of a dead friend. He lay like that for a while before he finally opened them again. "Well, *amigo*, you really know how to cheer up a sick friend, eh? So I'm finished. I guess I always knew it'd have to end like this someday."

Farrell was tired and sad, but he tried to inject some optimism in the words he chose. "Most of the people we knew in the old days are dead, except for a few who ended up serving long terms in the pen. With good behavior, you'll come out in five or six years and still have something. Money you laid aside, and a few friends to give you a hand. It could have turned out worse."

Martinez forced a smile. "How the hell did you find me, anyway? I made myself pretty scarce the past few weeks."

"You can thank several people, including Margaret Wilde. She snooped around until she discovered the whereabouts of that shack you were hiding out in. We must've just missed you last night. She volunteered to stay there and wait to see if you'd return. I came back to town, and a friend told me about Doc Poe's new live-in patient. We need to get out to the shack and give Margaret a lift home."

"Sweet, sweet Jelly," Martinez said softly. "I was really gone on that girl once."

"She's older now, Louie. She wants to see you. That's something else you might have if you use your head."

At that moment Doc Poe wheeled in an old-fashioned teacart with three plates of eggs and bacon, a plate of buttered toast, and a pot of coffee. "Sorry it took so long, the kitchen help is off today," he said sarcastically.

"You're a prince, Doc," Martinez said. "I could eat a wet *burro*, hooves and all."

Farrell propped Martinez up so he could handle his plate, then picked up a plate and began to shovel the food into his mouth. As the food reached his stomach, some of the bone-deep fatigue began to leave him.

"What do I owe you, Doc?" Martinez asked when they were halfway through their food.

Poe wiped his mouth on the back of his hand and shook his head. "Every now and then I gotta do some charity work, Louie. Just get the hell out of here and don't tell anybody who patched you up. I don't want a steady stream of bums through here lookin' for freebies, you hear?"

"Sure, Doc. *Yo comprende.*"

They finished their breakfasts in silence then Poe got up to clear away the dishes. He returned to check Martinez's bandages and to give him instructions on how to care for the wound, including some morphine for pain. He found a shirt for Martinez and helped him dress. They were on the point of leaving when Poe stopped them.

"You're forgetting something, ain't you, Louie?" In his hand he held the shoulder rig and the Colt .38 Super.

Martinez looked at it for a long moment. "Give it to Farrell."

Farrell exchanged a look with Martinez, then he took the harness, wrapped the straps around it, and tucked it under his arm. With Poe's help, they made it to the street entrance. Farrell went alone across the street, where he stowed Martinez's gun in the trunk of his car before getting behind the wheel and driving across to where Martinez and the doctor waited. Poe wordlessly helped the wounded man into the passenger seat, then gave them a brief salute before turning his back and disappearing down the alley.

Martinez leaned his head back against the leather upholstery and closed his eyes. "What happened to the cream and red Packard you used to drive?"

Farrell shrugged. "I asked too much of it too many times. It was showing its age. This one's more powerful. I'll open it up once we cross the parish line."

"Swell. I could stand to kick up some breeze."

They drove in silence for a while before Martinez spoke again. "How does she look? Margaret, I mean."

Farrell grinned. "What do you think? The few years since you've seen her didn't do her any harm. She grew up."

Martinez grunted. "Funny. Funny world." He closed his eyes again, and drifted off to sleep. Farrell briefly envied him as he turned his attention to the road.

They made good time, and in about an hour and a half they were back at the pair of ruts that led down to Martinez's fish camp. Farrell honked the horn, snapping Martinez out of his nap.

"What the hell—?"

"Sorry," Farrell said. "I was just announcing our arrival to Margaret." He got out of the car and called out to her as he walked to the shack. As he got near the shack, he realized something was wrong. The cabin door was ajar, and one of Margaret's shoes lay just outside. Farrell kicked the door open and leaped through the opening. The cot was turned over on its side, and Margaret's other shoe lay nearby. Just under the cot he saw the little Colt revolver he'd left with her. He picked it up and broke the cylinder—it hadn't been fired.

He shot glances about the room, and finally saw what he was meant to see. He walked to the rude table and saw a rusty butcher knife pinning a scrap of paper to the top. He worked the knife out of the paper and picked it up. There were just a few words scratched on it:

The plates for the girl—I'll call you tonight

Farrell was still staring at the note when Martinez staggered into the room.

"What's happened? Where is she?" His eyes were large and startled, like those of a man waking up in a strange country where he doesn't know the language.

"Compasso's man. He found the place after I left. He's got Margaret and says he'll trade her for the plates." Farrell's pale eyes were like something from a nightmare. "Where are the plates, Luis?"

"I—I hid 'em. I didn't want to have 'em on me in case I got unlucky." He ran his fingers through his lank hair. "I can get them easy enough. They're back in town." He stared at Farrell as comprehension dawned. "This guy. He's the one killed Linda and Wisteria?"

Farrell nodded. "We'd better get back to town. I want to be there when he calls." He shoved the note into his pocket, then got Martinez under the arm and helped him back out to the car. He slid under the wheel and wrenched it savagely, tearing long trails in the grass and weeds as he gunned the car back out to the road.

⋙⋘

Marta Walker was finishing up a late breakfast in the Metro dining room as she thought about the strange turns her life had taken. She had come here on a mission, and now that the mission was almost fulfilled, she wondered how she could go home again. She had found New Orleans an exciting place to be, and Marcel Aristide's company had made clear that she could never be satisfied with Brownsville again.

She had signed the check and was preparing to go up to her room to read the paper when something she saw out the dining room window arrested her. She walked closer to the glass and stared across the street. A well-dressed young man was walking along the street with a familiar lilt to his stride. There was, too, something very familiar about the jaunty angle at which he wore his snap-brim hat. As she stood there, she became convinced that the man was Wilbur Lee Payne, alias Albert Chenier.

She rushed to the hotel entrance and walked out under the sidewalk awning in time to see Payne go into the pawnshop across the street with a small parcel under his arm. She remained under the awning, watching the pawnshop, wondering what she should do next. If she went to call Marcel, Payne would surely be gone by the time he got there. She could walk across the street and confront Payne, but what she had learned about her old boyfriend had left her feeling leery of that prospect. She elected to wait.

Payne was in the pawnshop for more than ten minutes, but her patience was rewarded. He emerged and continued north on Rampart Street. He was no longer carrying the small parcel, and had both hands in his trouser pockets as he ambled along. Fortunately for Marta, he seemed in no hurry, allowing her to follow him from across the street.

Payne continued until Rampart merged with St. Claude. This proved to be an even busier part of town, and was a bit rougher to her small-town eyes. The people were not dressed quite as well, and it seemed to her that some of the men eyed her rather too boldly. It made her uncomfortable, but she was determined to find out where Payne was going.

About ten blocks from where they'd started, Payne suddenly quickened his pace and merged with a group of shoppers and other pedestrians. She lost sight of him almost immediately. She quickened her own steps and dodged traffic as she crossed the street. She reached the place where she'd last seen him and continued to the corner, where she ruefully concluded that he'd given her the slip.

Feeling rather chagrined, she turned and headed back toward the hotel. She would tell Marcel what she had seen, and perhaps he could do something with the information. Perhaps the owner of the pawnshop could tell them something. She was imagining what Marcel might say or do when something hard jammed into her back and a hand grabbed her elbow.

"Don't make any sudden moves, darling," Wilbur Lee Payne said. "This gun would make a terrible noise and you would be very, very dead. Just keep on walking, like we're on one of those little outings we had in Brownsville."

"Let me go," she said in what she hoped was a firm voice. "You're in a lot of trouble over what you've done."

"Well, sweetheart, for that to happen, someone would have to tell on me, and I've got too much invested here to let you blow it up. Here, let's get into this car. And don't think you can yell or get away before I shoot you, dear." He opened the car and pushed her inside. He closed the door firmly, then walked around to the driver's side with his hand in his right coat pocket. He slid under the wheel, stepped on the starter, then eased out into traffic.

"Albert, you're making a mistake," she said, trying to remain calm. "People here know me, and they're looking for you. They know about your real name and your prison record. It's only a matter of time until they find you."

Payne nodded his handsome head. "I always knew you were a smart girl, Marta. If I'd detected a spark of larceny in your little heart, we could have had a wonderful relationship together. As it is, well, I'm going to have to put you where you can't do any mischief."

She felt all the courage begin to drain out of her as he spoke. For the first time, she realized that the gentle, courtly facade he affected was just an act. He was a ruthless and cold-blooded man underneath. If she didn't get away from him, anything might happen. She weighed the possibilities: she could scream, but probably no one would hear, or if they did the car was moving too fast for anyone to get the license number. She could try fighting him, but he was much stronger. With a sinking heart, she realized her only option was to jump out of the moving car. Her hand inched toward the door handle as she waited. When he next slowed for a turn that would be her opportunity.

He came to a corner and downshifted, and as the engine whined, she jerked the handle. It came open as she threw her weight to the side. She was halfway out of the car when his hand jerked her back. She cried out, tried to pull away, but a heavy weight fell on the base of her neck. A dark, oily pool opened beneath her and sucked her down.

Chapter 13

Margaret Wilde came back to consciousness in a room that was more shadow than light. Her vision was blurred, but she couldn't raise her hands to rub her eyes. It took her a moment to realize she was bound hand and foot. The small movements caused her head to feel as though it would split down the middle. A muffled gasp came from her throat, and she ground her teeth together until the waves of pain began to subside.

Gradually, she recalled having driven with Wesley Farrell to Luis Martinez's fishing camp. She had insisted on waiting there for Luis while Farrell returned to town to continue the search. Once alone, fatigue quickly overwhelmed the tension that had kept her going for so many hours, and she'd fallen asleep on an old army cot.

Something had happened after that, but she was unsure exactly what had transpired. She'd heard a noise, and imagined it was in a dream. Had she stirred, or had that been her imagination? There had been a bright light and a moment of sharp pain inside her skull before she'd plummeted back down into unconsciousness.

Fully awake now, she understood that Farrell's fear had come true. Compasso's men had found the fish camp, too, and finding her defenseless, had knocked her unconscious.

As her vision cleared, she could fathom that she was no longer at the shack. The heat and odors that had made the shack so sultry and ripe were gone. This place was cool, dim, and musty. Not much light was getting in here. It was almost totally dark. Wait—was something—? No, it couldn't be. There it was again—movement of some kind. A man, but in the shadows, where only a vague shape was discernible.

"Welcome back to the living, for the time being, my sweet Jelly." Santiago Compasso stepped out of the shadows. "I did not mention that I was having you followed, did I?"

She licked her lips, and with an effort, forced words through her dry throat. "What are you doin', Spanish?"

He laughed, a full-throated laugh of triumph and cruelty. His cold blue eyes had harsh points of light in them and his wedge-shaped face seemed more demonic than ever. "What am I doing? I am going to grind Luis Martinez to powder, and I am using you to do it." He roamed about the room, his movements like those of a fierce cat. "I can bear the fact that you are a lying, treacherous slut, but I will not tolerate you treating me like a fool. Did you think I did not see you hating me with your eyes whenever we were in the room together? Did you?" He reached down, grabbed her by the shoulders, and pulled her off the bed until they were nose to nose. "Yes, you thought I was a fool. You thought I didn't see the little glimmerings of excitement in your eyes when you realized I had hired Luis Martinez and that he had betrayed me. Oh yes, *chica*. I saw." He opened his hands and she fell backward, striking her head on the wall as she bounced on the mattress.

A sickening hatred clotted her throat, but somehow she managed to keep the words from rising to her tongue. She knew him. She knew he would beat her insensible at the least provocation. "What are you going to do with me?"

A lock of yellow hair had fallen out of his widow's peak over his forehead, and perspiration gleamed on his pale skin. "I am going to get my engravings back, and I am going to kill Luis Martinez. I'm going to keep you alive just so long as you help me do that. By now, he and his friend, Farrell, will know that I have you, but they won't know where I am. Thanks to Martinez, the police know of us, and we had to abandon the house in the city. Believe me when I tell you that no one knows where you are, *gelatina dulce.*"

Her eyes burned with the rage she felt for him, and for herself. She had tried to make amends to a man she had wronged, and now she was contributing to his death. "I'll see you dead, you son of a bitch."

Her words had a peculiar effect on him. He seemed to enjoy her insult. He smiled, pulling his belt from his pants, and doubled it, swinging it from his hand like a dandy's cane. He moved toward her with excruciating slowness until he was even with the bed. Then his face changed, and he lashed her with the belt, again, and again, and again until she slid back into a dark place where fear and pain didn't exist.

※※※

Marcel Aristide tried several times that morning to reach Marta Walker, each time meeting with failure. Arthur Bordelon had taken the day off, and the assistant desk manager seemed to know nothing about the young woman. On his last try, Marcel hung up the telephone with the distinct sense that something was wrong. Fred Gonzolvo came into the office and saw the expression of trouble on his face.

"I know that look, li'l brutha. What's up?"

Marcel looked up into Fred's dark brown face. "Marta's missing from the hotel. Has been all day."

"Thought Arthur was gonna look after her."

"Arthur took the day off. His assistant hasn't paid any attention to Marta. She was seen in the dining room for breakfast before 9:00 AM, but not since."

Fred ran a thumb over the edge of his broad jaw, his eyes thoughtful. "Think she went lookin' for Payne alone?"

"I'm afraid she might've found him." He picked up the telephone receiver and asked the operator for a number in Carrollton. After two rings a man with a heavy bass voice answered. "Yo, this is Mickey."

"It's Marcel. I need you and five other men pronto."

"Okay. Then what?"

"I want you to get them down to Rampart Street in the vicinity of the Metro Hotel, then fan out. We're looking for a girl about twenty-two years old. Five feet seven, weight about one-ten. Honey-gold skin, wavy shoulder-length light brown hair. Her name's Marta Walker and we need to find her."

"Damn, this sounds like trouble, li'l brutha."

"I hope it isn't, but I'm going on that assumption. You man your phone. Tell your men to call in every hour with a report on where they've been, and what they picked up. I'll call you for a report at a quarter past."

"What if we find her?"

"Bring her to Soraparu Street and watch over her until I show up. Fred and I are gonna go out and look, too."

"You're the boss, boss." Mickey hung up.

Marcel put his receiver back on the hook and turned to see Fred slipping his arms through the straps of his shoulder harness. He drew his worn old .38 Colt, checked the loads and holstered it. He got his coat from the tree and looked at Marcel with a curious smile.

"If we goin' to a party, boss, we want to be in our party clothes, don't we?"

Marcel hated guns. They reminded him of a time when he'd been a criminal, and of people he'd shot at with every intention of killing. He was proud of carrying himself in such a way that he didn't need a gun. But this was different, and he knew it. He unlocked the bottom drawer of his desk and took out a small mahogany case. When he lifted the lid, a nickel-plated .38 Colt Detective Special with ivory grips gleamed in a bed of green felt. It was a gift from Farrell. He took it from the case, loaded it, and slipped it into his coat pocket along with a small leather pouch containing six extra cartridges.

He stood up and got his hat. "I'm ready now."

It took them about twenty minutes to reach the Metro, and another ten for Marcel to interrogate a pair of waitresses he knew. From them he was able to glean that Marta had left the hotel dining room about ten minutes past nine that morning. One had seen her under the awning, staring across the street at the pawnshop, but hadn't seen her go in. Marcel thanked them and met Fred in the lobby.

"I talked to the shoeshine men and some bellhops, but none of them seen anything," Fred reported.

Marcel scratched his neck and stared across the street at the pawnshop. "Couple of gals in the dining room said they saw Marta staring across the street at the pawnshop."

"They see her go in?"

"No," Marcel replied, "but that doesn't mean she didn't. Marta's a smart girl. If she was looking over there, she must've seen something. Let's take a stroll."

The two young men left the hotel and crossed the street to the pawnshop. Marcel didn't know the pawnbroker, but thanks to underworld gossip, he knew that Theron Oswald was a fence. He spoke a few words to Fred and was acknowledged by a nod as they entered the shop.

At the tinkling of the bell, Oswald looked up from a ledger he was writing in. It was plain from his glance that he didn't know them. "Help you gents?"

Fred grinned broadly. "Hey, man. I'm lookin' to go huntin' this fall and I wondered if you had any shotguns."

"Got a few," Oswald replied. "Got a real nice Remington pump, got a couple L. C. Smith double barrels, and I think I got a Savage."

"Sounds like good stuff all around," Fred said. "Lemme see the Remington, okay?"

"Sure." Oswald cast a look at Marcel. "I'll be with you in a minute, mister."

"No hurry," Marcel said. "I'm just lookin' around."

Oswald went to a rack at the far end of the shop where he hauled out a ring of keys, and began going through them for the one that would open the rack padlock.

As Oswald's attention was focused on the rack, Marcel's eyes made a quick circuit of the room, looking for what, he didn't know. It seemed a perfectly ordinary pawnshop with the requisite glass cases of old watches, diamond rings, pistols, and other paraphernalia that people hock for eating money. He was about convinced there was nothing there when he spotted a small white paper sack on the edge of the counter where Oswald's ledger lay. It reminded Marcel of the kinds of paper sacks pharmacies use to bag customer purchases. He slid toward it, listening to Oswald mutter as his ring of keys slipped from his fingers to the floor.

With the sound of the keys jangling in the background, Marcel spread the sack open and looked inside. There was a bottle of pills with the name of the drug typed on a label bearing the name and address of a doctor. Marcel made a mental note of each before gently pinching the bag closed and moving soundlessly to a case full of ladies' watches.

"This here Remington pump is like brand new," Oswald told Fred. "It sells for $42.95 in the Sears Roebuck catalog, but I'm lettin' it go for $33.75. Here, see how it feels." He handed the shotgun across to Fred, who threw it to his shoulder and worked the slide.

"Bang," Fred said as he depressed the trigger. "What you think about this, man? Could we blast some duck dinners outa the sky with this iron?"

Marcel was thinking about the drug in the bag. It was called trioxalen, and for some reason, he remembered reading about that drug somewhere. "What? I was day-dreaming."

"The gun, man. I was askin' if you thought it'd be good for huntin' some ducks. Duck season starts in just a coupla months. We could bag some for Thanksgivin' dinner."

"You're the outdoorsman, Freddie. If you think it will, give the man some money."

Fred practiced throwing the gun to his shoulder a few times, making shooting noises with his mouth while Marcel drifted closer to the man.

"Say, mister. My girlfriend said she might come in here to look at a diamond ring—which she hopes I'll buy for her." He leered good-naturedly at Oswald. "She didn't happen to come in this morning, did she? Tall, good-lookin' girl with dark honey-gold skin and long light-brown hair?"

Oswald grinned. "Reckon not, friend. If she had, I'd probably remember a gal like that. Sure it was this shop?"

Marcel shrugged. "I thought so, but you know how women can be with their directions. Could well've been someplace else. You got some nice stuff here, though. Might be I'll bring her in here to take a look. Man wants to buy the right ring when he buys one, you know?"

Oswald nodded seriously. "No lie, man. You got to keep a gal happy to make her stay around."

"You ready, Fred?" Marcel asked.

Fred looked at the shotgun longingly. "Dunno, man. This is one fine piece of iron." He shot a look at Oswald. "How's about I give you ten bucks to hold it until tomorrow? That be all right?"

Oswald showed all of his teeth in a big grin. "Sure. Lemme write you out a receipt, brutha." He got out a pad of printed receipt blanks and quickly wrote some information on it. "What name?"

"Fred Gonzalvo. Here's your ten bucks, man."

Oswald took the money and handed Fred the receipt. "See you tomorrow, my friend."

"Right." Fred flashed a grin before following Marcel out of the store. He didn't speak again until they'd walked a half block up Rampart. "Well? I seen you pokin' around in there. You find somethin'?"

Marcel frowned. "Something, but I don't know what. He had a prescription lying on the counter and it had the name of a doctor I didn't recognize on it."

"You told me that Payne could be posin' as a doctor," Fred replied.

"Yeah. If Marta saw Payne go in that shop, that may be why she was staring at it. He might've dropped off the prescription to Oswald and left, with her following."

Fred scratched the back of his neck. "That's a hell of a lot of supposin', li'l brutha."

Marcel cast a glance back at the store. "Yeah, don't remind me. I'm grasping at straws, Goddamn it. I should've moved her someplace where I could keep a better eye on her."

Fred listened silently. He knew from experience that no one was harder on Marcel than Marcel, himself. He dropped a comforting hand on his partner's shoulder and squeezed it lightly.

Marcel looked up at the larger man and grinned. "What the hell are you gonna do with that shotgun? You've never been hunting in your life."

Fred shrugged elaborately. "Maybe I wanta give it a try. I might be good at it. What we gonna do now?"

"I'm going to call Mickey to see if any of his boys have called in with news, then I'm going to call a cop who was looking something up for me."

"Let's hit the Oleander Café. I can eat somethin' while you're doin' your callin'."

"You and that stomach. Let's go."

It took them five minutes to reach the café. Fred took a seat at the counter and engaged the brownskin waitress in conversation while Marcel went to the phone booth. He quickly had Mickey Rawls on the line.

"Most of the boys done called in awready, boss, but so far nothin' doin'. You know we lookin' for a needle in a haystack."

"Yeah," Marcel said. "I know. Keep trying and I'll be back with you later." He hung up, dropped in another nickel, and asked the operator for Police Headquarters. When the desk sergeant answered, he asked to speak to Officer Eddie Park in the Negro Squad.

"Negro Squad, Officer Park speaking."

"This is Marcel Aristide. Have you had any luck with that favor I asked you about yesterday, Eddie?"

Park's voice dropped an octave, but his tone was friendly. "How ya doin', Marcel? Yeah, I got something for you, but I don't know what good it is."

"Were there many new office listings for doctors in the past two months?"

"Well, hardly any. Three. And two of 'em are obviously white doctors, 'cause they're Uptown exchanges."

Marcel felt the hair prickle on the back of his neck. "And the other one—is his name Abraham T. Rodrigue?"

There was a silence at the other end of the line, then, in an awed voice, Park said, "Man, have you taken up mind reading or what? That is the name, but how'd you know?"

"Call it a lucky guess."

"Well, his office is located at 7923 North Villere. Phone number there is Claiborne 3375. I checked to see if there was a home number, but no soap. What's the story on this guy, Marcel? He owe you a gambling debt or somethin'?"

"Eddie, if he turns out to be the guy I think he is, I'm gonna call you up and give you a chance to be a hero. I'll be talking to you, hear?"

"Okay, brutha. Play it close to your vest. One day you'll want to play with my catnip mouse."

Marcel laughed and hung up the telephone. On an impulse, he dropped in another nickel and asked the operator for Claiborne 3375. It buzzed three times before a woman picked up.

"Dr. Abraham Rodrigue's office. How may I help you?"

"Say, miss," Marcel said in a cracked old-timer's voice. "I got me a turrible pain in my sacroiliac. Could Dr. Rodrigue see me this aft'noon?" He coughed wetly for effect.

"Well, I don't think so today, sir. Dr. Rodrigue's out on a housecall just now, and I don't know when to expect him. I could give you an appointment first thing tomorrow morning. Would that do?"

"Don't think so, missy. I'm in turrible pain. Reckon I better try somewheres else. Thankee now, hear?" Marcel hung up the telephone before the young woman could reply. He left the booth with a thoughtful expression on his face and joined Fred at the counter. His friend was chewing an enormous bite out of a hamburger.

Fred cast a glance at his friend as he climbed up on the adjoining stool. "What's the verdict, li'l brutha?"

"Something's goin' on, Fred. But what, I don't know."

Fred bit into the hamburger again. "What now?"

"I want you to watch the pawnshop. Use the hotel lobby, because I want you to call into Mickey every hour at a quarter past. There's a booth in the lobby where you can still see the pawnshop."

"Okay. What're you gonna do?"

"Talk to a couple of people, then go see a doctor."

Fred frowned as he chewed. "You feelin' okay?"

"I'll let you know after I've seen the doctor."

⚭

It was nearly 11:30 AM when Farrell eased his convertible to a stop behind the Café Tristesse. Martinez had again fallen asleep in spite of his worry. Farrell had to shake him gently by the shoulder to arouse him.

"C'mon, pardner. I've got a nice soft bed you can snooze on after you make that telephone call."

Martinez grunted, and allowed Farrell to help him out of the car and up to the apartment. Inside, they went to Farrell's office, where Martinez sat down at the desk.

"You could've told me where they were and we'd have them by now," Farrell said.

"It's not that simple," Martinez said. "I left them with a guy, and he's got to hear from me. The way things are, I couldn't go there in broad daylight, either. It could be bad for him, bad for me, too."

Farrell took off his hat and hung it on the tree beside the office door. "So where are they?"

"Ozzy's got 'em. I sent them to him by Railway Express messenger day before yesterday."

Farrell's jaw tightened. "You picked a nice guy to play footsies with."

"He's all right. We been friends for years," Martinez replied. "At the time, he was the only person I knew I could trust."

Farrell bit back the words that rose in his throat. "Call him. Let's get them before any more time goes by."

Martinez picked up the receiver and gave the operator the number for the pawnshop. After a brief wait, Martinez was speaking.

"Oz? Can you talk? It's Louie." There was a pause as Martinez listened, then he said, "Look, I need to get my hands on the plates. Yeah, it's important. I need them this afternoon. What? What do you mean they ain't there? Where did you put 'em? For the love of Christ, Ozzy. When can you meet me there?" Martinez paused to look at his wristwatch. "Okay, okay. Yeah. I'll be there." Martinez put the receiver back into the cradle.

"What's the story?" Farrell asked.

Martinez looked up at him, trying to keep the chagrin from his face. "I thought he was gonna stash them somewhere in the pawnshop, but he says he's moved them."

"Where's the hiding place?" Farrell was feeling his temper start to fray. Knowing that Oswald had lied to him made it that much harder to keep his anger under control.

"He said for me to meet him in a commercial building off Tulane Avenue. It's a place he owns and it hasn't got any tenants in it now. Second floor." Martinez gripped the arms of the chair and tried to stand, but his face went immediately pale and sweat broke out on his forehead.

"You're in no shape to go anywhere," Farrell said. "I'll have to go for you."

Martinez sagged in the chair. "He ain't expecting you, Wes. He'll get spooked."

Farrell bared his teeth. "Let him. I'm gonna have a word with that lying rat after I get the plates from him."

Martinez smiled, shook his head. "*Chivato*, the trouble with you is you got no sense of humor. Sure, Ozzy's a rat and a coward, but at least he's straight about it. How many honest, lying, yellow rats do you meet in this life?"

Farrell was in a bad mood, but he couldn't be mad at Martinez. They had been through too much together. "What time will he be at the meeting place?"

"He said he'll close the pawnshop at 12:00 noon and be there at 12:45. The building's north of Tulane on Cortez. You can't miss it. There's nothing else in that block."

Farrell looked at his watch. He had better than a half-hour to get there and it wasn't very far away. "You need anything? Food, drink, coffee?"

"Nothin', man. It's good to just take it easy."

"Glad to see you, Louie. Why didn't you come around when you'd hit town? It would've been like old times."

Martinez looked up at Farrell, who had eased a hip over the edge of the desk. "The truth is, you got too respectable. I figured you wouldn't appreciate having a crook knocking on the door while you were doing all this honest toil. Maybe I was wrong about that."

Farrell nodded. "Dead wrong, you knucklehead."

The two men chatted amiably for a while, exchanging stories and exaggerating them the way men will to evoke a laugh. Finally Farrell looked at his watch. "Time to go, Louie. I should be back soon."

"Think I'll take you up on the offer of that bed, Wes. I ain't slept much lately."

Farrell smiled. "Same here. Funny thing, isn't it?"

It took Farrell less than ten minutes to reach Tulane Avenue, and another three to arrive at South Cortez Street. He made the turn and found himself in a block with a few empty houses and a vacant commercial building that was in a state of disrepair. Some of the windows were boarded up and others had broken panes of glass. It had clearly not been occupied for some time.

Farrell left the car and walked across the street to the building. Something about it bothered him, and without thinking he unbuttoned his jacket, letting his fingers brush the butt of his gun. The door was unlocked and slightly ajar. He stood looking at it for at least a minute before slowly mounting the stairs to the entry way and walking through the door.

Inside the empty vestibule, he listened, straining for the slightest sound that might betray where Theron Oswald might be waiting. He didn't like the quiet. If Oswald was expecting someone, why didn't he make his presence known?

Farrell found the stairs to the second floor and he mounted them slowly, keeping to the edge to minimize the number of creaks and groans the dried-out risers made. At the head of the stairs he was faced with a hall leading off to the left and right. Oswald had said nothing about that, nor in which direction he might be found. Farrell flipped a mental coin and went to the right. There were a series of doors on his left, and he paused at each one to push the door open. Each yawned into a dim, empty room.

He had reached the last door on the hall when he heard a sound behind him, a scuff of leather on wood that was so faint that another man might not have heard it at all. He threw himself through the last door on his left, hearing the explosion of a heavy gun as he did so. He rolled on his shoulder into the room, losing his hat as he came upright. He flattened against the near wall, his Colt cocked in his right hand.

He eased along the wall to the open door, forcing his quickened breathing back under control. His assailant was as quiet as cat. One harshly drawn breath could mask his slightest footfall. Farrell knew a good man when he met one, and this was one of the best.

He dropped to one knee and crept to the opening. He darted his head around for a quick look, and was rewarded with another explosion. The bullet took a chunk out of the doorframe, scattering splinters everywhere. Farrell shook his head, shoved his .38 around the frame and fired blindly, twice. The gunman returned fire twice more, each time chewing up a piece of the doorframe. This is getting me nowhere, he thought impatiently.

He cast a quick glance around the room, and saw a door in the wall behind him. He grabbed his hat and put it on, then gripped the knob of the door. He tried it, and it opened soundlessly into the next room. Farrell crept across the room where another door awaited him in the opposite wall. He opened that one. It was one more empty room with another door opposite. Each time he crossed a room, his risk increased. The gunman had to be in the next room or in the hall waiting for Farrell to show his head.

"Come on out, Martinez," a voice said. "I'm tired of huntin' all over creation for you, boy. Reckon you're gettin' tired, too, particularly if that useless fuckin' cop put a slug in you the other night. Gimme the plates and you can go on your way."

Farrell understood now. For some reason, Oswald had set Martinez up to be killed. He must be planning to make some deal with the plates, himself. He felt his skin grow hot as anger quickened his blood and caution dropped away from him like an unneeded garment. He crossed the room in a single bound and kicked the connecting door open. As it slammed back against the wall, he stepped through, saw a half-concealed figure just outside the room. He fired three shots from the hip as fast as he could squeeze the trigger.

The man was not only good but lucky, too. Even as the sound of the shots thundered against the walls and ceiling, the man was moving backward through the blizzard of wood splinters and burst plaster. He fired at Farrell as he ran, each shot missing by no more than a hair's breadth.

Farrell moved through the noise and destruction like a hot wind, his rage and blood lust blotting out all but the faceless shadow that retreated down toward the opposite end of the building. His gun jumped in his hand until the hammer fell on an empty chamber. Farrell ejected the spent magazine on the run, slamming the fresh one in with the heel of his left hand. A door slammed ahead, and as he grew near, chunks of wood exploded outward as the other man fired through the door to slow Farrell up.

He flattened against the wall beside the door, grabbed the handle and twisted it. It was locked. Sparks jumped from his pale eyes as he pointed his gun at the knob and fired twice. As the hardware flew from the wood, he kicked the door open and went in behind it. It took a moment for him to realize the room was empty. He crossed it, saw an adjoining room and passed into it.

A breeze fluttered a rotting curtain over an open window. A fire escape lay beyond, and below he saw an empty back lot that opened onto a neighborhood of shotgun cottages. Nothing moved on the quiet street but a pair of mongrel dogs scrounging through an overturned garbage pail.

He lowered the hammer on his gun and retraced his steps back into the hall. He saw spent cartridge cases and he stooped to retrieve one. It was a Western brand .45 auto. He felt a nerve pulse in his jaw as he remembered how close those shots had come. Farrell dropped the cartridge case into his jacket pocket and left the building. His next stop would be the pawnshop, and he grinned savagely as he anticipated the look on Theron Oswald's face when he walked through that door.

Chapter 14

It was early afternoon when Frank Casey and Treasury Agent Paul Ewell were ushered into the office of A. J. McCandless. The hard-faced old man sat behind his desk, his cigarette holder jutting up from his mouth like a naval gun. He greeted the two lawmen with a grunt and a nod.

"Thanks for seeing us, Mr. McCandless," Casey said. "We realize you've got a lot on your mind just now."

"We're terribly sorry about the death of Mr. Leake," Ewell added. "That must've been quite a blow."

"What do you know about it so far?" McCandless asked, ignoring their sympathy.

"Well," Casey began. "There are things we know for a fact, and then there are the things we surmise."

"Don't talk to me in riddles, Captain. I'm not in the humor for it. Marston Leake worked with me for twenty-five years, and he helped make this bank what it is today. I want his murderer on the gallows, and sooner, not later."

Casey had suffered the bluster of rich men more than once in his career. He had learned to ignore it. "Let's take what we know for starts. Two men leave here in the late afternoon yesterday to go to dinner. A Negro gunman jumps out, threatens them, and according to the only witness, shoots Leake. He then turns and shoots the second victim before he runs off."

McCandless made a dismissive gesture. "What of it? The fellow was either frightened or under the influence of some narcotic. His erratic behavior certainly suggests it."

"Or maybe we're meant to think that," Ewell said.

"What the devil do you mean by that?"

"We've got evidence that the gunman lay in wait in that alley. That's not the work of a drug addict, Mr. McCandless. That's the work of a seasoned hunter, calmly waiting for his prey to walk past his stand. You're enough of a hunter to know that." Ewell gestured toward a wall decorated with antlers and trophy heads.

McCandless ignored the observation. "What should he have done, struck a pose against the side of a building and then pulled his gun? Of course he lay in wait."

"Mr. McCandless, you're a banker, and we wouldn't dream of trying to tell you the complexities of banking," Casey replied. "What we understand is criminal behavior, so let us tell you what we know from experience.

"For a Negro gunman to have been in that part of the city," Casey continued, "in broad daylight, under the influence of drugs or stone cold sober, is not only completely out of our experience, but it's pretty unbelievable. To make it even more unlikely, the gunman executes one man, then only manages to wound the other before fleeing the scene."

"So what are you saying? That the Negro meant to kill Marston Leake? That it wasn't an armed robbery?" McCandless pounded his desk, his face red with fury.

Casey almost smiled at the fit of temper. "Mr. McCandless, if I were you, I'd calm down. We're investigating a murder, and we'll ask any question we think pertinent, and advance any theory we think plausible. Right now, I'm inclined to see this as murder, and not a robbery."

"And if I can put in the U. S. Government's two cents," Ewell added, "I think Casey's right. We're in the middle of a counterfeit currency investigation, a case that's covering a six-state region so far. And in the middle of it, an important banking executive suddenly gets killed. My boss would have my head examined if I didn't look into that."

"Which leaves us with two possible theories," Casey interjected. "One, either Leake was involved with the counterfeit ring and suddenly became a liability—"

"I've never heard such rot," McCandless exclaimed.

"—or he knew or found out something that made him dangerous to the operation." Casey leaned forward in his chair, his eyes fixed on McCandless's. "Did you know that Leake had been carrying a pistol?"

"What?"

"That's right. When he was shot, he was reaching for a pistol he'd bought a couple of weeks before. If he'd been faster on the draw, he might still be here. Why should a bank executive start going around armed unless he had become unsure of his world?"

Before McCandless could reply, Ewell broke in. "It struck me the other day that Leake was considerably more concerned about this counterfeit situation than the rest of you. Had he said anything to you that was out of the ordinary?"

McCandless, still scowling, eased back in his chair, his eyes shifting nervously between the two policemen. "Leake was a worrier. It made him a valuable man because he left no T uncrossed, no I undotted. On the other hand, he was given to fits of worry, even flights of fancy at times."

Ewell reached into his inside pocket and removed a letter. "I've got something here that Mr. Leake must've written just before he was gunned down. It's on First National stationery and it's dated yesterday afternoon. It was delivered to my office in the morning mail."

McCandless lurched in his chair, and his eyes got suddenly large. "What this?"

Ewell removed the letter from the envelope and unfolded it. "It's not a long letter, but in it, Leake offers a theory as to how the counterfeit money has been released into the currency stream, and suggests why we haven't found any of it in local banks."

"I've probably heard it before," McCandless said. "He was bothering me with it a couple of days ago. I thought it was ridiculous."

"Well," Ewell said, tapping the letter with a finger, "Mr. Leake isn't such a neurotic knucklehead as you might think. For example, he suggests a reason why none of the counterfeit money has been found locally—that the counterfeiters are using New Orleans as a base. We found evidence out near the airport yesterday that bears that contention out. We've even got a lead on who some of the gang members are."

McCandless bit down hard on his cigarette holder and puffed smoke from it. "Incredible," he muttered.

"The fact that he was so completely correct about the location of the gang makes me take the rest of his theory seriously," Ewell went on. "It may be too much to believe that employees of the Federal Reserve are directly implicated in funneling the phony money into the currency stream, but I can think of a few scenarios in which other people with temporary access to the money could, for example, switch genuine currency with fake while the money is in transit from the Federal Reserve to member banks."

Casey tugged thoughtfully at his earlobe and smiled at McCandless. "Mr. McCandless, Mr. Leake also said in his letter that you had taken to going to Atlanta by private plane several times a month on private business. That's interesting in light of these revelations."

"How many people do you think Leake may have spoken to about his theory?" Ewell asked.

McCandless was stiff and pale, his fingers tapping restlessly on the desk. "I—I have no idea. Why do you ask?"

Casey leaned back comfortably in his chair and crossed his legs as he held McCandless's eyes. "Because those people are all prime suspects in Mr. Leake's murder. We'll need to investigate everyone here with whom he had regular contact. Beginning with you, sir. Now, would you care to begin by explaining those trips to Atlanta?"

❧

Theron Oswald felt that with each passing moment he was aging several years. He had done business with a couple hundred criminals in his day, but none of them frightened him as completely as Dixie Ray Chavez. Oswald could still taste the oily hardness of that .45 in his mouth. He remembered how he had sucked on it, praying it wouldn't go off, hoping he wouldn't vomit on Chavez's shoes. He'd soiled himself like a child, and the memory sickened him.

He'd had to betray a friend to keep on living. The recognition of that was like a lump of lead in the pit of his stomach. He knew in his heart that Luis was no match for Dixie Ray Chavez, and that he had gone to his grave defiant. His hatred for Compasso was such that he'd never have given Chavez the satisfaction of giving him the plates.

Now Luis was dead, and Oswald was the only person who even knew where the plates were. He refused to look at the desk, but they called to him, like the heart of a dead man buried beneath the floor. He wanted them out of his store, out of his life, but where would he find the courage to bring them into the light, even to dispose of them?

Oswald felt an overwhelming urge to pray to God, to ask for His mercy, but he had forgotten how long ago. Somehow, he doubted it would do any good. He had heard that Catholics could confess their sins to a priest and receive absolution. He wondered if it was possible for a man raised Southern Baptist to work himself a deal like that.

He sat behind the display case, waiting. He almost welcomed the customers who came in to pawn or redeem some item. He served them in an impersonal, unemotional way, glad for the distraction, fearing the moment when Chavez would return. Whether he had the plates or not, what use would Chavez have for him now?

It was edging toward the middle of the afternoon when he heard the bell over the door sound. He turned and watched Chavez lock the door and pull down the shades. Oswald's mouth and throat were like the tail end of a dust storm. He couldn't even work up enough spit to speak.

The killer turned, his eyes gleaming in the shadows of the shop. "You're real cute, Oz. I figured you for just another two-bit sticky-fingered fence, but you got some balls, even some brains."

"M-man, I don't know what you talkin' about."

Chavez's mouth opened and that peculiar giggle escaped. "There you was, settin' up your buddy, and there I was, thinkin' it was gonna be like shootin' fish in a barrel."

"You d-done killed Luis, I guess."

"You guess? You *guess?*" Chavez laughed like a hyena. "You li'l beauty you. You set *me* up. You waited until I was gone and then you sicced Farrell on me."

Oswald was shaking his head dumbly. "Naw. Naw, man, I never—Why would I do that? You think I'd double-cross you? Naw, man. I ain't crazy. Only somebody wantin' to commit suicide would do that." Somehow he modulated his voice so that it didn't tremble with the overwhelming fear assailing him. Chavez had taken out his gun now, and was shaking it the way a teacher shakes a finger at the class cut-up.

"Naw, Ozzy. You act scared and you act dumb, but you ain't. You sent Farrell, and the sonofabitch nearly got me. He's good. He's every bit as good as they say he is. I am one lucky bastard today." He reached down with his left hand and jacked a cartridge into the breech of his .45. The metallic clash was like the crack of doom in the dim room.

Ozzy sank to his knees, and without thinking his hands came together in that same prayerful attitude as before. He couldn't pray to God, but praying to Dixie Ray Chavez was easy. "P-please, man. I—I swear, I didn't sell you out. I don't know why Farrell showed up. Maybe—maybe Luis was hurt. Maybe he couldn't make the trip and sent Farrell. They's friends from way back. Yeah, yeah. That's it. That's gotta be how it happened. I—I wouldn't— man, please—listen, I'll give you—"

"Shut up, Ozzy." Like a snake striking, the .45 leveled and a lance of fire leaped across the room. A slug struck Oswald in the middle of his chest and slammed him against the display case. He slid slowly down then keeled over on his right shoulder. His eyes were open, and they seemed to be staring at his bent knee.

"Lyin', shit-faced punk. You won't sell nobody else out." Chavez walked to the body and kicked it until it slid over on its side. He let down the hammer on his gun and slipped it into the holster under his arm. He half turned, then saw the white paper sack on the counter. He walked over, looked inside, then closed the bag and shoved it into his coat pocket. He passed between the display cases to the back of the shop, unlocked the alley entrance. He checked to make sure the alley was empty, then left the store.

⁕⁕⁕

After leaving Fred at the Metro, Marcel called a Negro doctor named Livaudais and asked him if he knew anything about Dr. Abraham Rodrigue. He quickly learned that no one had ever heard of him. There was no record of his having contacted the state or local Negro medical associations, he was unknown at Flint-Goodrich Hospital, nor could Dr. Livaudais find such a doctor registered anywhere in the state of Louisiana.

Marcel called Rodrigue's office again, but the story was the same. He hadn't returned and might not for the rest of the day.

Having tried every line of inquiry he could think of, Marcel drove Downtown to check with Fred and try once more to talk to the pawnshop owner.

A short time later he parked a half block down from the Metro and hiked toward the shop. He was surprised to see Farrell approach from the opposite direction. Even from a distance, Marcel saw the expression on Farrell's face that meant trouble. He hurried to meet him.

"What brings you down this way?" Marcel asked.

"I'm about to have a talk with a pawnbroker," Farrell said. His face was dark with suffused blood, and his eyes glowed with malice.

"Me, too. What's your beef with him?"

The question brought Farrell up short. "You're talking about Theron Oswald?"

"Yep. I'm looking for a missing girl. I think she's in the hands of a con man posing as a doctor. I believe Oswald's got a connection to this con artist."

Farrell almost smiled. "Ozzy's a busy boy. He's also holding some counterfeit plates that a murderer wants in exchange for another missing girl."

"Wes, I learned from you that there's no such thing as a coincidence. There's gotta be a connection here."

Before Farrell could answer, Fred stepped up behind them. "Afternoon, Mist' Farrell. Marcel, I been watchin', but nobody's come or gone from that place in a while, and so far none of Mickey's boys has found a damn thing."

Marcel glanced across the street. "It's still closed."

"Ozzy lives upstairs, and there's a service entrance in the alley," Farrell said. "Let's go calling." He turned and walked to the end of the block with the other two men behind him. It took only a few minutes to reach the alley.

Farrell paused and drew his gun. "It's unlocked. Let's go—but be careful. I've been shot at once today already."

Fred gave Marcel a wide-eyed glance, then jerked his Colt from under his arm and followed Farrell into the shop.

The back of the shop was poorly lit, but they were able to pick their way past shelves of musical instruments and a myriad collection of items until they reached the front.

"Well, now we know why the place is closed," Farrell said. "The owner's taken a permanent vacation." He walked to Oswald's body, knelt down and shoved his fingers against the carotid artery. "Dead, and not all that long ago. Shot once by some heavy artillery." He sniffed the air. "You can still smell the cordite. We just missed him."

Fred bent to pick up a shell casing. "Looks like he used a .45, Mist' Farrell."

"Let me guess, it's a Western brand .45 auto, right?"

"You called it, boss. How'd you know?"

"That's what the killer used on me earlier today."

Marcel took off his hat and ran his fingers through his hair. "Why?"

"It's a complicated story. An old friend of mine, Luis Martinez, is mixed up with a counterfeiting gang. He had a falling out with the boss and stole the plates. Later he gave them to this fellow for safe keeping."

"So why is he dead?"

"A little while ago, Martinez called Oswald from my office to arrange a pickup for the plates so we could give them to the man who has the girl. Oswald arranged the meet in an abandoned office building he owned. Martinez is shot up, so I went in his place. The killer was waiting but he wasn't good enough. My guess is the killer figured Oswald set him up for me, instead of setting Martinez up for him."

"Jesus, what a tangle," Marcel said. "You think the killer has the plates now?"

"I'm going to make a wild guess and say no. Oswald always played both ends against the middle. He and Martinez were friends, but Oswald's main concern was his own skin. I'm betting he didn't have the nerve to tell the killer that he had the plates. He had to figure the guy would think he was partnered up with Martinez and kill him for that."

"Damn," Fred said, shaking his head. "They had the poor bastard comin' and goin'."

"Now he's just gone," Marcel said. "And he can't tell us a damned thing."

"That's tough," Farrell said. "I wish I knew how to help you."

Marcel rubbed his face, trying to stimulate his brain as he looked about the room. There had to be an answer somewhere. "The medicine bag. It's gone." He strode to the counter where he'd seen it before. "It was right here."

"If that's true, then the killer took the medicine," Farrell said. "What kind of medicine was it?"

"I don't know. Just pills of some kind."

"Let's not waste any more time," Farrell said. "Fred, go upstairs and go through everything you can find. We're looking for some metal plates with the engraved fronts and backs of twenty and fifty dollar bills on them. Marcel and I'll look down here."

Fred turned and walked toward the stairs while Marcel took the back of the building and began to work forward. Farrell began with the display cases, looking for false bottoms or secret compartments. Each man knew that time was slipping by at an alarming rate.

An hour passed and Fred returned to the ground floor with a shrug and a shake of his head. He went to help Marcel. Eventually the three men converged on the area Oswald obviously used as an office.

Fred sighed heavily. "We're runnin' outa places to look. Think he's got a trap under a loose floorboard?"

"Give it a try," Farrell replied. "Oswald was a fence, so there's no telling what he may have used to hide things."

Marcel found a locker with a large padlock on it, and while Fred prized at the floorboards with the blade of a huge clasp knife, Marcel went to get the ring of keys on Oswald's belt. The locker was filled with watches, rings, and other valuables, along with a couple of smaller strong boxes, but no plates emerged from the clutter.

Farrell had turned his attention to the desk, but quickly discovered it was locked. He took the keys from Marcel and found one that unlocked the drawers. He systematically pulled each one out and sifted the contents. It was only after pulling out three drawers that he noticed that one was almost a foot shorter than the others. He unclipped a pencil flashlight from his inside pocket and shined it in the opening. There, at the back, lay a parcel. He grinned at it. "Paydirt."

"Man alive," Fred exclaimed after Farrell unwrapped the package. "So this is what all the fuss is about." He picked up one of the engravings and held it to the light.

Farrell carefully wrapped them back up. "They're going to send some people to jail, if I play this just right."

"You going to give them to Casey?" Marcel asked.

"Not yet. Not until I see if they'll buy Margaret Wilde back from Compasso. Let's get out of here. You two follow me back to my place."

Marcel said nothing. He tried not to think that Marta might already be beyond the reach of anything he and Farrell could do to rescue her.

Chapter 15

Farrell arrived at his apartment to find Martinez awake and drinking coffee in the kitchen. Martinez raised his eyebrows as Marcel and Fred entered behind the bronze-skinned man.

"It's okay, Luis. They're with me. Marcel Aristide's my business partner and Fred Gonzalvo works for him."

"*Buenos tardes, amigos.* Coffee for anyone?"

"Nothing for me," Marcel said, "but you can answer a question. Do you know a Dr. Abraham Rodrigue?"

Martinez shook his head. "Never heard of him."

"How about a man named Wilbur Lee Payne. Or maybe he called himself 'Keys.'"

"Sorry, no. Who is he?"

"A con artist passing himself off as a doctor. I think he's kidnapped a girl."

"Why would you think I know this man?" Martinez asked warily.

"Because he made a delivery to Oswald's shop," Farrell replied. "And there's bad news, Louie. Oswald's dead."

Martinez's tired face drooped a bit lower. "By who?"

"Louie, I think he tried to set you up for Compasso's killer. When I got to the meeting place, a man was waiting—with a gun. I traded shots with him, but he got away. Later I met up at the pawnshop with these two and we discovered Oswald dead. The killer used the same kind of gun and ammunition he fired at me."

Martinez had aged ten years in the past few days. Large patches of bruised-looking flesh lay under each of his eyes, and his skin was grainy with fatigue. His mouth worked until something resembling a faint smile lay across his lips. "Poor Ozzy. It's my fault. I knew the guy was a *cobarde*—a coward. I put him in a place where all he could do was turn on me." He looked up at Farrell. "I know you hated him, but he couldn't help what he was. When he knew he was going to die, he suffered twice over for every sin he ever committed, I tell you truly."

Farrell held up the parcel. "He did one good thing. He kept the plates safe and sound. I don't know why he didn't try to use them to save his life, and I guess it doesn't matter. We have them, and Compasso wants them."

Martinez held out his hand and took it from Farrell. Clumsily he removed the chrome-plated nickel engravings, unwrapped them, and lined them up on the table. "These were going to make me a *haciendado*." He bowed his head and shook it. "They ended up costing me everything that matters."

"And they might cost more yet," Marcel said. "We're no closer to finding Marta Walker than we were this morning."

"If this phony doctor of yours is mixed up with the gang in some way, maybe he can tell us where to find Margaret," Farrell said. "What do you know about him?"

"Other than the fact that he's as phony as one of those counterfeit bills, not much. I was able to track down his office, but he hasn't been in all day. His receptionist doesn't seem to know very much, and it's a cinch she won't give out the doctor's private address."

"Then we'll have to convince her. Fred, you stay here with Luis and keep him out of sight. I'm going to tell Harry no one's to come up here, but just to be sure, keep your eyes open, okay?"

"I hear you," Fred replied solemnly.

"Luis, get as much rest as you can. I may need you and when I say 'move,' you've gotta move, *entiende?*"

The Mexican offered a tired smile. "I hear you, too, *Patron*. *Buena suerta*, okay?"

⚭

Marta Walker lay on a cotton matelassé bedspread with feather pillows under her head. It was a better bed than the one in her hotel room but she was prevented from experiencing full satisfaction by the handcuffs on her wrists, the rope around her ankles and the gag in her mouth. Albert, or rather Wilbur, had left nothing to chance. She looked about the room and saw that it was furnished with an oak bureau, a couple of night stands, and a small bookcase full of books. There were no pictures on the wall, or any personal items on the bureau, suggesting that she might be in some kind of furnished rented house or apartment.

She attempted to wriggle off the bed, but found that her bound legs were further secured to the bedposts. As she lay there, panting from her exertion, she felt defeat nibbling at the edges of her spirit. How would Marcel find her when she herself didn't know where she was?

The door opened without warning, and Wilbur Payne stood there in his shirtsleeves. He stared down at her without affection. "Well, the pretty little gal's decided to wake up. What am I gonna do with you, sugar?" He came to the bed and dragged the gag from her mouth.

Marta licked her dry lips, her eyes wide with fear. "Let me go, Albert. Whatever you're up to, I don't know anything about it. I just came looking for you because I thought something had happened. I—I thought—"

"Aw, you thought I'd been forced to give up our love because of some deep, dark secret." He snickered nastily. "Baby, you're sure a dumb li'l small town gal, aren't you?"

His contempt angered her. "Sure, I'm small town and stupid. That's no excuse for you being a rotten, lying creep. I suppose it made you feel big to trick me."

He looked down at the nails on his hand as he buffed them on his shirtfront. "Baby, you were just something to help me pass the time. I was hiding out down in Brownsville, breaking my ass for peanuts in that drugstore where you worked. You gave me something more interesting to think about. I am sorry about one thing, though. That I had to leave before I got you on your back once or twice."

She growled at him in frustration and thrashed against her bonds while he laughed at her.

"Better be good, sweetheart. I'm gonna be drifting away from here pretty soon, and I don't have to kill you, unless you make me, you hear?"

The words chilled her and she sank back on the pillows, gnawing her lower lip to keep the fear from bursting out of her. "Please let me go. I can't do a thing to hurt you."

He nodded. "Maybe not, but I still got business around here, and until it's finished, you stay put. I'll feed you in a little while. Until then, be still and keep your mouth shut." He bent down, stuffed the gag back in her mouth, tugging at it experimentally until he was satisfied. He turned on his heel and left the room, shutting the door behind him. She heard the key turn in the lock, but her anger at Payne had awakened something in her. She began working her legs inside the rope, telling herself that if she could just get her feet free, there was some chance she could escape the fix she was in. It was better than considering the alternative.

⚬⚬⚬

Farrell drove with reckless abandon through the late afternoon traffic. Marcel rode beside him in silence. Each was weighed down with worries that neither wanted to confront.

Farrell turned off Elysian Fields to Villere and coasted to a stop a half-block down from Rodrigue's office. From the street, they could see the receptionist on her way out. She paused on the porch to check her hair and makeup in a small compact mirror before continuing to the street.

"You want to get out and talk to her?" Marcel asked.

"She's a very pretty girl," Farrell said thoughtfully. "And she knows it."

Marcel scratched his neck as he cocked an eyebrow at his cousin. "Yeah—so?"

"Let's follow her and see where she goes."

The young woman crossed the yard and walked through the gate to a well-preserved '32 Ford Tudor, got in, and started the engine. As she pulled away from the curb, Farrell put his car into gear and fell in behind her.

"Why are you following her?" Marcel asked. "Why not break into the office and see if we can find Rodrigue's address?"

"Call it a hunch," Farrell replied. "Aside from his knowledge of medicine, what else do we know about this character?"

Marcel shrugged. "He's a crook."

"Besides that. He was living in a small town, working in a drugstore, and he just happens to latch onto a pretty girl who works in the same drugstore. I'm guessing that Payne made it a point to hire a pretty, impressionable girl to play secretary to his doctor. I'm also guessing he didn't waste any time cuddling up to her. I'll lay you five bucks to three that she's on her way to Payne's crib for a little afternoon rendezvous."

"I'll take that bet."

The girl led them across town to North Broad, Farrell keeping a discreet distance behind. The young woman gave no sign that she was aware of the tail. Twenty minutes after the tail had begun, the girl eased her car to a stop in front of a two-story frame house with a fresh coat of white paint and gray slate roofing tiles. The yard was elaborately fenced with wrought iron at the front and a high board fence at the back. Farrell turned at the corner, continued down the block and cut his engine in front of a tree-shaded bungalow.

"We don't know if he's armed, but it makes sense to assume he is," Farrell said. "The best thing would be to go in from both the front and back. You take the front. Find some way to keep him busy. I'll go in from the back. I'll get between him and the girl if he gets past you."

"Okay. Let's go."

They got out of the car and advanced on the house. Farrell split off into a service alley while Marcel continued to the front. He walked slowly, giving his cousin plenty of time to find a way into the back yard.

Marcel heard the muffled chime of the doorbell as he pushed the button, and a moment later came the thump of footfalls on a wooden floor. The door opened, and the object of his search stood in the opening. "Yeah?" His shirt was unbuttoned and his hair was a bit disarranged. He didn't look happy at being disturbed.

Marcel nodded. "Wilbur Lee Payne?"

Payne's demeanor changed almost immediately. His body stiffened slightly. "You said which?"

"Payne. Wilbur Lee. That's you. Ernie Le Doux said I should look you up. He was in the joint with you."

Payne raised his eyebrows and shook his head. "You got me confused with someone else, cousin. My name's Rodrigue. Says so there on the mailbox, see?" He pointed.

"Hey, man," Marcel said, offering a dismissive wave of his hand. "I ain't here to crowd you or nothin'. You can call yourself Marcus Garvey for all I care. Le Doux said you were a good guy to know. Said you might be able to fix me up. See, I been down on my luck for a while and—"

A crash sounded from the back of the house, and Payne jerked in reflex. Understanding bloomed in his eyes, and he flung the door forward in an attempt to slam it shut. Marcel, expecting that, shoved his right foot into the opening. The heavy door bounced off his shoe and Marcel went in behind it, throwing a hard right at Payne's chin.

The blow connected, knocking the taller man back into the foyer, but he recovered quickly. He feinted with his right then threw a left jab that struck Marcel's jaw and knocked him to the floor. Marcel, his blood racing, rolled to his feet and launched himself at the fake doctor's legs. The two men went down in a tangle, kicking, punching and grabbing at each other. Marcel fought his right hand free and clouted Payne on the right ear, and as he flinched from it, Marcel smacked him on the hinge of the jaw. Payne collapsed, his eyes rolling up in his head.

Marcel struggled to his knees, pushed Payne over on his stomach, and got his arm in a hammerlock. Behind him a woman shrieked, and he jerked his head around to see the secretary standing at the open door to the parlor, dressed only in her slip, her hands up over her mouth.

Farrell stood just behind, smiling at her. "Better get dressed, miss. We're about to close up shop."

"Who are you? Why are you hurting the doctor? Get out, before I call the police."

Farrell nodded amiably. "That's okay. You see, this guy is a con man and a kidnapper, and that's just what we can prove. He might be some worse things, too."

Her eyes grew large, and she crossed her arms protectively over her bodice. "You're lying. Stop saying those dreadful things about Dr. Rodrigue."

Farrell sighed. "Sweetheart, you're lucky we got here when we did. You were about to give something away you couldn't get back." Farrell grinned down at Marcel. "Nice work. Sorry about the noise.

I had to come in through a kitchen window and I tipped over a pitcher he had on the table."

Marcel grabbed Payne by the collar and dragged him to his feet. The con man's legs were like stalks of rubber.

Farrell slapped him lightly until Payne was alert. "Where's the girl?"

"Wha—what girl?"

"Wrong answer." Farrell slapped him again, harder. "One more time. Where is she?"

"Man, fuck you—"

Farrell's swift hand cracked like a pistol shot against Payne's face. The con man's eyes crossed and he sagged in Marcel's grip.

"Upstairs," Payne gasped. "She ain't hurt, I swear it."

"You better hope not," Marcel said through bared teeth.

Marcel pushed Payne up the stairs with Farrell right behind. The secretary, still vainly trying to hide her state of undress, gave ground before them, watching as Farrell opened one door after another until he found one that was locked. He stepped back and planted a hard kick next to the doorknob. As the bedroom door flew open, they found Marta lying on the bed, muffled cries coming from behind her gag. Farrell went to her and removed the gag from her mouth.

"Marcel!" she gasped. "I thought you'd never find me." She looked bedraggled, but relieved.

Marcel held out a hand to Payne. "Key—now."

Payne withdrew some keys from his pocket, selected the handcuff key, and handed them to Marcel. It was the work of seconds to unlock the handcuffs and cut the ropes from Marta's ankles with a penknife. As Marcel helped the girl from the bed, Farrell twisted Payne's wrists behind his back and snapped the handcuffs on them. He grabbed Payne's shoulders and twirled him around violently.

"Now, let's hear some straight talk about the man who killed Theron Oswald. Who is he, and where is he?"

Payne showed no sign of recognition. "Who? Sorry, brutha, I don't know what you're talkin' about."

"Who was the medicine for, then?" Marcel demanded.

"What medicine?" That question shook Payne's *sang froid*, but he recovered quickly.

"The trioxalen you left in Theron Oswald's pawnshop. And don't tell me you don't know what I'm talking about, because I looked at the label. It had your phony name and office address on it." Marcel grabbed Payne's shirtfront, shaking him until his teeth rattled.

"It was just somethin' I got for Oswald."

Marcel didn't know what trioxalen was for, so he couldn't dispute Payne's answer. He released Payne's shirt and pushed him away. "Then what happened to it? We searched Oswald's shop from top to bottom less than two hours ago and it's not there now."

"Man, what the hell do I know? I dropped the stuff off there and that's it. I don't know what he did with it."

Marcel knew somehow that the man was lying, but he didn't know how to prove it. He glanced quickly at his cousin, and saw that glitter in his eyes that told how close he was to the edge. If Marta hadn't been there, Marcel would have been content to let Farrell do his worst. "Let's take him to the police. Marta can press charges against him for assault and kidnapping. That'll keep him on ice until we get this untangled."

The secretary stood in the open door, wriggling back into her dress. Her eyes blinked uncertainly. "W—what are you going to do with me? I didn't know anything about that woman, I swear it."

"What's your name?" Marcel asked.

"Phyllis. Phyllis D'Abadie. I started working for Dr. Rodrigue— I mean, him—about a month ago. I didn't know anything, I swear it."

Marcel shook his head. "If they put people in jail for bein' stupid, Miss D'Abadie, you'd get a life sentence. Since they don't, get on out of here and tell your folks the doctor had to close his practice and go on a long trip for his health."

Phyllis D'Abadie disappeared with a startling alacrity. Seconds later they heard the front door slam shut.

Marcel grinned. "I guess we're finished here."

"Then let's go," Farrell said. "We've cleaned up your half of this, now let's see what we can do with my half."

Max Grossmann left work early and went home by taxi. The past few days had been difficult for him. He was, by nature, a confident man, but it was difficult for him to maintain any feeling of optimism the way things stood now.

The cab had him at his front door within fifteen minutes of leaving the bank. He paid the driver and tipped him an extra fifty cents, then went inside. His houseboy was waiting for him with a smile. "Everything's been taken care of, Mist' Grossmann. They delivered your ticket an hour ago and I got your bags all packed and ready to go."

"That's fine. I'll have dinner at the usual time, and that'll give me plenty of time to make the plane. I'll go to my room and clean up a little, I think."

"Yes, sir."

Grossmann went upstairs to his room, taking the sling off his arm as he walked. He flexed it several times, and found that other than a tightness where the flesh was healing, the arm was as good as new. Inside his room, he took off his coat and loosened his tie, then went to his private line and asked for an Uptown number. It rang three times before Dixie Ray Chavez answered.

"This is Grossmann calling. Things have begun to come unglued, I'm afraid."

"That's tough, Mr. Grossmann. I been arranging things for people for quite a few years now, and I've seldom seen so much bad luck in an operation. I got wind of how the Treasury people found the half-burned money floatin' around out by the lake. Hot damn—I made a joke—'wind.'" He giggled while Grossmann bore it stoically. "What was it you called about, Mr. Grossmann?" he asked finally.

"Have you had any luck getting the plates?"

"It's mostly been bad, Mr. Grossmann. I had a friend of Martinez's in my grip, so to speak. Had that boy so scared I was positive I could get him to turn Martinez up for me. Had him lure Martinez to a place where I could ambush him, but the boy— Oswald was his name—had more spine than I thought. He betrayed me to Wes Farrell, and I just escaped with my life. Had to kill Oswald, of course, but that didn't get me no nearer to the plates."

"Perhaps you should fold your tent, Mr. Chavez. It seems that our friend, Compasso, caught his lady friend working with Farrell. He found her at Martinez's hideout, and I suspect he plans to trade her for the plates very soon, if he doesn't kill her. He's a vengeful man."

"You have more faith in Santiago than I do, Mr. Grossmann. I admire loyalty in a man, but Santiago's a prideful fella. He's more worried about his ego than he is about business. He ain't gonna last the long haul, I'm afraid. You'd do well to get shut of him, while you can."

"Well, as difficult as it is for me to admit a mistake, I'm forced to agree with you. At the very least, he is unlucky in the extreme. I am, in fact, about to leave the city. I would enjoy working with you again, Mr. Chavez, and I'm certain another opportunity will present itself very soon. My associates are only getting started."

"That's white of you, Mr. Grossmann. A telegram sent to Josiah Huntsville, Esquire at the Goldwasser Hotel in Silver City, New Mexico will always reach me promptly."

"Good. I'll make a note of that. We'll undoubtedly have need of your talents later on."

"I'll certainly do that, sir. Have a safe trip, hear?"

"Yes. I shall. Goodbye." Grossmann hung up the phone, then he went to his bureau and opened the top drawer. From it he removed a 7.62 millimeter Walther automatic. He made sure it was loaded, worked a cartridge into the breech, then let down the hammer. He slipped it into his inside coat pocket and patted it into place. He disliked guns, but America seemed obsessed with them. A barbaric place, America.

Putting his coat back on, he walked downstairs to see to his dinner. He was feeling lighthearted at the prospect of returning to South America. Buenos Aires was a particularly lovely place this time of year. There was a café he frequented that brewed the most delicious chocolate he'd ever drunk.

"How is dinner coming?" he called. He turned the corner at the stairs and found two men standing there. They were thick through the shoulders and had brutish faces. One had hair the color of gunmetal. The other had a wild head of red hair, and a long-tailed red mustache to match it.

"Mr. Compasso said you're to come with us," the gray-haired man said in a flat voice.

"There's been some mistake," Grossmann said reasonably. "I'm not going anywhere."

The red-haired man brought a hideous knife from his side and pressed it gently to Grossmann's throat. It was a long splinter of steel with a carved handle, the traditional weapon of the Argentine *gaucho*. Grossmann had seen them before. He looked into Rojo's eyes. He saw nothing there. Rojo had been told to bring Grossmann, and he would do it, one way or another.

Chapter 16

Grossmann endured the ride into Jefferson Parish sullenly, sharing the back seat with the taciturn Rojo. He still had his gun, but there had been no opportunity to use it. He knew he would only get one chance with either of these men, so whatever he did must be decisive. "You wouldn't mind telling me where we're going, would you?"

"To a place," Tink replied laconically. "Take it easy, okay? The boss wants all of us in one place before we head to Mexico."

"I can't go to Mexico. My associates are in another place entirely." Tink shrugged. "Take it up with Mr. Compasso. I just take orders."

Grossmann turned to Rojo. "I suppose you only take orders, too, so it would make no difference for me to plead my case with you."

"Rojo don't talk much English. He understands when he's been told somethin', though. I remember we was havin' some trouble with a guy and the boss told Rojo he was tired of listenin' to the guy run his yap. Rojo comes back from seein' the guy with his tongue in a pickle jar. Funniest Goddamn thing I ever saw."

Rojo looked at Grossmann with a big smile.

"Charming," Grossmann muttered.

The Huey P. Long Bridge's east bank ramp was located in an area known locally as Jefferson Heights. However, there were no actual heights, and the surrounding land was largely undeveloped. A forest of pine and old oak gave the area a wild, untamed look.

Tink skirted the highway leading onto the bridge and drove down a marl road until he reached a three-story farm house and outbuildings located in a clearing a few hundred yards distant from the banks of the Mississippi. The house was in something of a state of disrepair, the original owners having left it years before.

Tink stopped in front of the house long enough to let Grossmann and Rojo out, then he took the car into the barn. Rojo pointed to the front door and grunted. Grossmann took the hint and walked into the house. There were a couple of men lounging in the living room. One played solitaire while the other read a racing form. Each favored Grossmann with a bored look before returning to his hobby.

Rojo pointed to an adjoining room and Grossmann walked into it. He found Compasso sitting at a wooden table, his eyes glittering dangerously. Grossmann knew he was in trouble, so he went on the offensive.

"I hope you've got a good reason for kidnapping me this way. I have things I must do, and I can't do them here."

"Shut your mouth. I don't like you, fat man. I particularly don't like you trying to run out on me."

Grossmann put his hands on his hips. "And what should I be doing? The police and Treasury Department are investigating the bank's senior personnel to find out who killed Leake. I had a day at the most to clear out and that's what I was doing. It's bad enough that you single-handedly destroyed an operation that took months of preparation. Must you jeopardize me in the bargain?"

"I did not have the banker killed. That was your doing. If you had kept your nerve, that would not have been necessary and we would not be forced to run from here with our tails between our legs."

"I should have had Leake killed sooner. The very day of his death he communicated his suspicions to the Treasury Department. They're now investigating the Federal Reserve in Atlanta. It is only a matter of time before they catch some of my people in their net."

"You are not much of a gambler, Grossmann. You must know when to take risks and when not. At any rate, you are staying with me. That way when we arrive in Buenos Aires together, I will not have to defend myself from the slander you would make behind my back. Our friends will know from me how you stupidly brought in that *gringo rustico*. I would have found Martinez my way, and caused far less trouble."

Grossmann considered flying into a rage, he considered attacking Compasso here in this room. But he realized he was in a weak situation. Compasso could order him killed and then plead ignorance of what had happened to Grossmann when he reached Argentina. No, this was a game that must be won by stealth, and Grossmann was a past master at that. He turned and left the room with an idea forming in his head.

∞∞∞

Margaret Wilde returned to consciousness slowly, like a swimmer paddling up from the depths. It was hard work, and she was very tired. She moved one of her arms, and the movement sent off a wave of pain that made her breath catch in her throat. She tried to open her eyes, but they were badly swollen, and a slit was all she could manage.

She was still in the same room where Compasso had beaten her. She wondered how long the beating had gone on—she couldn't remember because she'd passed out several times. Each time she'd returned to consciousness, Compasso had been there to resume his torture. He'd wanted to know where Martinez was, but since she didn't know, all she could do was bear the beating until she passed out.

Her body was a mass of bruises and welts, and it seemed to her that there were some broken ribs. She couldn't breathe through her nose very well, or lay on her right side at all for the sharpness of the pain there.

Eventually she was able to move enough to realize that her bounds had been loosened by the beatings. She gently shrugged them clear of her body, and tried to sit up. The pain in her side brought a muffled cry from her, but she managed to swing her legs over the edge of the bed and hug her body until the sharp pains subsided.

There was a small sink in the corner of the room. The sight of it brought a desperate thirst into her. Standing hurt as badly as sitting had, and the pain was more persistent. Using a chair as a crutch, she made it to the sink and turned on the tap. A trickle of rusty brown water came out, but eventually the color disappeared. She began bringing handfuls up to her face and mouth. She couldn't remember champagne tasting any better, nor recall a cool shower that was any more refreshing.

She staggered back to the bed and gingerly lowered herself down to it. She gathered the ropes she had shrugged off earlier and wrapped them haphazardly around her ankles and wrists, then lay back down. She was too tired to invest in much thinking and in too much pain to worry about staying alive. She had heard that deaths came in threes. Two women had already given up their lives for Luis Martinez. She would round things out. She didn't want to die, but she didn't want to give Compasso any satisfaction, either. She concentrated on that single idea until fatigue and pain drove her back into oblivion.

❈

Farrell and Marcel took Payne and Marta to the Negro Squad room at Police Headquarters. One of the senior detectives, Merlin Gautier, had the day watch. He listened intently as Farrell and Marcel, with asides from Marta, told their story. Payne, his legs shackled to a bolt in the floor by Gautier's desk, maintained a sullen attitude, volunteering nothing.

Gautier called up to R and I and asked if they could locate fingerprints and a mug shot for Payne, suggesting a call to Angola to expedite things. As he listened, Payne began to slump in his chair and his eyes took on a faraway look. Farrell stared at him pitilessly as Gautier interrogated him.

"You could do yourself a favor, Payne. We know that the killer's name is Dixie Ray Chavez. You know him, and you know where to find him. Spit it out and it might get you a reduced sentence."

Payne ignored Gautier and looked at Farrell. "If I go to prison, at least I'll still be alive. You damn fools think you know what you're dealin' with. You haven't got an idea in this world. You don't cross Dixie Ray Chavez but once. He sees to that mighty damn quick. Yeah, I knew him when we were in Huntsville Prison together. We got to be friends, but he'd kill a friend as quick as an enemy if you crossed him."

Two uniformed officers came to take Payne to booking and then to the Parish Prison. Payne allowed himself to be led quietly away.

"That was a big help. We'll be lucky to ever find this Chavez guy," Gautier said.

"He's been busy today," Farrell said. "You'll find his bullet in Theron Oswald and several more in the walls of an abandoned office building on South Cortez where he almost got me. Say, where's the rest of the squad?"

Gautier shook his head. "Half the department's out lookin' for Compasso and his gang. They broke out early this morning after knockin' out the surveillance team. Most of this squad's out lookin' for the triggerman who killed the banker yesterday."

"Banker?"

"Uh, huh. Negro, the eyewitness said. Not very tall, brown in color, wearing a green jacket and cap. He uses a .45 automatic and Western brand ammo. That's about all we know."

"A .45 and Western ammunition?" Farrell said. "That's the caliber and brand used on Oswald. And the same fired at me."

"Was the shooter a Negro?"

"I wish I could tell you for certain. That office building was pretty dark inside. All I saw was an outline, but I heard the voice. He sounded like a west Texas cracker to me."

"Well, I know one way to find out. We'll get the lab men to those two locations. The cartridge cases will confirm it for sure." He got the crime lab on his telephone and relayed instructions to one of Delgado's technicians.

Farrell looked at Marcel as Gautier spoke on the telephone. "If you've had enough gumshoeing for one day, you can see the young lady back to her hotel, make sure she's all right. She's had quite a scare."

Marcel looked at Marta, who was sitting in a chair studying her face in her compact mirror. He grinned, thinking how resilient she was. "I better stick with you until we see this through. Like you said, we've only taken care of half of this job. We can drop her at the hotel, and this time I'll make sure somebody there takes care of her."

They left the police station at mid-afternoon, weaving in and out of the late day downtown traffic until they reached the hotel. Marcel left Farrell in the car to help the young woman inside. Arthur Bordelon, the hotel manager, met them in the lobby, a look of concern on his face.

"Somebody called me and let me know about what happened, Marcel. I'm sorry as I can be."

"Please," Marta said. "Don't blame yourself. It was all my fault, really, going off alone like that."

"Okay," Marcel said. "Let's all take some blame and then be done with it. Marta, I've got to help Mr. Farrell find the people behind all this. I hope you don't mind staying alone for a while. I'll be back as soon as I can."

"I'm not leaving my room tonight," she said. "I know already that a small-town girl has no business roaming around the big city." She smiled impishly. "Thanks for saving my life. I've never been so happy to see someone as I was when you pushed Wilbur Payne through that door. I'll remember it all my life." She put a hand on his face and kissed him lightly on the mouth.

Marcel felt a pleasant flash of warmth at the touch of her mouth on his. He smiled, squeezed her hand, then left the hotel.

"What's the matter?" Farrell asked when the youngster returned. "You look like you just hit the big number."

"Uh, huh," Marcel said.

Farrell parked in front of the Café Tristesse and they went in through the front door to check for messages. Farrell was somewhat surprised to see Father Maldonar perched on a leather setee in the lobby, his crippled leg stretched out in front of him. He looked up with a broad smile on his brown face.

"Mr. Farrell. I was hoping to catch you in. Have you any news about Señor Martinez?"

"Afternoon, Father. This is my business associate, Mr. Aristide. Father James Maldonar, Marcel."

Maldonar stretched forth his mottled hand. Marcel unhesitatingly took it and gave it a warm shake. "Glad to meet you, Father." He glanced at Farrell to see what he would say about Martinez.

"I've been in contact with Luis, Father, but there's been no time to tell him about his mother. Frankly, he's been wounded and in a pretty bad way emotionally. I'll tell him just as soon as I can, and bring him to you."

Maldonar looked unhappy. "Don't you think he deserves to know the situation, Mr. Farrell? His mother is in a serious condition. I'm very worried."

Farrell nodded. "I appreciate your concern. I'll tell him just as soon as I can. I don't think it'll be much longer."

The priest saw that Farrell would not be moved, and he nodded a bit dejectedly. "So be it, then. I'll pray for Señora Martinez's health and soul, and hope for the best." He pulled his crutches to him and attempted to get up. He seemed more tired than when Farrell had last seen him. Farrell put a hand under Maldonar's left arm and lifted him easily to his feet.

"Can I get you a cab, Father? It's quite a trek to the mission."

"I have one waiting outside. If you'll help me to the door, I'll be on my way."

Farrell and Marcel helped the frail man out the door to the sidewalk. Farrell spotted a Chauncey Brothers Red Top cab and whistled at the driver. The Negro cab driver eased up to the club canopy, got out and helped Maldonar into the back seat.

"Good afternoon, gentlemen. I'll pray this situation will soon be over." The priest shook hands with both of them through the window just before the cab rolled down Basin.

"What was that all about?" Marcel asked.

"He's a Josephite priest who runs a mission for poor people over in Carrollton. He came here with a message that Luis's mother is dying from lung cancer in El Paso. There wasn't any time to tell him, and with all that's been going on, I just decided to keep it to myself."

Marcel nodded. "You're probably right."

After a brief word with Harry, they took the stairs to the second floor where they found Fred reading a magazine in his shirtsleeves.

"All quiet here?"

"Like midnight at the North Pole," Fred replied. "How'd it go?"

"We followed the secretary to Payne's hideout. The girl had already become his new sleepy-time friend, which was a break. Marcel got through the door and knocked him down while I came through the back. A few minutes later we found Marta upstairs bound and gagged."

Fred slapped Marcel's shoulder. "Awright, li'l brutha. Where's Marta now?"

"After we took Payne to the police, we dropped her off at the hotel," Marcel replied. "Where's Martinez?"

"In bed, asleep. That man's been through the meat grinder. It's a wonder he's able to walk." Fred stretched his arms and yawned. "What now?"

"We're at a standstill," Farrell admitted. "Compasso's gone underground and he's got Margaret Wilde. Until we can figure out where he is, all we can do is wait for the telephone call to set up a meet for the trade. We can't trust him. The meet's liable to be an ambush."

"You haven't told the cops about having the plates," Marcel commented. "They're not gonna kiss your cheek when they find out you've been withholding evidence."

"Or for harboring a fugitive," Farrell replied. "But I can't take the chance of giving them everything until I know whether or not we can get Margaret back." He looked at his watch. "It's 5:00. The note said they'd call tonight. Maybe we haven't got long to wait."

Marcel looked at Fred. "Why don't you call Mickey and tell him to call in the boys. We might need them later."

Fred nodded and went to make the call.

Farrell looked at Marcel. "You did good today, kid. You can cover my back anytime."

Marcel smiled. A kiss from a beautiful woman and a laconic compliment from his cousin held the same magic for him today. He nodded his thanks. "Think I'll make some coffee. You hungry?"

"No," Farrell replied. "But it's been a long week. Some food in our stomachs wouldn't be a bad thing. I think there's some cold cuts in the refrigerator."

"I'll see what I can throw together," the younger man said as he walked into the kitchen.

※※

Daggett and Andrews, along with Eddie Park and Detective Landry, worked the taverns, corner grocery stores, and other points of congregation in the Negro neighborhoods in their search for a medium-sized brown man who kept to himself. Even in that neighborhood, a place known to nurture highly individualistic traits of character, the man was relatively unknown.

"What now, boss? We musta talked to two hundred people in this part of town today and nobody's seen a man in a green jacket and cap. Maybe that's just the costume he wears when he's downtown shootin' people."

Daggett shook his head. "This is real pick and shovel work. I wonder how the others are making out."

They returned to their car in time to hear their call sign coming from the radio. Daggett got inside and responded.

"Inspector Fifty-one, please meet Detective Gautier at Blue Note Pawnshop on North Rampart, over."

"Fifty-one to Dispatch. What's the nature of the call, over?"

"Homicide involving pawnshop owner, over."

"Roger. We're on our way."

It took them about thirty-five minutes to make it downtown with their siren wailing. They arrived at the pawnshop just as the coroner's wagon pulled up in front. Daggett and Andrews held up their badges so the uniformed officers would make a path for them into the shop. They found Gautier beside the crumpled body of Theron Oswald.

"Somebody finally took care of that stinkin' piece of rat meat," Andrews said as he stared at the body.

"What you got so far?" Daggett asked.

"It's a pretty complicated story," Gautier replied. "Wesley Farrell and that kid, Aristide, who works for him, came into the squad room this afternoon with a guy in handcuffs and a girl. The fella has been impersonating a doctor, and he'd kidnapped a girl earlier today."

Daggett scratched his head. "What's the punchline?"

"The phony doctor's name is Wilbur Lee Payne. He's an ex-con who served time in Huntsville with Dixie Ray Chavez. Farrell believes that there's some connection between him and the man who killed the banker yesterday."

Daggett felt a humming deep inside him. "Tell me more."

"Oswald was killed with a .45 automatic and Western brand ammunition, same as the bank killing. The guy fired several at Farrell in a building on South Cortez earlier in the day. I've had slugs and cartridge cases sent to Delgado for comparison, so we oughta hear something pretty soon."

"If that's a coincidence, it's the biggest damn coincidence in the history of the world," Daggett said. "Where's Farrell now?"

"He said he was goin' to his place on Basin. He knew you'd wanna talk to him."

"Hell yes, I wanna talk to him. Let's go, Sam."

Daggett turned and ran out the door before Andrews could react.

"Here we go again," the heavy-set man complained.

⊗⊗⊗

As the shadows lengthened in the clearing near the Huey Long Bridge, Max Grossmann pretended to make himself comfortable in the large downstairs room. As time had gone by, he had managed to deduce that there were six men in the house, including Compasso. There appeared to be a woman held captive in a room upstairs that Compasso visited from time to time. Muted cries reached his ears during those moments. The fat man shuddered as he realized how easy it would be for Compasso to subject him to mistreatment if he so chose. He still had his gun, but he could never outshoot all six men, nor could he hold them at bay for very long. It would take help from outside to free him, and he was in a poor position to expect help from the police.

He had been in the house long enough that the other men had become used to him. They no longer even bothered to look up when he'd walk about, peruse books on the shelves, or stare out the window. In that time, he had thought of a plan. It was a reckless, insane gamble by most logic, but logic seemed to have no place in this set of circumstances.

He put his book down on the floor, rubbed his eyes, and stretched. He got up, walked to the window rubbing his back. As he looked about him, only one man was in earshot, but he was busy with a crossword puzzle. Slowly, Grossmann worked his way into the small room where Compasso had received him upon his arrival. There was a telephone in there, out of sight of the man working the puzzle.

Grossmann reached the room with his heart pounding in his chest. Casting a quick backward glance, he slipped around the entrance and crept to the telephone. He gave the operator a number then stood quaking as he listened to the clicks and pops in the line before it finally began to ring.

Chapter 17

Farrell was walking up and down the floor, looking at his watch, wondering when the call would come. Marcel, who had been downstairs to use another phone, appeared at the stairway door. One look at Farrell's tense face and the brooding expressions of the other men told him nothing had happened. He had learned things from his call, which he wanted to discuss with his cousin, but behind him he heard the footsteps of men mounting the stairs. He turned and immediately recognized Israel Daggett and his partner. He stood aside to let them in. "Evening, Sergeant. We've been expecting you."

Daggett put a hand on the younger man's shoulder and gave it a good-natured shake. "Mr. Farrell, you've been busy today. How much can you tell me about Theron Oswald and the man with the .45 automatic?"

"Have a seat," Farrell said. "I'll tell you what I know. Maybe you can make some sense of it."

Daggett and Andrews found seats and looked at Farrell expectantly.

"When I started looking for Luis Martinez, I discovered he was in trouble with a gangster named Compasso. About what, I didn't know. I found out pretty quickly that Compasso had brought in a man from outside, a Texan named Dixie Ray Chavez. Chavez had two goals: to hunt Martinez down and recover some engravings to make counterfeit fifties and twenties. When Chavez couldn't find Martinez, he began going to his friends. Linda Blanc was first. Somehow he found her cousin, Wisteria Mullins, the next night. When they couldn't tell him anything, he had to kill them.

"Martinez only had so many friends," Farrell continued. "A fence named Theron Oswald and a nightclub owner named Wisteria were just about all. Oswald was easy to find and probably easy for the killer to manipulate."

"And now he's dead. How did that happen?"

"Here's where it gets complicated. Martinez declared war on Compasso after his woman was killed. He hit on the idea of caching the plates with someone who'd keep them safe. Oswald was his obvious choice, because Oswald was already sitting on top of a fortune in stolen goods he was fencing. I'm guessing that sometime after Oswald received the plates by messenger, Chavez arrived on the scene. He saw Oswald was weak and easily scared and it gave him an idea. Instead of torturing or killing him, Chavez forced him to set Martinez up for a shakedown and execution."

"But Martinez is alive, right?"

"He's asleep in the other room. He was shot while he was burning Compasso's boat near the Third District Ferry."

Daggett's eyes widened at the news of Martinez's close proximity. "That was Matt Paret who shot him. Paret took some slugs, too, and later Captain Casey forced him to sing his lungs out about Compasso's operation."

"That explains why nobody can find Compasso, I guess," Farrell said. "Anyway, when Martinez phoned Oswald to set up a meet to get the plates, Oswald was already under the gun. In order to save himself, he had to give up Martinez. He was probably hoping that Martinez would die before he gave up the plates, which would get Oswald off the hook."

"But that backfired."

Farrell nodded. "Martinez was no in shape to make the meet, which Oswald set up in a building he owned on Cortez. I went there instead, found Chavez waiting for me. We burned a lot of powder at each other, but he got away. He probably figured Oswald had tried to turn the tables on him, so he went back and paid him off, not knowing the plates were less than ten feet away when he squeezed the trigger."

"You found them?"

Farrell nodded. "Marcel, Fred and I met up there. Marcel was looking for a young girl who'd come here from Texas after a runaway boyfriend. The fellow turned out to be an ex-con with a tie to Chavez, but we couldn't get him to talk. He's down at the jail now and the girl's safely home in bed."

"So now all we need is Compasso and the triggerman," Daggett said. "Any ideas?"

"Uh-uh. But we hope to hear from him. There's another complication."

Daggett gave an ironic smile. "Isn't there always? What's this one?"

"A woman named Margaret Wilde. She's been mixed up with Compasso, but years ago she was Martinez's girlfriend. She went out looking for Martinez on her own—maybe to turn him over, maybe to help him—I don't know. I met up with her while I was looking, and after I told her about the two women Compasso's man had killed, she changed sides. Thanks to her, I found a hideout Martinez was using over in Saint Charles Parish. When we didn't find Luis there, she insisted on staying behind while I came back to town. I found Luis getting doctored for a gunshot wound, but by the time we managed to return, Compasso's men had found it, and her. They're offering to swap her for the plates."

Daggett grimaced. "I ought to call Captain Casey right now before this gets out of control."

Farrell almost smiled. "It's already out of control. I should have called him myself by now. The phone's on the table if you want to do it."

Daggett stretched out a hand to pick up the phone, and as he did so, it began to ring. Every eye in the room was riveted on the instrument as Farrell reached past the Negro detective and lifted the receiver to his ear. "Hello?"

"Is this Mr. Farrell?"

"It is. Who's calling?"

"My name is Max Grossmann. I'm Vice President for Foreign Investment at First National Bank of New Orleans. I am a prisoner of Santiago Compasso. There's a woman held here, too, and she's being tortured brutally."

"Where are you calling from?"

"It's a bit hard to explain. You know, of course, of the Huey Long Bridge?"

"Of course. Are you near there?"

"Yes, near the foot on the New Orleans side. We're in a rather undeveloped area, but there's a marl road leading toward the river off Highway 90 about a mile from the bridge. It's a farm or some such with a large house and several outbuildings."

"I can find it. How many men does Compasso have with him?"

"Six, including Compasso. They're heavily armed. I'm terribly frightened, Mr. Farrell. Please hurry." He hung up the telephone before Farrell could reply.

Farrell put the phone down on the cradle then looked up to see every eye on him, including those of Luis Martinez, who had come silently into the room.

Daggett felt something electric emanate from Farrell. "What's the pitch?"

"That's our invitation to the dance. Compasso and five men are at a farm just off Highway 90 not far from the Huey Long Bridge. That's where they've got Margaret Wilde and a banker named Grossmann prisoner."

Daggett snorted. "Don't be so sure Grossmann's there against his will. He's wanted for questioning in the murder of another executive at that same bank."

"That may be, but he sounded plenty scared enough." Farrell looked around the room at the other men. "Daggett, you're sup-posed to play this by the numbers, but by the time you get your troops mobilized, it might be too late for Margaret. Grossmann says they're torturing her."

Martinez said something that might have been either a curse or a prayer, but no one seemed to hear.

"It's out of our jurisdiction, boss," Andrews said softly. "But if you go, I go."

"What if Compasso calls with instructions?" Daggett asked.

"It won't be dark for an hour, and that's probably the soonest Compasso will call. I'll have Harry stick by the phone and take the instructions, just like we've been waiting for them." Farrell looked at the Negro detective, seeing the hesitation in his eyes. "If you want to come along, there's nobody I'd rather have. We might need a policeman before it's all over, even if he is out of his jurisdiction."

"I'm no good at talking about stuff like this. Let's go and get it over with," Daggett said. "I can radio our position after we get over the parish line. Maybe I can think of a story that'll keep me from getting fired after it's over."

"When it's over, you'll be a hero. Fred, you go with Daggett and Andrews. Louie, you're with Marcel and me."

None of the men said anything. They moved from their seats or places along the wall to follow Farrell down the stairs. He took a moment to fill Harry in, then he led the men outside to the waiting cars.

"What are you doing in here, Grossmann?" Compasso asked as he stood in the door to the study. He was in his shirtsleeves and his hair was in disarray. Grossmann fancied he could see flecks of red on the rolled sleeves of his shirt and on the pale skin of his arms.

"Looking for another book. A rather poor selection here, if I may say so." He pulled a mildewed volume of some forgotten Southern poet from a shelf and blew dust from the top edge.

"We won't be here much longer, so don't get too engrossed in it." Compasso walked past him to the table and sat down.

"Oh? Leaving soon, are we?"

"In about another hour I'll phone Farrell and Martinez. We'll arrange a meet to get the plates, and then it'll be over. We can leave and reach the Texas border before tomorrow morning."

"I really wish you'd reconsider forcing me to accompany you. I'll be no use to you at all. And driving south through Mexico this time of the year is singularly unappealing."

Compasso looked up at him. "If you prefer, I can leave you here. Rojo will see to your comfort with great pleasure."

Grossmann's face was impassive but he quailed inwardly. As frightened as he was of Compasso, he was that much more afraid of Rojo. Without bothering to reply, he took the book of poetry back into the living room. He consulted his watch. It was nearly twenty minutes past six.

He was feeling hungry, having been deprived of his dinner, so he walked to the kitchen. On the table he found the remains of a roasted chicken. It had been pretty well picked over, but there was a leg, a wing, and part of the left breast still on the bones. He sat down, wrenched the leg from the carcass, and bit a hunk out of it. It was wonderfully flavorful and juicy. He wondered as he chewed it if his proximity to violent death had anything to do with the heightened sense of taste he was experiencing. After a moment, he gave in to his senses and let his brain lie fallow. There was nothing he could do but wait, so he made himself as comfortable as he could. He still had his pistol, and help was coming. He would survive. He was convinced of it.

∞∞∞

It was nearly dark by the time they had the gargantuan Huey P. Long Bridge in sight. It soared into the sky at a greater height than the tallest steamship mast, and boasted lanes for automobile traffic as well as railroad tracks. Farrell never went over it without experiencing an attack of vertigo.

They had driven through the semi-rural environs of Jefferson Parish without impediment. Marcel looked at his cousin, examining his face in an effort to know what went on in his mind at such times. He had seen Farrell in many moods, but whenever a fight loomed, some kind of inexplicable calm always took Farrell over. It was as though he had no fear of his own death, or perhaps he simply couldn't imagine it. With his vivid imagination, Marcel could imagine it all too easily. Only once had he been in the kind of fight they were approaching. All he could remember of it was the explosion of violence at the beginning and the eerie calm at the end.

As they passed the entrance ramp to the bridge, Farrell spoke in a low voice. "It won't be far past here. It's mostly trees and undeveloped land between here and Harahan. You got a gun, kid?"

"Yeah," Marcel replied. He could think of nothing else to say.

"Yours is still in the trunk, Louie, but I don't think Daggett would like me giving it to you. Maybe you'd better hang back on the outside. You're still pretty weak."

"I can still kick your ass, *chivato*. Margaret is in this mess because of me. You think I'm just gonna take a seat at ringside?"

Farrell laughed softly. "It's your funeral—*viejo*."

They drove a short distance before Farrell picked up the beginning of the marl road in his headlights. He slowed to a stop and cut his lights. Off to the west, he could see a glow of lights. "That has to be the farm Grossmann was talking about. There's nothing else out here to make that much light." He got out of the car and motioned for the men in Daggett's car to come up.

The lights to the police car shut down along with the engine. Daggett's party got out of the car. Daggett and Fred approached

Farrell's party while Andrews went to the trunk of the Dodge. He brought out a shotgun and two heavy flashlights. He handed one each to Fred and Marcel.

At Farrell's word, they started down the marl road until they came to the edge of the clearing. Lights were on in most of the downstairs windows. In the open door of the barn, they could plainly see the grillwork of a Lincoln limousine.

"How do you want to work this?" Daggett asked.

"Grossmann said Margaret's being held in an upstairs room," Farrell said. "I'm going to find a way to get up there so I can set her free."

Daggett grunted. "They'll fight if we give 'em much of a chance. There's too many of them to simply lie down. I'll give you ten minutes to get up there, then I'll have Fred and Andrews cover the back. Marcel can enter from the left side. I'll take the front and try to surprise them."

"What about me?" Martinez asked.

"Martinez, you're under arrest. It's only because of Mr. Farrell that you're in this at all. Stick with me and watch my back. By the time cars get here from Jefferson Parish, you'll already be in my custody. That's all that'll keep them from arresting you, understand?"

"I understand."

Daggett drew his .38-44 Smith & Wesson from under his arm as he looked at Farrell. "It's your party. Go blow out the candles."

Farrell touched two fingers to the brim of his hat and disappeared into the trees. His disappearance was so sudden and complete that it took some of them by surprise.

As Farrell went deeper into the woods, he heard the unaccustomed sounds of insects, the slither of reptiles as he made his way past them. It was different from the cool, dark alleys of the city where the night creatures all moved on two legs. As he reached the northwest end of the house, he paused to study the structure. There were no lights on at that end, but there was a drainpipe to climb. He went to it, his footfalls silent on the dry grass and pine needles.

When he reached the drainpipe, he listened intently. The muffled sound of music from a radio was the only human noise he heard. He grasped the pipe and tested it gingerly—it was loose, but it was the only avenue available. He planted a foot on the lowest bracket, gripped the galvanized metal, and began his ascent.

It shook and groaned as he made his way up, each sound grating on his ears like fingernails on a chalkboard. He couldn't imagine the inhabitants not hearing the sounds. He made the roof and knelt on it, listening again. His luck was holding so far. He cast a look at the clearing surrounding the house, but could see no one in the yard or anywhere near the outbuildings.

The roof was nearly flat here, providing him easy access to the upstairs windows. He crept to the first one, found it open, and peered inside. Nothing. The next nearest window was a dormer projecting from an attic room. He climbed to it slowly, his leather soles threatening to slide from under him at each step. He hooked his fingers into the windowsill and pulled himself to the open window.

Margaret slumped in a wooden chair, bound and gagged. In the moonlight he could see her clothes were in rags. He climbed over the sill and crept into the room. As a board creaked beneath his feet, she made a noise of alarm in her throat.

"Quiet, Margaret. I've come to get you out."

She whimpered, and as he drew near her, he saw the bruises and welts on her skin. He pulled the gag gently from her mouth and she gasped with relief. "Get me out of here before he comes back. He's been—"

At that moment there was a terrific crash of broken glass downstairs, followed by two gunshots and a scream. Farrell pulled his razor from his coat and began to slice through the ropes binding the woman to the chair. She was nearly free when a shrill scream erupted from her. The door to the hall slammed open and a rectangle of pale light fell across them.

In a single fluid motion, Farrell dropped the razor and drew. He fired twice at the silhouette in the doorway, saw it fall toward him. Before he could recover, another man launched himself across the room, knocking Farrell to the floor.

The man's weight and sheer physical power bore Farrell down and all but overwhelmed him. He lost the gun as he grappled with the man. He saw light glint from a long dagger in the man's fist, saw the dagger fall toward him like a blade of lightning. Somehow he got an arm free, checking the fall as he grabbed the man's wrist. It bought him a moment, but no more. His other hand was trapped between his body and that of his assailant. As the blade began another slow, inexorable descent, he fought his trapped hand lower, found the man's testicles, and squeezed them as hard as he could.

A bellow of pain erupted from the man as his body bucked in shock. Farrell used that moment of weakness to heave the man's bulk from him. He rolled to the side, bounced to his feet like a cat as the other man struggled to his knees. Farrell kicked him in the face, felt things break under his toe. The man shuddered with the impact, dropped the knife. Farrell stepped in, grabbed him by the hair and hit him on the hinge of his jaw. He hit him again, and a third time. Light from the hall showed Rojo's eyes were glazed, unseeing. He fell forward on his ruined face and didn't move.

Farrell felt himself trembling all over but refused give in to it. He grabbed the dagger from the floor and used it to slice through the rest of Margaret's bonds. He retrieved his gun and jerked the wounded woman to her feet, pulling her toward the dimly lit hall.

Below him, guns continued to explode. Daggett had caught two men by surprise when he destroyed the parlor window, and his first two shots had taken Tink in the chest. At the rear, Andrews' shotgun made bloody smears of another man who ran out the kitchen door in an attempt to escape.

Marcel entered through an open window at the opposite side of the house. As the gunfire began, a man went past, the back of his head exposed to a smashing blow with the flashlight.

Daggett entered the house through the door with Martinez behind him. At some point in the battle, they became separated, but Daggett had no time to think of that. It was only when he saw Farrell appear on the stairs with Margaret Wilde in tow that he realized the fight was over. He began calling out to the other men, counting them off as they replied to his hail. "Martinez? Martinez? Anybody seen Martinez?"

"I saw him run back out the front door," Marcel said, pointing. "He picked up that man's gun from the floor."

Farrell and Daggett looked at each other, then simultaneously broke for the door.

"Let me go," Grossmann cried. "Can't you see it's finished? Let me go before the police kill both of us."

"You will die, of that you can be certain," Compasso hissed. "I don't know how you did it, but I know you did this thing to me." He jerked the fat man's arm sharply up between his shoulder blades as he pushed him through the woods.

Grossmann whimpered with pain as he slipped and stumbled through the underbrush. He still had his gun, but Compasso had him by the right arm and he couldn't reach it. *All my planning, all my study and it has to end like this.* His thoughts were almost of a wondering kind. It was far too late to be frightened.

They were nearing the highway when a man stepped from behind a tree. "*Hola, amigo.* Were you planning to go without saying *hasta luego?*"

Compasso stopped short, bracing himself against the bulk of the fat man in front of him. He laughed as he recognized Luis Martinez. "Put down your gun, Luis. You can't get a bullet through this bucket of lard." He laughed again, aiming his Astra automatic past Grossmann's meaty shoulder.

"What you can't go through, you must go around," Martinez said philosophically. He fired twice at their legs. The first shot hit Grossmann in the left thigh, and he collapsed, screaming. Compasso fell with him, tangled in the fat man's flailing limbs.

Martinez walked slowly toward them as Compasso fought to free himself from his prisoner. Martinez laughed now, as though he were watching something comical on a movie screen. "Hey, Santiago, I got your plates. Want them back?" The gun in his hand bucked and roared four times, the muzzle flashes illuminating the violent spasms of Compasso's death throes. Martinez continued to fire until the hammer on his revolver snapped dryly on an empty chamber. He was still snapping the empty gun when Farrell and Daggett arrived.

Farrell went to him and gently plucked the gun from his unresisting fingers. "It's all over, Louie. You can't make him any deader."

On the ground, Grossmann groaned as he moved his heavy body away from Compasso's. "Help me, for God's sake. I'm grievously wounded. That lunatic shot me. Help, before I bleed to death."

Daggett bent over him and ripped open his trouser leg with a pocketknife. Blood welled in a hole, but it was clear the bullet had only drilled through the fat of his thigh. "You'll live, Mr. Grossmann. Which reminds me, you're under arrest for suspicion of murder."

"You—you can't do that."

Daggett got out his cuffs and snapped them on one of Grossmann's wrists. "No? I just did it."

"I claim diplomatic immunity. I demand to be taken to the German Consulate in New Orleans immediately. I am a German national traveling under a diplomatic passport." He pulled it from his pocket and waved it at Daggett.

Daggett looked at Farrell. "What the hell is he talkin' about?"

Farrell shoved his automatic back into his waistband and looked down on the fat man. "I'm not sure, but I think he's telling you he's a wolf in sheep's clothing. Maybe we ought to shoot him right here and now, because I think he's responsible for this whole damned mess."

Grossmann's round face paled. "You—you can't do that. It's contradictory to diplomatic agreement and a violation of international law."

Daggett grabbed Grossmann by the lapels and jerked him to his feet. He felt the hard weight in Grossmann's jacket, reached in and found the Walther automatic. "Since when do diplomats carry guns? You're comin' with us, Mr. Grossmann. Passport or no passport, I'm gonna lock you up for carrying a concealed weapon. At least until I can find something better."

As Grossmann howled with pain, Daggett pushed him down the path leading back to the farmhouse.

Farrell and Martinez fell into step behind Daggett and the protesting German. "Let's go back to Margaret, Louie. She went through a lot to see you again. Daggett'll let me drive the two of you back to town."

"What'll they do with me, Wes?"

"I don't know. I'll get you a good lawyer and we'll see what can be done for you if you help the Feds. Frank Casey seems to think if you offer to turn state's evidence with the U. S. Attorney that the local district attorney may waive prosecution on the other charges."

Martinez grinned sourly. "He 'thinks'? *Amigo,* he's shovin' my head into the lion's mouth."

"No, Louie. You did that a long time ago. You should have quit when you were ahead."

"Hey, *compadre.* You won't give me a gun and a head start?" Martinez tried to inject humor into his voice, but it had a hollow, empty sound.

"I wish I could, but those days are gone for me. They're gone for you, too. You just didn't see it."

Martinez was silent as they made their way back to the farmhouse. They found the place surrounded by Jefferson Parish sheriff's cars and two from the New Orleans police. His father stood on the front porch talking to Lieutenant McGee, and Margaret Wilde sat on the steps with someone's jacket over her shoulders. When she saw Farrell and Martinez approach, she got up and stumbled over to them. Farrell stepped away as she put her arms around Martinez's neck. After a moment, he gently slipped an arm around her waist, and they walked slowly back to the house.

Farrell got out his cigarette case and put one in his mouth. As he set fire to it, his father and McGee approached.

"Farrell, is this your doin'?" the Jefferson Parish deputy demanded.

"I told you I'd bring Martinez in. This was what it took to make that happen. You ought to be happy, McGee."

"Happy, my ass. I—"

"Before you get too wound up, let me fill you in on something. These guys were all guilty of Federal crimes. What's more, that fat banker from the city claims he's a German in the country on a diplomatic passport. He's yelling for the German counsul."

Casey's eyebrows shot up. "What?"

"He's mixed up with Compasso's gang, and I've got a hunch that if you squeeze him hard enough, you'll find out he's the mystery man behind the counterfeiting racket and the one who wrote the contract on that dead banker Downtown. Daggett's got cuffs on him, but he's in your jurisdiction, McGee. Take him in and put him on bread and water until the New Orleans police can work the transfer. If he's talking straight, it's all you'll get to do to him."

"He's right," Casey said. "Foreigners on diplomatic passports are immune from prosecution. Get him out of here, McGee. I'll take my time getting back to you on his disposition."

McGee looked from Casey to Farrell, doubt written all over his face. "Casey, I'll buy this on your say-so, but you—" He glared at Farrell. "If I find you in this parish two hours from now, I'm gonna arrest your miserable ass for withholding evidence, assault with a deadly weapon, and anything else I can think up." He turned and walked away, his back and shoulders stiff.

"You better go, son. I wish you'd done this a different way."

Farrell nodded. "Me, too. But I promised to turn Luis Martinez in and I've done it. He's ready to spill his guts to the U. S. Attorney and he'll take what the judge dishes out."

"You sound sorry."

"I don't know what I feel."

Casey felt many things, but what he could say as a father, he couldn't say as a police captain. "Go home. I'll talk to you tomorrow."

"Is it all right if I take Luis and Margaret back to town in my car? I'll bring them to you tomorrow."

"Fair enough." Casey turned and walked back to the cluster of police cars, leaving Farrell standing alone.

Marcel saw him, saw the way he held his body and the way he looked up at the sky. He was almost reluctant to bother him. When he thought he had waited long enough, he joined his cousin, and stood looking up at the stars with him.

"You all right, Marcel?"

"A little shaky, but all right. What's gonna happen now?"

"The cops will clean up the bodies and take the rest to jail. I'm gonna take Luis and Margaret back with me in a few minutes. They need each other now, and he's already agreed to turn state's evidence. Maybe I can get him bail later on."

"Mind if I go back with you? I've got some things I need to tell you."

Something in his voice made Farrell look at him with a curious expression. "If you want."

Epilogue

Early the next afternoon, Luis Martinez drove a borrowed car to St. Swithan's Mission on Joliet Street. He was bathed and shaved and wore new clothes over the bandages. His left arm was still in a sling, but he managed the car without difficulty. He parked, then walked into the old church and saw the two pretty young girls manning the desk.

"I'm here to see Father James Maldonar. My name is Luis Martinez."

"The Reverend Father's in the sanctuary, Mr. Martinez. I'll go and announce you," the taller of the young women said. She ducked under the makeshift counter and led him to the back of the church. She knocked on the door and at the sound of a voice she opened it.

"A Mr. Martinez to see you, Father."

"Yes, Rosary. Send him in, please," the priest replied. He turned off the sun lamp he'd been sitting under, and with some difficulty got to his feet with one of the crutches. He hobbled painfully to the center of the room as Martinez entered the sanctuary.

"Wesley Farrell said you wanted to talk to me, Father, so here I am. Something about my mother?"

"Yes, my son. Please sit. I've been hoping against hope that you'd be found at last, and here you are. I wish I had good news about your mother. She is not well."

Martinez looked stricken. He put his head in his hand. "*Aiee.* I haven't talked to *mamacita* in such a long time. Tell me what is wrong."

Maldonar leaned on his crutch and dragged his lame leg to Martinez, placing a comforting hand on his shoulder. "Prepare yourself, my son. The news is hard. She has cancer of the lung, and is not long for this world. Even now, it may be too late, but one never knows. She wanted very much to see you before—before the end came."

Martinez shuddered, and a wail escaped his mouth. "*Dios*— Mama, you are being made to pay for my sins."

"Come, come. God doesn't work that way, my son."

Martinez choked, shaking his head. "No, I've done bad things. Terrible things. This is how I'm being paid for it." He felt the priest's comforting hand leave his shoulder, as though he was being repelled by Martinez's confession. "Tell me more, my son. I can grant you absolution."

"I'm a thief. I've killed some men. I helped a counterfeiter spread phony money into banks."

"Then you must know where the plates are, right?" The priest's words were punctuated by the sharp metallic sound of a hammer rolling back on a gun.

Martinez looked up slowly, found himself at eye level with the bore of a .45 automatic. "I didn't know you could get absolution from a gun. Who are you really, *Padre?*"

"I'm the one who's hunted you from Hell to breakfast, Luis. Now you tell me where the plates are, and maybe I won't shoot you in the guts and leave you to die." Dixie Ray Chavez's dark face split into a pearly grin, his eyes hot and mad looking. A peculiar giggle came from between his clenched teeth.

Martinez's face hardened as he looked from the dark bore of the Colt up into the killer's eyes. "So it's true. You're the one who tortured Linda and Wisteria. You killed them."

Chavez giggled again. "You shoulda heard that first woman. The whole time I was killin' her, she was beggin' me to stop, tellin' me stuff I didn't even want to know just to let her go. She offered to lay down for me, and don't think I wasn't tempted, lookin' down on that fine, hard body of hers. *Uhmm—uhmmmm.* But I was hired to get the plates, so I kept burnin' her with that hot iron. Y'know, it's funny the way human meat smells like chicken when you're cookin' it."

Martinez slowly stood up, clenching and unclenching the fist on his good arm. A vein stood out in his forehead and pulsed like something alive under his skin. "You think I'll give you the plates?" He stood up straight, shifting his feet, watching the muzzle of the gun ape his movements, not caring at all whether he lived or died in that moment.

Dixie Ray Chavez licked his lips hungrily. "Oh, you'll talk, Luis. See, I ain't gonna do nothin' to you here. We goin' out that back door yonder to a place I got. That's where I'll go to work on you. The hot iron don't work so well, but I bet a carvin' knife'll work. I'll just take li'l slices out of your arms and legs. After while, the pain'll be so bad you'll sing your lungs out. You'll beg to die."

"No," Martinez said slowly. "I'll make you kill me here."

Chavez giggled again as he raised the .45. "I ain't got to kill you. A slug in the arm'll do it, then you'll behave. I'll lay this gun across your head, then I'll just tell the young gals out front that I dropped somethin'. Once I get this Goddamned brace off'n my leg, I'll carry you out." His arm was stretched at full length, his finger heavy on the trigger as Martinez walked toward him.

Harsh light brightened the room starkly as the back door to the office swung open. Chavez jerked around, his turn hindered by the brace. He desperately threw the muzzle of his gun at the silhouette of a man standing there, struggling to squeeze the trigger as the man's gun spurted yellow flame at him. Chavez screamed as Farrell's first two shots took him high in the chest and spun him around. He was falling when a third shot struck him in the middle of the back. He hit the floor hard, his body strangely numb to the impact. His fingers scrabbled clumsily over the floor toward the fallen gun. Just as he touched it, a foot trod viciously on his hand. A shoe stabbed into his ribs and turned him over on his back. His nerve endings felt dipped in acid, and a high-pitched feminine scream escaped his mouth. Each breath was like a hot iron stabbing into him, and it took a while for the red and yellow lights to stop flashing in front of his eyes. When he could see clearly, he found Wesley Farrell staring down at him with hot red eyes, his lips drawn back from his teeth in an animal snarl.

"You sonofabitch. How—?"

"You were good with that brace and crutches, Dixie Ray," Farrell said. "I bought that hook, line, and sinker. That kid who shook hands with you yesterday, he doped it out. He saw the skin on your wrists. He had seen the medicine on Theron Oswald's counter when he went in there. When it wasn't there after you killed Oswald, we figured out that nobody but Dixie Ray Chavez could have taken it. It took a call to a pharmacist to help him remember that trioxalen is the most effective cure for vitiligo, and Father Maldonar was the only person in the picture who had vitiligo."

Martinez listened as he stooped and picked up the .45 from the floor. He straightened up, holding the heavy automatic down beside his leg, his finger just touching the trigger. "This is Dixie Ray Chavez? It can't be, Wes. Chavez is a white man. I saw him once in El Paso." He shook his head, his eyes staring confusedly at his friend.

"That's the cute part," Farrell replied. "Marcel's scientist said it was possible for a white man to turn himself dark with heavy doses of trioxalen and a sunlamp." He pointed at the light still burning in the corner. "We found out from Wilbur Payne, who was Chavez's buddy in Huntsville Prison, that even with Payne's sources of supply they'd had trouble getting enough of the drug to keep Chavez's skin pigment colored all over. That's why he's got the white patches on his wrists and neck. It was wearing off even with the help of the sunlamp."

Martinez shook his head. "How long has this been goin' on?"

"People in the neighborhood told Daggett's men that Chavez turned up here just about the time you went on the lam with the plates—five weeks. He set up the mission and used it as a base to look for you. When he couldn't flush you by himself, he began looking for your friends."

Martinez's face flattened as he looked down at the killer's twisted dark face. "And you found them. The helpless ones." His voice was soft, almost awed.

"The neighbors also told Daggett that he's had trouble with his skin pigment all through that time," Farrell continued. "They thought he was a saint who was sorely tried by God. That the patches were like stigmata."

"A counterfeit *negrito*. That is the cutest trick of all." Martinez sounded amused, but his eyes were flat, his fingers white around the butt of the .45.

Dixie Ray Chavez stared up at Farrell, grinning to cover the pain. "Y-you're good, boy. B'lieve you done broke my back. I—I can't move."

Farrell stared pitilessly at him. "I guess I need a bigger gun. I was doing my best to kill you."

Chavez tried to grin, but his eyes had a desperate gleam. "Man, I—I'm h-hurtin' real b-bad. Help—me—please."

Martinez stepped back, raising the pistol muzzle until it centered on Chavez's inert body. "I'll help you, *hombre*. I'll sell you a ticket on the night train to hell."

Farrell saw the sudden move and countered it. "Louie—put the gun down. It's over now." He saw the look in Martinez's eyes, and felt suddenly afraid.

"Wes, don't get in my way. I've gone along with this *fandango* as far as I can. I kill him and the debt's paid. I walk out the door and disappear. Forever."

"I gave my word, Luis. I said I'd bring you in."

Martinez shot a tired look at his friend. "I can't take ten years in prison. Not for you. Not for nobody." He half-turned to face Farrell, his gun at waist level, but not pointing it at Farrell yet. It would take only a snap of the wrist to bring the heavy automatic to bear.

"Don't be a fool. You think the cops can't find you? Where the hell do you think you could go?"

Martinez shrugged. "Mexico, maybe. I get deep enough into the country, and nobody can find me. I can find myself a village and just become another old *peon*. I'm sorry, Wes. I don't want to cause you any grief, but you see how it is. I won't just turn myself in and give up. I never said I would. I was just goin' along until I could even the score for Linda and the others."

Farrell felt sick in his stomach. He felt his hand grow sweaty around the butt of his gun, tried to find the strength to turn it on his friend. "Use your head. I'll do everything I can to help you. Walk out of here, and nobody can help you ever again."

Martinez nodded miserably. "Yeah." The automatic in his hand snapped up and the roar of a shot filled the small room. Martinez stared at Farrell, then down at the gun still cocked in his hand. It was only then that Farrell noticed the red stain spreading across his old friend's shirtfront. He caught Martinez as he sagged and gently lowered him to the floor. Martinez grinned up at him, the old cocky grin from the days when he and Farrell had made their own rules and owned the dark streets of the City that Care Forgot. "*Chivato,*" he said in a whisper.

Farrell lost track of time as he stared into Martinez's glassy eyes. He eased the dead man to the floor and stood up. Marcel stood beside him with an expression on his face Farrell had never seen there before. The boy looked sick and old. The .38 Detective Special hung limply in his grasp, the hand trembling.

Farrell put an arm around his cousin's shoulder and hugged him, trying not let out the scream of rage and grief stuck in his throat. It seemed an eternity passed before he could trust himself to speak. "Let's go home, kid." He pulled Marcel to the door leading into the church and they walked out into the afternoon sunshine.

※

September 14, 1940

FINNS PRESSED BACK, ASK WORLD AID; CALL BATTLE WORSE THAN WORLD WAR.

SENATE VOTES BILL FOR HELSINKI AID

RECORD NAVY BILL CUT BY $111,699,699. PUT UP TO HOUSE

NAZIS USE RED CRY IN PLEA TO LABOR

PRESIDENT DECIDES ON VACATION AT SEA IN AIR OF MYSTERY

Frank Casey paused at the newsstand inside the Louisville and Nashville Railroad Station to scan the headlines as he and Treasury Agent Paul Ewell waited for the arrival of FBI agents who were flying in from Washington, D. C. Surrounded by plainclothesmen, Max Grossmann sat in a wheelchair off to the side.

"Any word on how the investigation in Atlanta is going?" Casey asked.

Ewell shook his head, his expression sour. "I'm not sure we'll ever know the whole truth. They've rung the curtain down on this like it was a bad play. People I know there have told me confidentially that there have been a couple of low-level arrests. A mid-level Federal Reserve employee committed suicide at his desk last week. He was found to be a member in good standing of the German-American Bund, although he'd kept that a secret from his bosses. Two other employees have simply disappeared. They've got a dragnet out for them."

"Sounds like the Reserve's Board of Governors is making an effort to keep this quiet. I can't say I blame them. It's a pretty embarrassing mess."

"They won't be able to pull this trick again," Ewell said. "After Grossmann spent a few days in the Jefferson Parish lockup, he was willing to cooperate. We also picked up a master engraver named Michael Hardesty and Abe Appleyard, a top-notch chemist, and they sang like sparrows. Between the three of them, we figured out that they sent disguised boxes of phony money by Railway Express to a non-existent business set up by the Federal Reserve employee in Atlanta. He bribed some drivers and guards with the armored car firm that transferred money from Atlanta to the banks in other states, and they made the switch with the phony money before they left the Atlanta city limits. They got a nice payoff, while it lasted."

"Pretty slick work," Casey said. "As well organized as anything I've seen in thirty years."

"And how," Ewell agreed. "It's taught me a lesson, though. We think we're immune to all that's going on over in Europe and Asia, but we're sitting ducks for anybody who wants to come here and throw a monkey wrench into our gear box. We've been given orders from upstairs to open files on certain people and to step up surveillance activities. They won't admit it, but they're scared."

Casey nodded. "I don't blame them. I'm getting so I can't stand to read the newspaper or listen to the war news on the radio. There's trouble coming, Paul. We're big, but we're gonna get hurt."

Ewell nodded. "I've got a son in college. I hate to think of him going to war." He paused until the silence between them became too heavy. "You figured out all the connections in this mess?"

"After they operated on Chavez, he admitted that Grossmann had hired him to come to town and track down Luis Martinez. He used a drug to disguise himself as a Negro and trussed himself up in a brace to pretend he was a cripple. He said it all made him invisible. If he hadn't had so many bases to cover, things might've worked out better for Grossmann."

"What do you mean?"

"Chavez was trying to keep an eye on both Farrell and Oswald, and he was managing it pretty well. But when Marston Leake virtually figured out the counterfeiting conspiracy in front of Grossmann, Grossmann panicked and pulled Chavez in long enough to kill Leake. He didn't know Leake had already sent that letter to you just before his death. Once we spilled the beans to McCandless and ordered the interrogation of senior bank officals, Grossmann decided to cut his losses and make a run for it. If Compasso hadn't grabbed him, they all might've gotten away, and Chavez might actually have been able to recover the plates." He took off his hat and ran his fingers through his hair. "I thought McCandless was in it up to his neck until he admitted his trips to Atlanta were to spend time with a mistress." He laughed. "I'd love to hear what his wife had to say when that all came out."

"And now everybody else is dead or in jail—except Chavez and Grossmann," Ewell said sourly. "Grossmann we can't touch, and Chavez is paralyzed from the chest down so he'll escape the death penalty. Hell of a note."

Their conversation was interrupted by the arrival of a carload of FBI agents, crisply dressed young men with dark suits and serious expressions. Their leader took out his shield and identification card and held it so Casey and Ewell could see it.

"Special Agent Mark Deane. Are you Captain Casey and Special Agent Ewell?"

Casey and Ewell took out their own identification and held them for Deane. "That's us. We've got your man over there." Casey jerked a thumb at the fat man and his three plainclothes baby sitters. "Do you know what they're going to do with him when you get him to Washington?"

Deane shook his head. "Hush-hush. I could tell you if I knew, but I don't. Since he's got diplomatic credentials, they have to turn him over to his ambassador—according to the law. After all, we're supposed to be on good terms with the Germans." Deane almost smiled.

"That's what I figured. Pardon me if I don't give three cheers. Let's get this over with." He turned and led Ewell and the FBI agent to the wounded German. Grossmann looked up, mildly curious.

"Is it time for us to go, gentlemen?"

"If it were up to me, you'd be taking a much shorter trip, Mr. Grossmann, if that's your real name. When the doctor examined you prior to surgery, he discovered you weren't Jewish. This is FBI Agent Deane. You're his problem as of now."

"Well, I'm ready to go. I'm rather homesick, if you must know the truth."

Deane handed Casey some documents, which Casey signed with Deane's fountain pen. When it was over, Casey nodded to his plainclothes contingent and they withdrew so the FBI agents could take Grossmann in charge. As they got ready to leave for the special private car on the outgoing eastbound train, Casey asked Deane for a moment to speak to Grossmann.

The agents withdrew a few feet, and Casey squatted down so he could speak confidentially to the German. "I've got a message for you from Wesley Farrell, Grossmann. He said if you ever come back, he'll find you and leave your bones in the swamp. Take him at his word, because the law won't help you again. Not in New Orleans." Casey nodded to the FBI agents, then stood as they wheeled Grossmann to the train. The German cast one last look back at Casey before he disappeared from view.

"What did you say to him?" Ewell asked. "He looks like he swallowed a bad oyster."

"I told him to have a safe trip and to come back and see us some time."

⚛

Marcel found Farrell packing suitcases in his bedroom when he came calling that afternoon. Marcel noticed that his cousin seemed tired and withdrawn since the death of Luis Martinez.

"You look like you're going somewhere."

"I got a wire from Savanna. She found a place in Havana she wants me to look over before we sign the purchase agreement."

"You lucky dog. I want to go there one day."

Farrell smiled. "Your day is coming. By the way, I told Harry that you're running the show while I'm away. I think you're ready for it."

Marcel felt pleased, but a bit hesitant. "Harry's okay with that?"

"Harry and I have been together for a long time. I talked it over with him, and he's okay with it. Let him run the bar the way he wants, and he'll be a happy man."

Marcel went out to the living room and built a couple of rye highballs and had them ready when Farrell came out of the bedroom with his suitcases. He took one of the drinks and toasted Marcel. "To you, kid. As of now, you're all grown up. You did good in the last few weeks."

"Thanks, Wes. I'm still shaking from that fight, though." He looked about awkwardly, obviously trying to find the words to say something that was weighing on his mind. "Wes, about Luis Martinez, I wanted to tell you—"

Farrell walked to the window. "Shut up," he said in a soft voice. "Just shut up a minute and listen. Luis made his choice a long time ago." He turned around to face Marcel, his expression hidden by the light coming through the window behind him. "We all have to make a choice, sooner or later. I did, and so did you. There's only one choice, really, Marcel. Never forget that."

There was a finality, certainty in those words that buoyed Marcel even though they were borne on a voice that sounded old, even diminished. He decided to change the subject. "I heard you gave Margaret Wilde a job."

Farrell seemed glad for the distraction. "That's right. She needed something to keep her mind off things, so I bought Wisteria's Riverboat Lounge from the estate. Margaret's going to run it for us. She's got a ready-made clientele, so we all ought to make money off of it."

Marcel finished his drink and put the glass on the table. "What about you? Are you going to be okay?"

Farrell shook his head. "I don't know. I looked up to him once. He was like an older brother to me. I could have ended up like him without too much trouble."

Marcel looked back over his own short life. He knew he'd be in jail, or dead, if not for Farrell so his cousin's words had a strong resonance for him. "But you didn't. You're not like him, no matter what you might think. If you don't know that by now, ask some of the people you've helped. Ask me, for Christ's sake."

Farrell smiled, but it didn't quite reach his eyes. "Almost time for me to go. Say, what became of the cute little girl from Brownsville?"

"She's still around. She took a job working for Dr. Sampson over at the university. She likes it around here for some reason."

Farrell laughed softly as he put on his jacket and hat and picked up one of his suitcases. "Looks like my cab is here. Walk me downstairs, will you?"

Marcel picked up the other suitcase as he followed his cousin. They paused on the sidewalk while the cabbie put the bags into the trunk. Farrell offered his hand to his cousin.

"Take good care of things, kid. I'll see you when I see you."

Marcel took his hand and squeezed it gently. "You'll be back. We've got a lot more business to take care of, and I can't do it alone."

Farrell nodded, gave him a smile, then got into the cab. Marcel watched it until it disappeared down the street. When it was gone, he cast a glance up at the distinctive neon sign of the Café Tristesse before he squared his shoulders and walked back inside. There was a lot of business to take care of.

To receive a free catalog of Poisoned Pen Press titles, please contact us in one of the following ways:

Phone: 1-800-421-3976
Facsimile: 1-480-949-1707
Email: info@poisonedpenpress.com
Website: www.poisonedpenpress.com

Poisoned Pen Press
6962 E. First Ave., Ste. 103
Scottsdale, AZ 85251